HIGH SCHOOL:
BUFFOONERY CENTRAL

ACKNOWLEDGMENTS

*I wish to thank all those in my personal and
scholastic lives who made this book possible.*

*A special thank-you to my close friends N.K., E.G. and J. Logg
for providing me with vital details for a few of the vignettes.*

MR. NICK PRODUCTIONS, LLC
©2020 by Mr. Nick Productions, LLC

Edited by my longtime friend and editor/writer,
Marilyn Milow Francis – Thank you

Front cover art – William Zach and Kristy Klein
Back cover and spine – Kristy Klein
Book layout – Kristy Klein | seeingistudio.com

Photo of typical twelfth grader – Anonymous
Published by Mr. Nick Productions, LLC ©2020

ISBN: 978-0-578-68046-0

Dedications

To Mr. L.H., my tenth-grade Biology teacher. I fell in love with Biology and most likely became a pharmacist and dentist because of you. And to Mrs. L.R., my high school Major Authors and Creative Writing teacher. Your savvy sense of humor and prodding often brought out the best in me. And thanks for listening to my complaints all those years ago. And to my irrepressible mother, who, while actively pursuing advanced collegiate degrees in languages, still found time to minister to her family's full-time needs. Thank you!

And to J. Logg, my enemy-turned-friend, confidante and unwavering, trustworthy, "posse-mate." You were always there for me and the rest of our "gang." Thank you, Jim – rest in peace.

Foreword

Those four years in high school weren't wasted, were they? They were the best four years of my life, right? It's hard to tell; it could have gone either way.

Before embarking on another addition to my current comedy books already in print, I took a pause, a long and hard reflective pause. Not a diapause, which suggests suspended animation or hibernation, but a mental break, so to speak. Not a mental breakdown, mind you, just a slightly prolonged period of contemplation as to the necessity of this project. Then a brief browse through my high school yearbook not only flooded me with yesteryears refreshed recollections but acutely reminded me of the often absurd and humorous situations and paraphrased conversations that transpired between me, my friends, teachers, family members and frenemies. Back in the day, lots of senior classmates signed my yearbook with a common thread: namely, that I was "funny" and should keep it up. Hopefully they were referring to my personality and not a Viagra moment. Besides, Viagra wasn't invented yet. Many former high school cellmates thanked me for not only interjecting often unnecessary and unorthodox levity during school time but for lightening up serious and depressing situations in their lives as well. Everyone had personal shit going on, you know. I have found new respect for those long ago, teenage

daze but was I really the class clown? It's such an ignoble and harsh moniker to bear. Did I really make people laugh as a quirky coping mechanism? Was my personal life super stressful and so devoid of "joy" that I lashed out at the outside world with snarky and humorous retorts? Not really. So why did I carry on the way I did? Was I mentally ill and didn't know it? I don't know. But it seemed effortless on my part and I'm glad I was able to help many appreciative fellow inmates douse some personal fires and put on some fleeting happy faces. As a dentist in the fourth quarter of my career, actually the two-minute warning with no time-outs left, I'm still putting out fires, albeit in patients' mouths. However, I'm probably entertaining them as well, knowingly of course. It has been a long and often frustrating haul for me as I'm sure it has been for most of my former high schoolers. "Aggravation Saturation" is not just my coined slogan, but a psychological fact of aging and putting up with life's bullshit for so long. You know what I mean. Hopefully this book will rekindle and expose some of that high school spirit, angst, and humor that I thought was appropriate to elucidate. Although loosely based on my memories and interpretations of twisted, funny events, this book is "technically" fictional. It is a book of humor and should be taken as such. There is no malicious intent; the only intent is to entertain!

Dr. I. Mayputz
My preferred pronouns are: he/she/it

TABLE OF CONTENTS

FRESHMAN YEAR

JUNIOR YEAR

SENIOR YEAR

Introduction

This book is about a slightly fictionalized account of my life in high school, inspired by actual events. Embellishments of strange happenings were unnecessary because human foibles ran rampant. However, most names and places have been changed so as to not embarrass the guilty, inept and downright scurvy. The stories are retold in a series of vignettes which best captured my mood at the time. Let's hope I can poke a little fun at my former classmates, friends, teachers, townsfolk, family members, and especially myself, without much angry backlash. But why even write this book? Why bother after close to five decades of elapsed time? Does anyone really care anymore? I don't know. But while slowly shuffling down my memory lane one day, and before embarking on this humorous writing journey, I sincerely searched my feelings and possible ulterior motives and decided that comedy still rules! Hopefully you will be entertained and laugh along with me. Maybe at me, as well!

Enjoy.

Dr. I. Mayputz

FRESHMAN YEAR

It's time to get serious

1

Here We Go Again

Junior high had ended on a sour note for me, at least by my demanding father's and family's unrealistic measuring stick. Because of the perceived blight of bigotry against my "foreigner" folks and paternal grandfather, they readily empathized with my plight but simultaneously ridiculed me for not living up to their lofty standards. I thought I had done just fine under the trying circumstances of junior high, what with navigating tough classes, putting up with the offspring of village roughnecks, and deciphering *weird* and prejudiced teachers. Let us just say that it was a strenuous summer that followed, with disgruntled undercurrents swirling around me for three long months on the home front. I continued to learn and play high level tennis with my old man, collected and raised "bugs and slugs" as usual, rode my racing bike regularly, and tried not to engage family members in any meaningful scholastic discussions. Nevertheless, the usual hand wringing and worrying of my parental units bogged me down bigtime. I could "feel" the anguish in their voices whenever my future was depressingly brought up. "What will he become some day? Why is he doing so poorly in school? He'll never amount to anything if this keeps up!" I heard that crap all summer long, and it stung. Even my old fashioned, superstitious and cynical live-in paternal grandfather would frequently chime in as if to reinforce my "obvious" shortcomings. How could his stupid grandson have his last name? He knew I was feeling low, but by his old-world upbringing that was the best time to hit me below the belt even harder, to shame me into doing better by intimidation, sarcasm and embarrassment. You know, the tried and true psycho-parenting methods of a bygone era where the self-esteem and fragile egos of children were openly devalued and laughed at. I took it but didn't like it. And I'm sure most of my friends had it just the same, or even worse. Well, high school that counted toward your college admissions was ready to start in a few days and I made up my mind that I had to do something extraordinary in the next four years to get EVERYONE off my back. Maybe extra studying would help, perhaps a tutor or two? Maybe not hang out with my nascent group of like-minded jokesters? Boy, it was a lot of anxious reckoning for a thirteen-year old who desperately wanted to please a lot of people, including him. However, I never figured out what I should do differently, and I couldn't use Woodstock, the Vietnam War or the moon landing as distracting episodes anymore. Those events had ended. So, what WOULD be my "winning game" as a new high schooler? I didn't know as I stepped inside that oversized, Roman-columned brick shithouse on a hilltop pasture at the end of Sheldon Drive for the umpteenth time, after I had gotten off Bus 57 for the zillionth time. My younger sister said goodbye to me as she and her friends hurriedly galloped to the elementary school wing, where I had been held prisoner just a few years back. It was all getting so old and yet there I was, a fresh freshman that wanted and needed to get a giant chip off his shoulder so he could further shoulder the world and ninth grade! What was I thinking?

2

"Peace with Honor"

Good old Tricky Dick and his cockamamie catchphrases. But in reality, after working on a peace initiative for months with Southeast Asian counterparts, president Nixon, his shills, and America finally witnessed the last U.S. soldier depart Vietnam at the end of March 1973. No more POWs, no more intentional lying by the Pentagon, no more war! We had not technically won, nor had we lost. But the resulting treaty was broken by a jubilant North Vietnamese communist ideology. Its eventual takeover of South Vietnam usurped democracy and united a country in a part of the world that our government had repeatedly pledged would remain pinko free. Oh well, at least no more of our conscripted boys would be in mortal danger and, more importantly, my immediate chums and I could stay home. Amen. However, as many of you will recall, the hippie movement, previous protest marches, and war moratoriums had soured the mood of the nation causing an anticlimactic return of our brave troops. And, also remember, no one back then discussed PTSD and other serious health problems (side effects of Agent Orange, for instance) that would dog the returned veterans for many years to come. For them the horrific battles fought on hostile and foreign soil were over but their ongoing "civilian battles" here in the states would continue to the present. Hopefully all the servicemen and servicewomen still alive who suffered during and after that useless and terrible conflict can find some type of physical, psychological and spiritual solace before the grim reaper finally comes calling for them. Let's hope.

3

Our "Gang"

Since junior high, a few like-minded and levity-prone students gradually coalesced to form a very loose confederation of "soul mates." And I use that term to impute true friendship, not to imply any lascivious or physically intimate relationships between the parties. There were originally eight of us, all in the same grade; some having met and bonded as early as grammar school, others coming aboard in seventh grade while two more joined the group as a sophomore and senior, respectively. So who were these pugnacious purveyors of laughs at our high school? Who were these unassuming jokesters that often hung out together and unofficially had their mitts involved in most school *dys*functions? Who were these sarcastic wiseacres that appreciated the same brand of humor and daily doled it out as needed to each other as well as to the myriad of hapless hayseeds in our soporific and uninspiring pastoral school? Well, I'll tell you: First of all, we were not a gang like the ones portrayed in *West Side Story* and did not always hang out together, or even eat lunch side by side. We each had an independent streak yet gelled mentally. Like certain molecules, our natural and organic gravitation toward one another resembled weak van der Waals forces rather than forced loyalty and constant comingling. And secondly, we were not a knock-off of *The Little Rascals*, that ragtag band of poor and precocious neighborhood kids led by Spanky and his faithful sidekick, Alfalfa. Was I the leader? Hardly, I may have been the lead instigator/provocateur and resident "funnyman," but I definitely was not the head honcho. Always on the lookout for nonlethal and fingerprint-proof mischief, I frequently suggested outings and play dates, and often masterminded our in-school monkeyshines. However, there was no life or death allegiance to me or to anyone else in our bunch; nobody went to anyone for a weapon or advice. Everyone was bright enough to figure things out for her/himself. Plus, we all had watchful married parental units at our respective domiciles for backup guidance if our own systems failed. Now, let's take a peek at my pals, my bosom buddies, my compadres, my …. You know what I mean. Me first: Although born in western New York State, I was the nonlocal, black haired and dark skinned "foreigner," with Estonian-accented immigrant parents and a younger sister. Early and consistently palpable prejudiced animosity toward my family and me from the inbred village yokels and their progeny abated with each passing grade and I was grateful. And my budding sense of quirky humor saved me from succumbing to bigotry and, ultimately, saved me from myself. E.G. and I went way back, to elementary school and Mrs. M.'s third grade class. Even though he was originally from NEW JERSEY, he and I sparked an enduring friendship in third grade that continues to this day. He didn't mind my outward appearance and we quickly became buds. We shared jokes, jibes and went to each other's houses for play dates and birthday parties. We both had myopia but refused to wear glasses in class, at least until eighth grade; we had much in common! We each played the violin poorly, had strict and overbearing parents yet could easily joke about the mutual anxieties and stressors emanating from our homes. And then there was our shared love of similar irreverent comedy. THAT was the real glue that bound us together. N.K. and I had gone even further back, to our Clinton Street and kindergarten *daze*. I practically lived on her front porch during those halcyon times in the late '60s. Our respective fathers both taught at the same junior college in town and her mother would someday be our high school German teacher. N.K. and I were always close, and still are. She was like a smart sister to me and more than alright for a girl! And then there was our shared love of similar irreverent comedy. THAT was the real glue that bound us together. J. Logg and I were paired as unlikely locker mates in seventh grade. We couldn't have been more different. It was like Tennessee Tuxedo (me) and Chumley meeting for the first time, before they became great zoo pals. Initially we disliked one another, with J. Logg bullying me around that damn gray locker we shared. We had nothing in common it seemed. He was not a sporty specimen while I already played outstanding tennis for my age. We were in vastly different classes and had differing views on careers, politics and adulthood. My father was a college professor, his ran a successful grocery store/Getty gas station at the edge of town. We were frenemies at best. However, gradually our senses of humor got the better of us and started to mesh and, by the end of junior high, J. Logg became my very close friend, confidante and go-to guy. You could always trust him to have your back, no matter what. And then there was our shared love of similar irreverent comedy. THAT was the real glue that bound us together. That feisty female L.B. and I started to share sarcastic witticisms during our time in seventh grade New York State history class with the beloved teacher Mr. K. We tried to be quiet and respectful, but our sardonic senses of humor usually won out during class time. However, Mr. K. never punished us for being humorously disruptive and we greatly appreciated that. L.B. was short, determined, often wore overalls to class, and was full of energy. Our friendship blossomed and she enthusiastically joined our incipient group of unorthodox and levity loving dissidents. And then there was our shared love of similar irreverent comedy. THAT was the real glue that bound us together. G.P. was next. Although something of a screwball early on, E.G. vouched for him as being a good egg. He was slightly soft boiled, but a good yolk, nonetheless. As a close neighbor of E.G., they often carpooled together to school in later years. He was already heavily involved in 4-H and the Future Farmers of America (FFA) club when I started to interact with him, although he vehemently hated crafts, agriculture and farming. Was belonging to those woebegone organizations, populated by underachievers, his ticket to greatness? Was he a big fish in a small cesspool? Perhaps. But, boy, did that *boy* have a gift for gab! He was a fantastic, natural born horseshitter/public speaker and I surmise that's what helped him get through high school and beyond. And I didn't mind some of his personal peccadilloes because I really liked the dude. And then there was our shared love of similar irreverent comedy. THAT was the real glue that bound us together. P.M. had transferred into our grammar school by fourth grade and we became close pals in sixth, sharing a love of science and humor in the same classroom. She and I just clicked. Our later high school antics would often be fomented at her folks' house, specifically in her home's finished basement, along with a few cracked brewskis between the underage participants. She became an integral part of our "posse." And then there was our shared love of similar irreverent comedy. THAT was the real glue that bound us together. I had never heard of the next member of our group until seventh grade. We kept missing each other in the early grades of our forced incarceration; he and I never played together on the kiddie playground or broke bread with each other at chowtime either. But he quickly became my ying to his yang, or vice versa. Both of our fathers were college professors, we had disparate personalities but were profoundly and deeply affected by British comedy in addition to a horde of other parodies that we uniquely found entertaining. We became best friends. That fellow joker named F. and I also bonded over orchestral rehearsals and violin lessons, and our unlikely pairing would stay unusually strong for years, endure past graduation and into the first two years of pharmacy college, which we both initially attended as roommates. Of course, there was a shared love of similar irreverent comedy. THAT was the real glue that bound us together. T.B. hopped on our bus as a sophomore transfer student. We were not an exclusionary group of misfits, but you know how it is…. It was a minor miracle that we let anyone "new" into our special sect, especially an "outsider" and dreaded transfer. However, he decided to "read" our unwritten script and comic credo and fit in beautifully into our band of slightly mischievous minions. He was very smart, low key and subtle with his many original subterfuges. What a pal! And then there was our shared love of similar irreverent comedy. THAT was the glue that bound us together. As I have already mentioned, the tenth and final cog in our comedic wheel came to us from Australia, as the foreign exchange student that lived with my friend F. during our senior year. It was easy for him to dovetail right into our bosom because F. was his pseudo brother in this country. But there was more to this story. I believe he genuinely was sincere in his dealings with us. He could have been an arrogant, sullen and discontent asshole like a few of our previous exchange students turned out to be; but not Dave W. who took great pride in participating in nearly all aspects of school life, both scholastically and extracurricular, and on the home front. Because "we" were so heavily involved in nearly all facets of school by twelfth grade, it was a natural fit for him. He thrived and we had added another dingo to our kangaroo court of jesters. And then there was our shared love of similar irreverent comedy. THAT was the real glue that bound us together. So, what did we eventual ten *wiseguys* and *wisegirls* have in common? Why, an ounce of brain, humor, sarcasm, a biting wit, and the uncanny ability to laugh at ourselves as well as others. Were we the funniest kids in high school? Maybe, maybe not. And did we monkeys solely hang out with each other? Not at all. On weekends we were on our own but during school hours we tried to intermingle regularly. We had different academic and athletic abilities along with varying familial backgrounds and values. But we found enough common ground to stick together throughout our high school tenure. Lunchtime and study halls would usually find at least a few of us huddled together, chuckling and gestating amusing future pranks, dissecting recent TV sitcoms, and purely enjoying our camaraderie. What started as a disorganized bunch of slightly nerdy, humor-enhanced adolescents in junior high morphed into a small, zany mob that eventually ran roughshod over our later contemporaries and school faculty with jokes, sketches, parodies and bushwhacking bullshit. Nothing injurious or suspension worthy; we were just a fun-loving and nonsexist troupe of wiseacres going through school and life as a loose embodiment of the Monty Python crew, with Benny Hill and other comics thrown in for good measure! Yes, we had fun in high school!

4

Why das Deutsche?

Even for such an ignoble high school, located in the middle of nowhere and attended mainly by the progeny of local dairy farmers, two European languages were offered. The rule was later changed allowing eighth graders to participate earlier, but for our class foreign tongue training began as ninth graders. French had been taught for years but was abolished just prior to our high school beginnings, leaving German and Spanish as the only choices. And they were choices, not mandatory requirements at the time. The majority of the class wishing to study a language took Español, which was widely acknowledged as an easy A, easy to learn and probably very useful for the future, especially when the U.S. Spanish-speaking Hispanics finally become the majority. Si? German (das Deutsche) was difficult, had an allegedly hard-nosed and hard-marking teacher (whom I had known since kindergarten), and was considered the elite foreign language in our *bovine-bred* school. It was "arrogantly" reserved for top students who weren't afraid of its rigors, memorizations and Frau K. I HAD to take it you know. Firstly, Regents German was taught by the mother of one of my longtime female buddies, fellow classmate and "crew" member, N.K.; secondly, supposedly only *smart* kids enrolled in it; and thirdly, we thirty or so signees had heard that there would be an annual competitive convention or festival of some sort by junior year which was so glorified by upperclassmen that it justified frosh taking such a demanding, tongue twisting parlance. We filed into the German room, which was at the end of the hallway in the 4-6 grades, first floor wing of our building, just as the elementary school librarian poked her devilish snout out of her door from across the hall and sneered at me. Although I thought my errant overdue book fiasco was resolved in fifth grade, it seemed as if she still grudgingly remembered the screw-up and relished giving me "the look." I was innocent, I tell you! I wagged my head in disbelief as I walked by her and took a wooden seat in the middle of the German room, near the rear. Frau K. addressed the class in das Deutsche, gave us our translated names and started right in. She also gave me a quick smile and nodded to her daughter before having us crack the antiquated textbooks to begin learnin' the blasted der, die and das (neutral) gender prefix articles that applied to most nouns; ones that we had to learn by rote. For example: der Mann (man), die Frau (woman), das Boot (boat). You get the drift. In addition, we quickly were ushered into a world of humongous words and sentences, with the verb (action) frequently at the end. Instead of saying "The silly and pockmarked boy ran with the spotted ball," the German equivalent would be "The silly and pockmarked boy with the spotted ball ran." Well, simplistic sentences were relatively easy to decipher if they were short in length; however, stumbling over twenty long words in a row often made one forget what was just said, even after saying the payoff word at the very end. But, hey, we brave lot signed up for this and had no one to blame but Frau K., I mean, ourselves. Endless listening to that same damn male voice on scholastic German tape recordings (Hören sie zu und wiederholensie – listen and repeat) resulting in mandatory class recitations was a pisser. And the proper pronunciation of words, translating sentences both ways, primitive attempts at speaking in class, and remembrance of vocabulary words also made that course a brute at times. And that was just German 1, in ninth grade. There was the potential of taking that "blistering brogue" for three additional years to really get immersed in the Teutonic language! Thankfully the Regents exam was offered after the junior year, leaving only Germanic diehards to partake in the senior iteration of the course. Now, a few words about Frau K. She was not mean, had a wicked sense of humor, and greatly appreciated having our "posse" in her classroom, although she would feign disdain during our frequent humorous interruptions, especially when F. and I got going. She was tough but fair and I considered her my second mom when in *shul*. Because Estonian was my first language, with English being second, my addled gray matter had already been forcibly trained to bend my tongue accordingly. So, for me, German was a no brainer to read and phonate correctly. It was the comprehension, grammar and vocabulary recall that frequently had me stymied. My good buddy E.G., being of German descent, intuitively prospered in the course as did my pal N.K., the teacher's daughter. Nevertheless, the rest of us, although often stumped, still managed and loved Frau K. anyway. And we still had a few more years to go. Sehr gut!

5

A Breath of Fresh Math

Just a quick and painful recap: Sure, I had micro aggressions foisted on me since kindergarten due to my funny sounding surname and brown skin. But I was used to it and sought to overcome the biases by working hard scholastically and athletically. I usually fared well and even excelled at most school courses, gym and sports, much to the ire of some of the bigoted, hometown teachers. But one subject in particular had managed to flummox me since the end of fifth grade: math! Darn it all. I couldn't blame the color of my epidermis or hair on my stupidity when it came to the numbers game. My lack of numerical brain cells in sixth grade caused me to slide and be demoted to the regular arithmetic section while most of my pals easily sauntered down the HIGH math group path and, skipped seventh grade math in lieu of pre-algebra. Meanwhile, I slogged through meaningless, worthless and often confusing junior high mathematics with a piss poor attitude in tow. My civil engineer/professor father was bewildered and frustrated that his supposedly "smart" son was floundering in something that he found exceedingly easy. His habit of belittling me to "get it" was not paying dividends for either of us. He was constantly on my case. I was envious of my friends. Why was I so dumb when it came time to figuring out equations, etc.? I don't know, I never quite figured it out. Nevertheless, I was determined to make a fresh start and take a fresh step into the world of ninth grade algebra. This was the beginning of high school, when grades started to matter. If I wanted to make any future dreams come true, NOW would be the time to get my ass in gear and really *put out* in all subjects, including you know what. I took a wooden seat in the row by the windows as Mrs. J.T. walked in, quickly introduced herself and launched into lecturing. She was short, middle-aged, had glasses, and a tight, short, black bob. She was even-tempered, no nonsense and persistent about teaching we greenhorns. And guess what? No matter what she talked about, regardless of the nuanced reasoning involved or her convoluted chalkboard renderings, I understood it all. But how and why; I don't rightly recall, but it happened. My heretofore mathematically impervious numbskull magically opened up and absorbed her teachings like a new sponge. Was it a positive attitude on my part or was she a genius teacher who finally got through to me? Perhaps it was both? Others in the class, including the bevy of smarty-pants eighth graders, seemed to struggle and never had a kind word for her. I, on the other hand, had the highest average in the class and greatly looked forward to the daily barrage of challenging numerology that spilled out of her mouth. I loved that course and Mrs. J.T. as well. Pop was off my back, I was off to a great start as a freshman and things were looking up. And believe it or not, things continued that way until the end of the year. I still possessed the highest GPA in the class and was looking forward to the Regents exam. Alas, after months of *Barron's Review Book* preparation, the state exam was abruptly called off for our year. It turns out that a buttload of various Regents exams had been stolen by some enterprising students downstate, so a bunch of the tests were canceled statewide, including algebra. We still got credit, though. The Regents "marks" that we received were the same as our final class grades, which was fine by me. I took my 97 final average and 97 Regents score and kissed my report card. Finally, I was algebraically vindicated, at least for ninth grade, that is. Thank you, Mrs. J.T.

6

"You Gotta Play Football!"

It was widely known to many classmates that coach K. and I did not see eye to eye. He knew it, I knew it; all my close pals knew it. So why did that DIMINUTIVE and prejudiced native son keep hounding me to play varsity football? He was the junior high and high school Phys Ed teacher besides being the coach of a myriad of sports teams in our DIMINUTIVE school, including JV and varsity football. Besides outperforming his many "jocks" in gym class, it became obvious that the paucity of athletic-type boys in the school made him come-a-calling to me. He had to eat crow and kowtow to a brown-skinned "outsider," but he had no choice. I was a fleet-footed sprinter, could throw and catch with the best of his future sports stars and had a killer instinct when it came to winning. He accosted me over and over in the hallways in the fall of my freshman year, and for four years hence. His beleaguered statement was always the same: "You gotta play football," he would implore me; as if he had just uttered something I had not heard before. Some of my best pals, such as E.G., were trying out for a coveted spot on the varsity gridiron team and here I was dragging my heels in disinterest. Football was big in my school, regardless of the abysmal win/loss record at nearly every season's end. Most of the "loco" boys actively participated as per a cultural continuation of rugged ball sports played by their likewise inbred and farm bred ancestors. It was an esteemed "honor" to play for the Bulldogs, yet, there I was, weighing a healthy buck fifty, but, bucked "tradition" by refusing to enlist in the corps. What was wrong with me? Well, for one, I strongly disliked coach K. and, for another, my mother emphatically put a kibosh on the whole darn thing. She would remind me that every year there was always a footballer hobbling around school on crutches due to a broken leg. She didn't want me to be that boy! She was right, though. My position as a potential running back would have exposed me to multiple hits and tackles on my lower extremities, especially my knees. I could have been a cripple by my sophomore year! Mr. K. got the brush-off from me and I stuck to that wimpy sport called tennis. It further infuriated him because tennis and track were held at the same time in the spring. I couldn't even run the 110 and 220 yard dashes for him (It was yards and not meters back then, remember?). Boy, he was continually mad at me. I recently heard that my former corn-fed high school graduated fewer than fifty total students as opposed to the one hundred-plus pupils in my commencement class.

Where did the new coaches find enough manly athleticism to even field a football team? There was also boys' soccer to contend with in the fall which was absent in my day, thereby further reducing eligible males for the pigskin sport. Yikes! I wonder if sturdy farm GIRLS try out now.

7

Lunchtime Longings

I was a freshman, she, a petite sophomore. I had sat down
next to her during lunch one day by happenstance. None
of my buds were around so I took a testosterone inspired
initiative and plopped into the empty seat adjacent to her.
It was obviously on purpose; well, to eat that is, but also to
possibly engage her in social intercourse. After all, at the
risk of being politically incorrect and in "violation" of
today's "newly" accepted standards of sexual deviances,
disorientations and identity procurements, I didn't suffer
from any sexual confusion back then: I was a boy and I
liked girls, period. There, I admitted it; now you all know
that the proverbial closet which I came out of was
heterosexual! But who knows if that noun can even be
mentioned in public anymore? Is it still in vogue? Perhaps
not. I may be a "straight" dinosaur…. Anyhow, M.D.
looked over her glasses at me and smiled; I grinned back
and then looked at my hot lunch of tomato soup and
grilled cheese sandwich. Hers was the same. Well, we
started conversing in short unmeaningful sentences as
other students seemed to fade from view. But she and I also
touched on some deep adult topics as well. She was fairly

attractive, smart and "into me," for some strange reason.
Now, mind you, I still sat with my chums on most days
but found myself next to her whenever she was alone. My
pals noticed this but said very little. No teasing, no
questions, no nothing. Perhaps they were at least a little
puzzled? Probably. I know I would have been, and I was,
with myself! Why was I getting a wicked crush on her, an
older girl that I had met in the cafeteria lunchroom? Was it
because she talked to me in an obviously flirtatious way? Is
that all it took for a gal to get me gaga? Just throw a few
soothing syllables in my general direction, feign interest
and bat your eyes at me provocatively? Was I that easy?
Was I really a horny chump and hard up for feminine
attention? I guessed so. How sad. But I did not care
because I greatly enjoyed the titillating feelings she aroused
in me. I think she was sincere and felt the same way about
me, but who knew? It might have all been a clever tease on
her part. I still didn't care. She was a good-looking woman
that spoke her heart and that's all that mattered. It was
strange that none of my immediate *home gurl* "posse
members" elicited those same strong male longings in me.
They were my gal pals, my humorous sounding boards, my
intelligent friends. And that's as far as it went. But M.D.
stirred up my mind in other ways and I liked it. But, alas,
things ended between us after a few months. I started to sit

with my buds again, and she with her girlfriends. We still acknowledged one another by nodding and waving but that fervent and unrelenting emotional pull between us was over, at least for me. I'm not sure how she felt. Nevertheless, other girls started to pique my interest in that same high school eatery as I daily surveyed the field of females in front of me. Puberty had hit me a few years back; however, I continually had nothing physical to show for it. However, at least my eyes and brain were appeased by all the "potential" surrounding me. Nevertheless, it was all fleeting romantic daydreaming, between bites of Salisbury steak and flaccid string beans, until the bell clanged, signaling the end of lunchtime. I often wonder if other adolescent girls of yesteryear had noticed me and my buds and secretly desired us? Perhaps? Maybe the primitive dalliance that M.D. and I manifested had been an aberration? I hoped not. Sparking cerebral pathways of future intimacy between willing high school partners was all part of growing up in my time. I presume it is much the same today, regardless of "mainstream" bizarre sexual orientations and the added bonus of genitally modified students. What the hell is going on in this world?

8

Ping Pong Prowess?

So, here was my chance to impress that biased "all-American" and hometown athletic legend Mr. K., who graciously returned to his alma mater to teach us physical education. He never took a liking to yours truly, be it the brown color of my skin, my *weird* last name, my parents' European accents, or whatever. He also didn't like me outshining his "chosen" jocks when playing football, softball or running track while in gym class. He begrudgingly started giving me well deserved A's, but only after a blowup with my mom years before at a parent/teacher conference arranged on her behest. But here was a chance to show him another sporty skill I possessed in spades, or so I mistakenly thought. There was a badly beat up ping pong table in the boys' locker room complete with shitty paddles and cheap balls that male students could use during study hall or just before the start of P.E. on given days. Seniors usually dominated the scene and paid no attention to would-be other players, if they were underclassmen. You know, manly hierarchy and all… Then I appeared one day with my expensive Stiga paddle with Yasaka Mark V rubber and a Halex three-star ball and caused a bit of a commotion at that chewed up table. At least the net was still intact and at the proper height. A cocky senior immediately saw my equipment and quipped that he wanted a piece of me. I obliged and wiped him out rather quickly. Next. Another older boy tried in vain, but my superior spins and slams got the best of him too. Then S.M. showed up. He was a smart fellow classmate, a son of a locally well-known lawyer and school board member, a lefty, and a baseball player. He picked up one of those slimy, ratty paddles, examined my tournament level ball and said, "Let's play, Mayputz." Obviously, he had played before as we tapped the ball back and forth to warm up. I happened to see Mr. K. walk out of his office to witness the table tennis action about to unfold. Good. My idea to showboat a bit was coming to fruition; hopefully S.M. would cooperate and tap out like the others had done. I was supremely confident and ready to play. Unfortunately, so was S.M. He thwarted my cunning plan to showcase my ping pong prowess by soundly defeating me in the two games we played. He had no Olympic style strokes or even a decent bat and yet he still managed to push the ball past me over and over again. I felt disgraced and humiliated as Mr. K. smirked in the corner while attentively watching our battle. Needless to say, I didn't sway anyone that day and sulked off to my gym locker after being so badly whipped. Mr. K. loudly congratulated S.M. on a job well done. Darn it, my one chance to show off in front of that dreaded, red-headed, hot-tempered gym teacher had failed miserably. At least S.M. did not rub it in. Nevertheless, our later matches proved to be lopsided in my favor as my formidable talent and nimbleness finally shone through. However, where was Mr. K. when you needed him? Alas, he never saw me win and I lamented that. The table was removed shortly thereafter because someone had physically broken it in half. And it was not replaced. I continued to play at home with my dad, who was a former New York State table tennis champion, during the winter months. He had taught me the game as a youngster and kept on giving me pointers to improve. I carried that skill set into college and greatly enjoyed beating up on unsuspecting students who thought they were "players." Too bad Mr. K. never witnessed a great match in that dank and rank locker room all those years ago. Perhaps a grandstanding victory by me would have impressed him; maybe, maybe not? C'est la vie.

9

Newtonian English

Did I finally flip my lid or did ninth grade English have something to do with Sir Isaac Newton and his mathematical/scientific discoveries? Well, nothing so obvious I'm afraid. The word Newtonian has also been used to portray an old-fashioned sense of order, logic and a well thought out doctrine that is relatively simple to follow. That is what freshman English was like with Mrs. N. at the rudder, steering young and impressionable minds through a bevy of subjects such as poetry, literature, public speaking, writing, and reading comprehension. And she did it with ease and grace. Mrs. N. was a middle-aged, slender and elegant woman with long, light brown hair and a placid disposition. She kept law and order in class due to our adoring respect for her and relief after experiencing last year's grammar debacle. Most of the class, including me, had suffered greatly under the tyrannical thumb of the demanding Mr. G., the eighth grade grammar teacher. I eventually prospered in his course, but most of my classmates and my fingernails had taken a bad beating before getting out. And I won't get into the opinionated progressive pablum which the seventh grade *feminazi* instructress had forcibly tried to instill in us in HER controversial English class. That was one horrible horror show, at least for boys. By contrast, Mrs. N. was a breath of fresh air. English was supposed to be easy and enjoyable and she made both happen. And we learned something in spite of ourselves, without her berating us daily for our alleged shortcomings. What a teacher: silent but *deadly*! She was THAT clever, teaching us English principles without us knowing it. The nerve of her! However, she was no stranger to me. I had known her for the past few years; she had been my homeroom teacher in seventh grade. The comely and smiling Mrs. N. was the perfect adult to calm down our nervous and scatter-brained junior high class as we were beginning our assault on seventh grade. She would calmly take attendance, never reprimand tardy pupils, and would matter-of-factly point to the loudspeaker when Principal *Shag* began his morning spiel. I quickly realized that she was hard to rattle; she was a pro at this teaching gig. I vividly remember telling myself that I could hardly wait until ninth grade so I could have her as my English teacher. It finally happened and I was not disappointed. I think she also fondly recalled me. And, instead of breeding contempt, our familiarity bred delight and gratitude, at least on my part. Thank you, Mrs. N.

10

Spitball Surprise

Boy was I ever grateful for a "new" history class in ninth grade! After last year's disaster with a disinterested and crummy American history teacher, coupled with my equally disinterested and lousy attitude, I greatly looked forward to Afro-Asian Cultures, the name of the new course. What? Afro Sheen? No, it was going to be a class studying the geography, geopolitics, cultures and religions of Africa and Asia, although with a condescending "colonial" U.S. viewpoint. But what did WE know at the time as freshmen grunts? It was a mandatory high school social studies class and we took it. The Vietnam War was ostensibly over, President Nixon was about to be ousted and Cadillac sedans were over nineteen feet long. You know, those were normal things back in the early '70s. So was this course I figured; however, the teacher was a bit "stuffy," to say the least. Mrs. G.S. was a middle-aged, no nonsense lecturer with hair in a tight bob, who usually wore stylish, colorful clothing, expressive earrings, and had a brown complexion, similar to my own. With a loud voice and perfect posture, she pontificated from day one and strutted around the room while educating we neophytes.

But was this class really that serious or did she just want some control over us? I mean, the subjects she covered were interesting and all, but she always had this habit of instantly quashing any dissenting opinions from the peanut gallery and glared disparagingly at would-be troublemakers. In other words, she didn't want to hear a peep out of us for the whole class period! She rarely smiled and had this withering gaze that suggested she had taught long and hard and would not tolerate any monkeyshines in her presence. She was a tough nut to crack, but we tried anyway. One such incident of pent-up tomfoolery happened during a film strip presentation on the ancient Saudis of Suez. The dorky AV nerds set up the film projector, put on the film reel, threaded the cellophane through the various spools and managed to fire up the works without much fanfare as I silently watched and waited. My pal G.P. was asked by Mrs. G.S. to tug down the white screen as V.F. and a few others pulled down the shades to darken the room. We were now all set to begin our juvenile hooliganism. We certain boys had known about the upcoming film and had armed ourselves with cheap plastic Bic Stic pens that could be quickly taken apart and converted to spit wad shooters; you know, similar to a straw. We had long barrels, tiny, wadded up pieces of saliva-coated paper in our mouths and used a forceful puff of breath to launch the sticky projectiles from our lips. Of course we could quickly put the pens back together again as if nothing was out of the ordinary should we be accused later. And so, after my buds and I surreptitiously ripped off small shards of paper and placed them in our cake holes, the barrage began. Every time I saw a camel appear onscreen, I covertly fired at it, first making damn sure that Mrs. G.S. was not eyeballing me or my cautious, surrounding friends. We were quietly chuckling and silently and sporadically spit wadding at the large canvas throughout the whole time period. Other boys started to join in the fun as the clock ticked. However, the girls did not participate in our folly. They stoically watched the shenanigans unfold around them and said nothing. Though not active participants, they nevertheless appreciated our senses of humor; no one tattled on us. Toward the end of the class, we rematerialized our "guns" into pens and just sat there, rather mute, as the lights were turned back on. In the previous darkness, we had mistakenly thought that our balls of paper/spit had harmlessly bounced off the textured screen but were instead horrified to see hundreds of spitballs stuck to it. We would be in major trouble for sure. But wait, before Mrs. G.S. realized what was happening, G.P. quickly took the initiative and pushed the awning back up into its holder as it spit out tiny bits of rolled up balls of paper onto the floor. Mrs. G.S. stared indignantly and tight-lipped at the littered ground, at our dour pusses and didn't know what to say. No one laughed as she suspiciously scanned our class. She probably figured it out too late as we perpetrators left the classroom, heads down, with nary a word spoken betwixt us. Only later in the hallway did we exalt and congratulate ourselves on a job well done. And she never said a single syllable about the affair, not one mention. I'm sure the other educators and school brass in the teacher's lounge got an earful from her, but not us. However, to be fair, we kind of liked Mrs. G.S. and not much "tainted fun" occurred in that course, except for when the dumbass student teacher came on board; that is another provocative story.

11

Tennis Great?

My above average athletic/tennis skills seemed to point to a glorious upcoming high school tennis career. I had picked up the sport because pop stuck a racquet in my hand at age nine. If he had been a football or basketball player, I most likely would have played that particular sport. But, no, tennis and ping pong were "IT" at my house. And having a former university tennis standout father who was a current professor and successful coach of the local men's college tennis team was convenient as well. And coupled with possessing the latest and greatest wooden Wilson Jack Kramer model racquet with new-fangled nylon strings, I was a future shoo-in to be the best player on my school's varsity team. Ha. As I later learned however, in addition to practice and determination there were also petty politics and favoritism to contend with. Anyway, my preadolescent hitting and serving abilities were great at the time, if you compared me to recreational Sunday hackers. I cockily thought I knew how to play and did not always listen to directives very well. Jimmy Connors was my idol in the early '70s and I mistakenly thought that merely watching him on TV was as good as hands-on training. Really? Not! But to be fair, it wasn't entirely my fault. I'm not sure how he coached his college boys to yearly championships, but my old man's idea of teaching ME was to enforce the old-fashioned, eastern grip stroking method and proper timing when hitting that fuzzy white ball. Yet, he never gave me strategic tips such as: how to play actual matches, how to stay tough and focused during a grueling game; or how to really set up winning points. Serve and volley technique, what was that? And our practice sessions did not have me blasting endless buckets of balls but a measly hour here and there of light rallying back and forth. And this was in the windy summertime only. We did not play tennis in the snowy wintertime, only table tennis. I basically struck those white hairy blobs for only three months. How can you get good at something when participating in it so sporadically? Oh, there were pricy indoor tennis facilities in surrounding cities but who would drive hours and spend hard earned moola just to smack a ball? Not us. Anyhow, pop had an uncanny and innate ability to rise to the occasion to defeat adversaries that were often younger and more talented than he. He was a natural and an extremely gifted athlete and had excelled in most racquet sports since a youth; as for me, perhaps a little, but not so much. Yet, somehow, he figured that his passed on genes alone would magically do the same trick for me, regardless of our paltry practice sessions and his indifferent instruction. Nevertheless, he wanted me to always win; I just wanted not to lose. However, my record was about even in the win-loss department when he arranged matches for me against other tennis-playing kids in town. The combination of my sporty arrogance and his unrealistic expectations, in spite of his lackadaisical style of coaching, made me a decent but not great junior tennis player. I wanted to quit many times but feared disappointing him; I did enjoy the game and stuck with it, through frustrating losses and all. Then came junior high. I had received a controversial and complimentary logoed duffle bag as a "bribe" in eighth grade from my upcoming new varsity tennis coach who had heard of my supposed prowess and wanted me on the team. The controversy was because I had received that crumpled maroon carrier in junior high, and I was not even on any varsity team yet. My bigoted baseball coaching, eighth grade history teacher had seen it under my desk in his class and rudely and embarrassingly called me out on the preposterous proposition of me owning such a highly coveted bag. Anyway, that fiasco quickly died down because I stopped bringing it to school. By the way, I had fully intended to "try out" for the varsity tennis team in spite of any "gifts" given to me. And I enthusiastically did.

12

A Dancing Fool

The above heading was used by Frank Zappa for one of his popular songs – *Dancin' Fool* - on his 1979 album: *Sheik Yerbouti*. However, that prescient title first applied to me in 1973. Please, allow me…. A high school fall dance was announced over the loudspeaker by Principal *Shag* one morn and got the whole 9-12 student body atwitter. Well, at least the "good" kids got excited. The known longhaired (guys and gals) stoners and heavy drinking hippie-types didn't seem to care one way or the other because every day and evening was a chance to party! However, the rest of us "normal" pupils greatly looked forward to a free Friday night of camaraderie and, hopefully, "dancing" with the opposite sex. You know, boys and girls. There was no obvious LGBTQ community to deal with in those days, although members of it may have always been present and the rest of us just didn't bother to notice or acknowledge them. Plus, it was politically incorrect to do so at the time, even if we had known better. My mother dutifully pressed my deep purple, polyester bellbottom slacks while I polished up my tan, leather, four-inch heeled, platform shoes. That was the party style back then, man, complete with an open V-shape neck, buttoned, tie-dyed shirt with frills around the collar. I looked like a junior Reggie Dwight (Elton John) clone minus the flamboyant glasses. Mine were just wire-rimmed jobs and coke bottle thick, definitely not sexy or provocative. Anyway, speaking of dressing up, none of us *home boyz* ever wore such cool clothing to school, it was reserved for special occasions, even though our "clubbing" consisted of an occasional date and school-sanctioned dances. We were fourteen at the time; we couldn't drive, had no dates, but like Boy Scouts, were prepared just in case. You had to dress to impress when you went out, at least to some degree. This was my second "dance" and I have to say that male accoutrements and wearable plumage frequently surpassed the attire of our *home gurls*. Blouses, bras, shoes, and dresses were often drab and dreary, even with the senior gals. Provocative female clothing and the baring of busty cleavages was not the feminine style in our high school, at least not in public. And with its idiotic pulsing and annoying beat, rising disco music was also rearing its ugly head in our dusty village, but no one seemed to buy into it whole hog. The townie redneck rockers were still the majority and were an effectual buttress to Donna Summer and the Bee Gees. Like the natives, I hated disco then and I hate it now. But at that time I didn't care about the flippin' sound system or

the tunes emanating from it. I was ready to rumble and
dance with a bona fide girl; maybe? At the last high school
dance, I stood around with some of my freshman buds,
mesmerized by the gyrating girls in front of us, and waiting
for something to happen. Nothing did. I have to admit
that we all failed the same Heterosexual Dating 101 class!
THIS time, however, I hoped to actually squeeze some
appreciative female flesh. My dad dropped me off at the
high school gym entrance in the back of the school and I
went in. I didn't have a girlfriend but knew enough ladies
from my class to at least banter small talk. Plus there
would be older girls there that knew me from lunch period
and study hall. I was all set. Was I, though? I entered; I
surveyed the field and my "male competitors" and meekly
retreated to a darkened corner and slumped against the
wall in defeat. Upperclassmen and their respective chicks
were hugging up on each other during slow dances while
we discouraged frosh dunces looked on longingly. Of
course, sometimes it was hard to tell the genders of the
couples because long hair was the norm for both sexes back
in those days. Anyway, I was about to leave the gym for a
breather when I saw fellow freshman D.H. on the floor,
dancing with the ultra shy twin sisters from my class. Wow,
she looked very pretty decked out in tight white
bellbottoms with a billowy, cuffed white blouse while

swinging her shiny blond mane in time to the tunes. I
knew her, I casually liked her, she was *fine*. Smart, tall (of
course most girls were taller than we adolescent boys at the
time), poised, and a minister's daughter; she was a looker,
even at that age. Well, this was my chance to horn in on
the action and perhaps make an impression on her. In
what seemed like an anguishing amount of time for my
brain to make up its mind, I slowly approached the trio
and boldly asked D.H. if she wanted to dance with me.
My heart was thumping, the music was throbbing, and my
hands were damp as she acknowledged my presence and
said yes in a soft-spoken voice. Her female partners got the
hint and moved out of the way as I sidled up next to D.H.,
face to face. My futile moves didn't seem to change her
demeanor and she never smiled at me. I was hot and
bothered; she seemed only a bit bothered, however.
Perhaps she was also shy or perhaps she really didn't like
me and had given me a shot out of politeness and
convention? I didn't care as a slow song began playing. I
really wanted to press up against her and put my arms
around that beautiful bod, and it nearly happened.
However, her idea of closeness was a foot of distance
between us, with hands on shoulders and arms, not around
the waist or anything so lascivious. Man, she was a prude.
But what could I do? I was dancing with a gorgeous girl,

wasn't I? Wasn't that enough? During our infantile mingling I had fleeting thoughts of D.H. and I as boyfriend and girlfriend. Maybe she felt the same? Was this going to be the beginning of a wonderful courtship with more than casual touching of sweaty palms? Ha, nothing further happened at that soiree or in the future. I left that teen dance perspired, satiated and full of testosterone enhanced anticipation. But I guess D.H. had left it with a more realistic and mature feeling, namely, that I was not the one. Sadly, we returned to our classes with our previous interpersonal dynamic intact: I would say hi to her and she would nod in return. There was no dating, no positive reciprocation of affection of any kind on her part, just as before. She left our school after our freshman year and I kind of forgot about her until recently. However, as I was perusing my 1974 yearbook, I noticed the uncanny physical similarity between my wife and D.H. And their personalities were also nearly identical. What the eff? I had dated a slew of ladies during my first three years of pharmacy college, with disparate hair styles, body shapes, eye colors and dispositions. Then, that hot, blonde haired, blue-eyed freshman babe (Hottie Blondie was her nickname in pharmacy college) came into my life and that was it. We dated, mated and have been married for close to forty years now. But wait a minute; did I end up with

D.H. after all? What a profound feminine imprint she must have left on me all those years ago. Wow.

13

Extra Credit Blues

Mr. A.G. had replaced the recently retired Mr. B., who was not only head of the bus garage but also doubled as the previous earth science teacher. We were newly minted freshmen and Mr. A.G. was a newly minted science instructor. I had him for Regents Earth Science, along with twenty-five other so-called brainy kids. Additionally, he taught other sections of regular earth science to the rest of the class. Now, I had heard that this particular course was demanding and difficult; wouldn't a brand-spanking new lecturer make it even more so? Yes, and that's exactly what transpired as if on cue from a higher power, or the devil down below. Mr. A.G. was long-haired, brash, handsome, and young, with an attitude of superiority from day one. Most of us didn't care about his personal mannerisms, his ways of teaching, or even the hardships involved in learning the oftentimes soporific material. Most of my chums and I were only concerned with our marks and passing the Regents exam at the end of the year. That's all. That was enough! Well, by midyear my immediate smarty-pants male buds and I had averages in the low eighties, you know, in the garbage can by my yardstick. What the hell was going on? Even the smart young ladies had trouble making heads or tails out of his course. It was troubling all around, to say the least. I tried to chat him up in lab on a few occasions and even blurted out once that I wanted to be a doctor someday, more as an idealistic affirmation of the future than a well thought out plan. Maybe talking to him about my sincere science aptitude would give me some Brownie points? No such luck. I also mentioned that I was Estonian and he was Polish; we would have practically been neighbors in the Old World. I recall him listening to me half-heartedly as if instantly realizing that he was being schmoozed. Then one afternoon my friend F. came to me and said, "Maybe if we did an extra credit project he would give us some bonus points to give our shitty grades a boost?" Wow, now that's one *smart* pal I had. So, F. and I stayed after class one day and pressed our luck by browbeating Mr. A.G. into giving us a chance to raise our averages with a "researched" science endeavor. To our limited knowledge, no student had successfully done this before on her/his own volition but there we were, begging him for a chance to get ahead. And it worked. A week later found us after school, in his classroom, ready to convince him of our scientific know-how. However, we were not alone, there was another adult present in that room – Mr. F., the new seventh grade life science teacher, who had taken the reins after the retirement of the beloved and Caucasian-challenged Mr. V.N. Well, it turned out that the two bachelor science instructors lived together as roommates outside of town. Whether they had previously known each other in college I did not know. So, Mr. F. pulled up a chair and had a bemused look on his face as F. and I proceeded with our dissertation. Suffice it to say that our subject matter was unimportant at the time. What was important was getting Mr. A.G. to give us those vaunted extra credit points. We talked over each other, we made jokes, and we tried various methods of explaining ourselves to the two laughing hyenas in front of us. Were they laughing with us or at us? Was the absurdity of the situation that funny? We couldn't tell. But I guess two asinine adolescents desperately gesturing and verbalizing plagiarized scientific jargon nonstop for an hour was worth something, at least for the entertainment value alone? I hoped they would take pity on us and Mr. A.G. would keep his promise. We finished our God-awful orations as they both clapped and cheered sarcastically. It was late, so they decided to drive us home, chuckling all the way at the audacity of our presentation. First though, Mr. A.G. dropped Mr. F. off at their pad, a tilted and grungy-looking double-wide trailer just outside of town that they were temporarily renting. I looked at my friend in the back seat and quietly remarked that teachers probably didn't make all that much money if they were forced to live in such humble accommodations. Anyway, we arrived at our respective houses without being kidnapped or molested in any way. This was 1973 you know, when things like that rarely occurred, remember? Plus, we were boys in a mostly heterosexual world back then. If they had been Catholic priests or Boy Scout leaders, perhaps things would have turned out differently, but, no, we were safe. And we got those additional points added to our second quarter grades. Yay! Finally, I could say that I had a solid B average, at least for one quarter. It wasn't great but not crappy either. F. and I had pulled off a scholastic stunt that was to be repeated in different forms for years to come. We made a great team, whether fiddling together in the orchestra, pretending to sing in the varsity choir, or cleverly bamboozling teachers and fellow students for our enjoyment and benefit. Our friendship only grew, and I was grateful for it, as was F.

14

The Artful Codger

I selected Studio in Art with Mrs. S. as an elective because I fancied myself artistically inclined, even after being browbeaten and demeaned by the previous junior high art teacher, Mr. L. You know, the long haired, mustachioed Salvador Dali-type who was addicted to Zotz and was probably frustrated teaching drawing and painting to unwilling and untalented fellow rednecks. That guy. I was his favorite "whipping boy" in seventh and eighth grades, although my final grades were A's, for both years. Anyway, I had signed up for art once more as a ninth grader. Why not? But what was that dufus SENIOR doing in our class? Most of the kids were freshmen and sophomores, why was HE lurking around and acting like a buffoon without taking a seat? Great, just great, he decided to sit next to me on the first day of school. Crap. He was a widely known loquacious bozo, full of bull and stories, mostly about himself and his idiotic ideologies. No one wanted to hear his tired *shtick*, especially me. I pretended not to listen or notice but it was just too late. And after the sultry and mellow Mrs. S. (our aged dentist's granddaughter) implored us to choose a partner for the year, I was doomed.

Why did he have to *platz* next to me? Why? And now I was his art-mate? Shit! I was a thin and immature frosh, he, a looming and grown man, with vestiges of a beard. I, on the other hand, hardly had any chest hairs at the time. He didn't belong in this class yet there he was, legitimately enrolled and artfully ready for action. Was he though? Well, yes and no. In spite of his flair for the dramatic, his limited artsy talents basically consisted of cribbing off of my creations and getting easy A's for the duration of the scholastic year. But wait; there was more to him and the course…. Mrs. S., the sullen and outwardly banal art teacher, was a hometown product and well-regarded graduate of our school. That may have explained her recent hiring. I guessed she knew about all things "artistic" because she was always prepared and seemed to give adequate demonstrations to the mostly unskilled labor in front of her. After the five-minute intro she would methodically put on Carole King's *Tapestry* album and play it for the entire period, flipping it as needed on the turntable, over and over again. This went on every day, mind you. Although kind and gentle, Mrs. S. had this sadness about her and when approached with suggestions for other vocal artists, she would look away in a melancholy manner and not respond to the query. But one day she surprised us by playing Terry Jacks' latest LP, with his famous cover – *Seasons in the Sun*. Jacks was okay, a troubled troubadour that seemed to resonate with the sorrowful Mrs. S. So, we painted, molded clay, drew, colored, played with plaster, fired porcelain, etc., all that while humming along to King and Jacks and deliriously immersed in our artwork. Unlike my older and glommed-on sidekick K.M., who continued his curious habit of singing *Doors'* songs to himself, most notably when stressed. He loved the *Doors*, especially lead singer/ songwriter Jim Morrison, and often waxed poetic about the band, as if its lyrics touched his very soul. Mrs. S. never reprimanded him and only increased *Tapestry's* decibel level as a counterbalance to his inappropriate vocalizations. My senior "partner" was full of boastful stories, one of which was his supposed prowess as a basketball player. He would often wear a Milwaukee Bucks jersey with the name Jabbar emblazoned on the back. Kareem Abdul-Jabbar (the former Ferdinand Lewis Alcindor Jr., before he changed his name and conveniently converted to Islam to avoid the Vietnam war draft as a "religious objector" in 1971), was his NBA hero and he patterned his "game" after him. Jabbar often used a patented skyhook shot but he was over seven feet tall. I doubted that K.M. used the same shot with effectiveness at five foot ten! Nevertheless, during virtually every art period, K.M. would regale me ad nauseum with fetching stories about his basketball skills and gamesmanship. I surmised it was a big part of his life and character. He told me that he diligently practiced nightly at his hoop at home and regularly played against stiff competition. He wasn't even on the varsity team at our school! What stiff competition: his brothers and sisters or the neighboring Guernsey cows in the field next to his house? Give me a break. But I listened politely and unintentionally validated his delusions of basketball grandeur. It was easier that way than arguing with a *madman*. However, one day he started a campaign to cajole our school's assistant varsity basketball coach, and soon-to-be head coach, into a one-on-one game against him. Mr. Fokay, the tall and talented former basketball stand-out alumnus, who also doubled as a coach and junior high math teacher, was unresponsive for a long time. But daily needling from K.M. and a groundswell of satirical and teasing support from his fellow male classmates eventually produced a "dream" high school matchup: Mr. Fokay versus K.M. in a clash of "basketball titans" at the gym during lunchtime. Mr. Fokay's pride had finally caved and he agreed to the competition. Wow, it was unprecedented, and most likely unwarranted. But the administration brass officially sanctioned the horseplay and it was Game On! Months of loud trash talking by K.M. had made this into a

David and Goliath adversarial archetype, and "it" would finally be settled once and for all. At least, that's what K.M. had been endlessly telling me for weeks. He had built up this epic battle in his mind whereas I'm sure Mr. Fokay just wanted to trash him and teach an unathletic, bragging bullshitter a lesson. And the latter happened as kids crowded the gym and stood in line to witness the one-sided spectacle. I did not attend the beat-down, but I heard it was ugly. Mr. Fokay won handily without K.M. sinking a single shot, regardless of wearing a headband, sweatbands and his favorite Bucks jersey. Of course, I had to hear the endless verbal repercussions from a visibly depressed and sulking K.M. for days after that embarrassing debacle, which I reminded him that he had brought upon himself. I had never envisioned being his juvenile sounding board, but it happened. He was prone to confiding in me as if he had no other close friends and I never betrayed his innate trust in me, except for now, exposing some of it for you readers. He eventually came out of his downward spiraling funk and sort of rejoined the here and now, but sometimes it was hard to tell. Because he was oftentimes very expressive in his many moods, they no longer alarmed me; I was used to his quixotic personality and started to befriend him by year's end. He was okay, a bit kooky and spooky, but okay, nonetheless; we ended up having a

Lennie and George (*Of Mice and Men*) kind of
relationship. Back then, all of us students were struggling
with self-esteem issues, acne, puberty, and how to best fit
into the bedraggled and confusing '70s. It wasn't only him;
I was included in that bunch as well. Even the so-called
"well-adjusted inmates" had problems on the inside; some
just effectively masked it or sublimated their feelings of
inferiority and perceived persecution with drugs, cigs or
booze. Sometimes it was all three. However, I did notice K.
M. emotionally hurting more and more as the year dragged
on, especially after being shot down by S.L. as a potential
prom date. Sophomore student and cheerleader S.L. WAS
arguably the hottest blonde babe in our entire institution
at the time and had her pick of male escorts and sexual
consorts. And as expected, I heard that she rather cavalierly
and openly burst K.M.'s overinflated bubble when he asked
her to accompany him. It was yet another devastating cut
to his already wounded psyche. But why did he set himself
up for constant failure and rejection? He never wanted to
stay in his lane and he got punished for it. But didn't all of
us want to upgrade and move upward and onward in our
lives? Unfortunately, only HE blatantly and repeatedly
stuck his neck out and tended to live in a fantasy world of
his own making. And he was often ridiculed for it. I often
wondered if psychological therapy would have helped

K.M. and to quiet the inner demons he was fighting. Perhaps he was getting professional counseling/medical treatment and that was the best that he could be? I don't recall having simple answers to any of those difficult questions. Anyhow, he ended up not going with any girl to that prized dance and I had to console him once again after yet another blow to his fractured and fragile ego. The academic year ended as K.M. and I glazed our last paltry pottery projects together and said our mutual goodbyes, which were tearful on his part. I was all set for summer vacation….and then I heard the unthinkable: K.M. had taken his own life a few weeks after graduating and the word on the street was that he was listening to his favorite *Doors'* eight-track tape ballad *When the Music's Over* when his life expired. The choice of tune was eerily appropriate and poignant; however his untimely demise remains a horrible tragedy. Rest in peace if you can, K.M. I still think of you, which is a lasting legacy in itself.

15

Florida or Bust

Holy moly, 1973 was turning out to be quite the year. Although a few positive accomplishments did grace our planet, such as ABBA, the Bee Gees, the Concorde intercontinental airplane, the disastrous Vietnam War "officially" ending, and the launch of Skylab, the vast majority of the "news" was in the dumpster. Vice President Spiro T. Agnew resigned, the Watergate scandal was gaining momentum, the Sioux Indians occupied Wounded Knee, abortion was now federally legal, OPEC cut oil production and raised the wholesale price of crude by 200% because of our and many other nations' support of Israel during the Yom Kippur War, the Bahamas gained independence from Great Britain (are you kidding me?), "streaking" became popular, and Basque freedom fighters had killed the Spanish prime minister. Whew! Yet there was my conservative old man, uncharacteristically plotting and planning our first family road trip to Florida as if oblivious to the country's distressful convolutions. But why go in the winter of '73? Perhaps his bon vivant optimism was instead fueled by a doomsday feeling: The opinion on the street was that America was going to hell in a hand basket so maybe we should go to the sunshine state for our Christmas vacation because we may never get the chance again! "Kids, get in the fuckin' car if you want to eat real Florida oranges, see a damn palm tree, and swim in the warm Atlantic," he seemed to be telling my younger sister and me, although he rarely swore. I added those curse words, sorry. Perhaps that former sentence was a bit harsh and unwarranted, however, it may have been the truth for my dad was always a very logical thinker and prided himself on usually sound decisions. Through pop's very wealthy cousin from Indiana, Aunt M., my mom secured an inexpensive room in a beach motel called Casa Juno. Aunt M., her husband, son G., and prissy mother-in-law traveled to Florida in style in their spacious converted van. And they went thrice yearly and like clockwork, irrespective of oil embargos, etc. We would be meeting up with them at their spacious three-bedroom beachfront condo apartment (not a time share) in Juno Beach when we arrived. Meanwhile, for us poor northern pikers, spiking gasoline prices and national fuel shortages hurt, and a worried W. Cronkite reminded us nightly about them. My parents were more than slightly concerned, and it showed. But at least there was the CB (Citizens Band) radio craze to look forward to on our trek southward. The oil crisis, coupled with the newly imposed 55 mph velocity

limit and fuel rationing, seemed to inspire and galvanize
redneck truckers into a loose consortium of
antigovernment protesters on the highways, with ordinary
citizens piling on. Although CB radios were in use since
the late '40s, the '70s fanatical fad caught on with non
truckers fed up with a lot of "things" back then. The
in-your-face, antiauthority, clandestine purveyors of dissent
ridden communications used popular channel 19 on the
free radio network to broadcast varied opinions regarding
political and driving displeasure, while cloaked behind
"handles" that did not reveal their identities. Actually, it
was mainly used to locate diesel sources for big rigs as well
as to narc on speed traps and cops (smokeys) lurking on
the newly speed-reduced roads. I'm sure that if the initially
inane radio correspondences had indeed turned into a
nationwide "revolution," the FBI, CIA and "deep state"
would have squashed any such movement by confiscations
of the *walkie talkies* and incarcerated the perpetrators. And
Radio Shack would not have been allowed to sell the CB
units anymore, period. But as things stood, it was just a
"harmless" exercise in freedom of speech "allowed" by
Nixon's paranoid goon squad at the time. Pop was ready, as
he expertly mounted the expensive, cream-colored, Pace
CB radio under the dashboard of his 1965, green colored,
Rocket V-6, F-85 Oldsmobile station wagon; the very car

that would carry us on that southern trek, a pilgrimage
similar to the future 1980's National Lampoon vacation
movies starring the fictional Griswold family, although WE
were the dysfunctional "originals." Mom was overpacking,
as if anticipating more than gasoline shortages in the Deep
South, while dad and I carefully attached two, ten-gallon
steel canisters containing regular Mobil gasoline (his
favorite brand) to the chrome-plated roof racks on the
station wagon. We used thin wood planks as a base, ropes,
and a wooden wind deflector shield that was placed in
front of the extra fuel jugs to negate wind resistance. Wow,
pop meant business. I guessed he really wanted to revisit
Florida again, in spite of the televised warnings by *CBS
News*, the only "fake news" that we "religiously" watched
back then. I mean, sometimes W. Cronkite would come
out with the truth, but his lies about Vietnam War
statistics, such as the seemingly small number of daily
deaths of American troops, were unforgivable. It was either
because of his political sense not to alarm the country or
from an order given to him from higher ups. Regardless,
we cynically didn't always believe him after that. So
perhaps this gas shortage was overblown as well? Pop
hoped for the best. Anyhow, my parents had been to that
wondrous tropical state once before as dating love-birds,
back in the late '50s (they had traveled there in a manual

transmission, 1950 Oldsmobile 88 sedan WITH my paternal grandparents), so they kind of knew the lay of the land and what to expect on the long journey. But it was all new to my sis and me. As pop counted out the cash for the two-week trip (my family did not use credit cards, traveler's checks or even possess a dining card), my sister and I excitedly packed our suitcases with clothing for all seasons, which proved to be excessive yet smart. Mom was doing the same thing, in addition to preparing and storing mounds of food rations for the ride. There was no way in hell we were going to foolishly spend a nickel on nourishment along the way, she seemed to imply. The car was loaded, and I mean loaded. Besides the usual, extra coats, hats, raingear, shoes, etc. were tossed into the back of the station wagon at the last minute as my father grew more and more agitated and exasperated. He could hardly see out the back, what with the fishing poles and metal containers of cookies piled up high in his line of rear view sight. And the weight of it all! He kept checking the rear tires and exclaimed that we were taking too much shit, but mom would always interject and remind him not to blame her later for forgetting "something." We left at four in the morn, during a raging snowstorm, with Grandpa Pete waving goodbye as pop slowly drove down our unplowed street and onto an unplowed county roadway. But the

weather improved and, besides the ice storm delay on route
81 in Pennsylvania, we were trucking and laughing along to
the CB banter and AM radio. I was too shy to talk on the
CB at first, plus I was sitting in the back seat. The
Oldsmobile did not have FM, just AM reception. So, in
between noshing on homemade snacks and endlessly
listening to the current pop songs such as *My Love* by Paul
McCartney and Wings, and Jim Croce's *Bad, Bad Leroy
Brown*, we kept motoring, however, we passed by many
closed Mobil gas stations and pop became slightly fretful.
God forbid he should taint his Olds with Esso excrement
or Texaco tar oil, as he put it. Sure, we had the back up
emergency fuel up on the roof, but that was for a real
emergency. So, while my dad drove and worried, my
normally intelligent and nonhearing impaired sister and I
kept on fighting while in the back seat. She insisted that
Helen Reddy's hit song was pronounced "Hilta Dawn,"
while I fought back and said it was in fact *Delta Dawn*.
And, she also misconstrued Maureen McGovern's tune *The
Morning After*, calling it "The Moaning After" instead. Of
course, being played virtually nonstop on all the AM
stations thus far made us bicker every few minutes, no
matter how many times pop turned the dial. Finally, we
saw an open Mobil station next to a Stuckey's, on the
border of Maryland. We were officially in the south, at

least that's what we thought after passing the Mason-Dixon
Line and Gettysburg. And Stuckey's must be a southerly
store, for we had never heard of it before. So, while dad
was swearing and filling up the tank with "inflated" 60
cent per gallon gasoline (39 cents was the norm back
home), mom, sis and I went inside the nearby store
because of the giant billboard on its roof advertising the
scrumptious Giant Pecan Roll. What the heck was that?
We had promised each other not to spend any money on
frivolous bullshit and out we walked to the car, each of us
smiling and clutching an unwrapped, foot-long, pecan-
encrusted, nougat filled, "log" of sugary goodness. Mom
gave my dad a bite and he became a convert on the spot.
At that moment, perhaps we should have discarded all the
tins of "dough" that mom had painstakingly made for our
pioneering excursion, and lightened the auto as well? We
did not, however. And then, the unthinkable happened.
No, I didn't get yelled at for buying a small confederate
flag at the Maryland Welcome Center, but something
worse. As the conscripted co-pilot, somehow my backseat
map reading and navigational skills had gone awry and we
got off-track. My father did not blame me because the road
signage was confusing. But it was getting dark and we were
disoriented and hopelessly lost in downtown Baltimore, in
a dilapidated and sketchy section to boot. Now what do we

do? My furious attempts at finding our way out of the maze of beltways and on-off ramps had proved futile. It was time to ask for directions on how to get back to route I-95 South. Dad inched into a darkened, barred up service station even though his gas tank was more than half full. We anxiously waited at the pumps and were about to drive away when a grizzled black man suddenly bolted out of the office and ran at us at full speed. I thought my mother was going to have a heart attack. Pop jumped out of the car and politely told him to fill-'er-up, and then asked for directions to 95. Things were going to be OK, nothing deleterious was going to happen, and then "it" happened: The attendant finished filling up our auto's tank with an off-label brand of gasoline, pop winced but nervously paid him, and we were about to leave when the dark-skinned gentleman remarked, "Check yo uhl, suh?" Of course, pop didn't know what he said and had him say it once more. "Check yo uhl, suh?" the man repeated, this time in an angry voice. My father still couldn't make it out and started to panic. It sounded like he said, "Check your ulcer?" Was that right? When the guy violently popped our car's hood, then it dawned on dad what he was going to do. "Oh, check your oil, sir" pop smilingly said in Estonian-accented English to a visibly offended and linguistically confused man who was probably as shocked to see a scared white family in a bad part of the city as we were in trying to comprehend him and his southern drawl. Our "oil" was fine, and my dad thanked him up and down for checking it as we slowly drove away, with him still standing there staring at us. That was rich considering that we were sometimes mistreated as "foreigners" up north in our own village yet here we were instantly labeled as those "damn Yankees." We were back on the highway but truly ready for some vittles and rest. But where? Good lord, not in a motel! My folks were allergic to them, even cheap ones. They still cost money ($19.99 per night at a Days Inn) and we could possibly get our stuff ripped off if the car was left unguarded all night. Hell no! Hello, rest areas. (My parents were way ahead of their time by knowingly practicing social distancing before it became a government edict such as during the CHINESE coronavirus pandemic of 2020). Pop decided to keep on driving while we all ate mom's yummy Polish sausage sandwiches. But then, just as I was about to fall asleep and abrogate my copilot duties, I saw that first funny sign that made me wake up my sister. It read, "Chili Today, Hot Tamale." There was a cartoonish figure of a guy named Pedro in one corner and the miles left to go to get to *South of the Border*, which turned out to be our new landing place. The comical and colorful placards started to appear regularly and frequently, in politically incorrect Mexican-speak, such as "No Monkey Business, Joost Yankee Panky." My sister and I stayed awake just to read the adverts out loud and to "force" my bleary-eyed father into stopping in Dillon, South Carolina, at the supposed stop of all stops. Dad only took a few pee breaks at the ensuing highway rest areas; he was also hell bent on making it to the Coffee Casa at Pedro's place as well. Meanwhile, I had switched seats with mom and sat next to the CB radio, and started timidly talking – "Breaker one nine, this here's the Purple Pansy on 95 heading down to Dillon; anyone got their ears on? Come on back." It was CB lingo and you had to use it to fit in. I had thought of that effeminate sounding "handle" all by myself and foisted it on the public! A few truckers replied, stated that they saw no smokeys (cops), had my back door closed (were behind our car and would warn me if they saw any), and asked me what my 20 was (location based on mile markers or closest towns/exits). I was a big shot but did more listening than speaking and finally just sat back and dozed as the late-night communications continued nonstop on that CB Radio. It was funny as hell, sometimes provocative and even my old man enjoyed it. Plus, it kept him awake, all the way onto the exit and the expansive parking lot at *South of the Border*. We had made it and were now officially about halfway to our ending place.

Hurray! And what a sight we beheld. Open 24/7, it had tons of glittery neon lights, a huge gaudy gasoline station, tacky Mexican-motif shops, multiple restaurants, and a large motel that graced the humongous property just off exit 1B. And the huge fireworks building immediately caught my eye. While pop caught some much needed shuteye in the locked car, mom, sis and I checked out every possible location, including the fireworks shop. I must have spent twenty dollars of my own birthday money in there, buying Black Cat firecrackers, bottle rockets, Roman Candles, cherry bombs, M-80s and specialty stink bombs. It was a boys' dream come true, to load up on stuff that was illegal in New York State. We also purchased a few Mexican trinkets that were made in Japan or China and then retreated to our car to eat our own food and rest for a few hours. The whole layout was basically a glammed-up rip-off. A pseudo "theme park" promising an authentic Mexican flavor yet chintzing out and delivering cheap, flimsy goods and meals at expensive prices. Only much later did I learn that an Orthodox Jewish family actually owned the joint, which started decades earlier as a kosher beer distributorship. From beer to burritos and through clever marketing, the "family business" stayed afloat and prospered one way or another. There was nothing Mexican about it, save for the racist stereotypical portrayal of lazy

Pedro, the sombrero-wearing and mustachioed "mascot" of the park. But still, it was a fun place to stop and visit. Before dawn, we filled up on "expensive" Phillips 66 gasoline (not Mobil) and got back to driving. Interestingly, there were plenty of stations open for business, regardless of the dire warnings that were continuously broadcast on the radio. At the border of Georgia, both pop and I started to hear a rhythmic thudding sound emanating from the left rear wheel. Uh-oh, trouble. And about this same time, route 95 abruptly ended, sending all cars onto route 301 and other "local" roads. It was a caravan of slow-moving cars with mostly New York plates on them, meandering through bankrupt-looking villages that had a token gas station and a Crazy Ed's or Crazy Tom's fireworks emporium along the roadway. Evidently route 95 was not finished in long stretches and the detours forced the long line of drivers, whose destinations were Florida, to bond with one another, at least for a short time. And some of the northern cars even had gas cans on their respective roofs, just like ours. Finally, we fit in! Now about that thumping noise. Dad had to pull into one of those dinky and dirty local service stations that people always warn you not to pull into, for fear of being charged an arm and a leg by unscrupulous locals looking for unwary suckers. Luckily, the attendant that helped us was honorable. Expensive, but honorable. It turned out that the wheel had a busted bearing and a piece of the tire had shredded off. It would have blown sooner than later and possibly caused a nasty accident. Now, while mom and sis went to a nearby boiled peanut stand to investigate the offerings, pop haggled with the serviceman about fixing our problem. About two hundred fifty dollars, a brand new wheel bearing, and a Dunlop tire later, we were back on the road again, with me sampling the bacon-flavored carton of mushy peanuts that mom had bought. At least the moon pie desserts washed down that nasty nutty aftertaste. Pop was down some serious cash and boisterously blamed two things: my mom for overloading the car which caused the bearing to snap, and Firestone, for making such shitty tires. After that ordeal, my father rightly or wrongly swore off Firestone tires for life. Meanwhile, my sister and I had caught a glimpse of our first palm tree, read the billboards for Piggly Wiggly Supermarkets, Starvin' Marvin convenience stores, and were ready for fresh orange juice at the Florida Welcome station just up ahead, on route I-95. At least that's what the sign on the highway said. But first we made pop stop the car on the right shoulder so sis and I could chase a nearsighted armadillo. It was the first live one we had ever seen and I'm sure locals laughed their asses off while watching us try to corral it against our car. We HAD to do it, you know. It was late morning, none of us had showered and had that disheveled look going on, however, we were in Florida. And we repeatedly kept going back at least thrice apiece for the free orange juice at that welcome station. Man, it tasted divinely. Dad promptly took a nice long rest as did we, until the sun started to bake us in the car. We were hot, sweaty and euphoric; we were finally in the Sunshine State! But wait, while we were needlessly dawdling, precious time was ticking away. We had at least seven more hours to go before we could crash at our reserved motel room. Crap. Florida was a long state, darn it. Dad put the pedal to the metal, started cussing under his breath, and drove like a champ, past Jacksonville, St. Augustine, Vero Beach and Jupiter. During that last bit of driving, dad kept on remarking in amazement about the Floridian transformation. Instead of shacks and dumpy motels dotting the seaboard like in the '50s, huge condominiums were now blocking the skylight and beach access areas. He lamented that he should have borrowed five grand back in the day to buy some cheap oceanfront property. By now he would have been an easy millionaire. Who knew that the scrubby and swampy, gator-infested, sandy land would be so valuable someday, and just because it kissed the sea? Who knew? But some enterprising people did. Just not pop. Oh, well. At last, by evening we had arrived at Juno Beach, exited off to route 1, followed by A1A and then, there it was, the grand and stately Casa Juno. Mom went in to register and came right back out flustered. What, we weren't booked there? What the hell? What do we do now? She went back inside and begged the staff to call Aunt M.'s number. Mom came out again and announced to us that Aunt M. had changed her mind and got us a reservation at a boffo motel closer to her condo complex. It was called Juno by the Sea. Pop was exhausted; just one more delay or snafu would have put him over the edge. He was ready to go ballistic a few times on the trip down and this last minute change of venue was almost the last straw. However, he drove a few minutes north and there it was, the right lodging, complete with '50s-era styling, an outdoor unheated pool, and a cracked concrete shuffleboard court. We had made it, and never touched a drop of gas from off the Olds' rooftop. I have to say that for such a seemingly pokey, cynical and pessimistic bloke, my old man was tough as nails and rather perseverant once the undertaking began in earnest. Not easily rattled in the face of adversity, he inadvertently taught me about being a manly man on that southern sojourn. It was unlike my own family treks years later, which usually involved passively flying, unlimited snacking, and mind-numbing computer games and cell phone usage by my children. I was no traveling role model for my son, or daughter for that matter. Anyway, back to 1973. We unpacked, ate the rest of mom's provisions, changed into bathing suits and hit the ocean at eight o'clock at night. The full moon looked great and gave us much needed light as we frolicked in the warm waves. I marveled that we were privileged enough to partake in such hedonistic and pleasurable activities while over a thousand miles away from snow, inclement weather and my grumpy grandfather. I'm sure there were sharks around in the murky sea, but we were stupidly fearless back then and splashed with abandon before turning in to finally shower and sleep. That first tentative winter trip with my parents turned into a yearly affair, with my young wife and kids joining us decades later for all the same treats along the way: Pecan Rolls, Stuckey's, Shoney's, *South of the Border*, and Publix grocery stores, to name but a few. The relatively short winter vacations usually found us hobnobbing with our filthy rich relatives, fishing for bluefish, and kicking back some sand after settling in along the treasure coast, be it in a motel at Juno Beach, a rented trailer at Nettles Island, or a condo unit at Port St. Lucie. The trips home were usually uneventful, with a *South of the Border* bumper sticker firmly affixed to whichever car we took that year, and a large bag of Indian River oranges proudly laid out on the rear window ledge as a bragging badge of honor for having made the arduous automobile ride down and back. However, we eventually stopped traveling by car. My parents got physically older as did my wife, kids and I; no one wanted to drive that far anymore. The hardships and deprivations along the way weren't worth the effort. Gone was the thrill of the trip; the ending was now the only prize. Flying became the new option, with my family and I doing the obligatory Disney, Universal Studios and Busch Gardens "routines" a few times. However, La Paz, Mexico and Great Harbour Cay in the Bahamas have been our destinations as of late due to my ownership of beachfront homes there. The travel time is much shorter, the beaches are much, much nicer, and the accommodations are first rate. In addition, we can fly down there whenever we like and stay for free. However, you just can't put a price on those automobile adventures of the seventies, the zeal and messianic machinations of the ride, and the exaltation on finally reaching Florida!

16

Squirt Gun Warfare

It was springtime, when, traditionally, men's fancies turn to the opposite sex. However, something completely different swayed the male ardor in our Podunk school for those two or three fleeting weeks, something that could not readily be explained. Yes, squirt gun mania grabbed hold of huge swaths of the boys as a yearly high school ritual. Girls did not usually participate in those sophomoric hijinks, and not just freshmen were involved. Grade 9-12 *boyz*, including me, willingly, covertly and maliciously engaged in shooting streams of water at other students in classrooms, hallways, the lunchroom, restrooms, etc. But why? No one knew for sure but all it took was one squirt of liquid during an uneventful day and before you knew it, you could be doused at any time, from around any corner. Teachers and the administration wonks were often blindsided by the sudden appearance of bovine hypodermic syringes, and all shapes and sizes of plastic devices to discharge water from. Of course it was illegitimate; of course it violated school policies and decorum. That's why we boys did it! Duh! However, if you "open carried" your "weapon" it was instantly taken away.

If the truly insolent or stupid were repeatedly caught in the act, harsher punishment was doled out. I remember concealing a Greenie Meanie in my waistband, just for defensive purposes, you know. If someone got me good in the hallway, they would get a return shot to the back of the head as they turned to leave. So I was a backbiter, so what; I did what I had to do to prevent from being disrespected by the older students. Sometimes, however, the guns would leak and give away the troublemaker with telltale water stains on his britches. Technical difficulties happened and the teacher would gain a free toy for her/his children. And the lines to the boys' restrooms were often long and not because of urinary urgency or to smoke a Marlboro, but to refill a discharged squirt gun. But, like all fads, it was over within a month, after much ado from the school officials. Hordes of water pistols were confiscated and mysteriously vanished. No one knew exactly where they disappeared to and none were ever returned to the owners. I reverently cleaned and put mine away for the following year, you know, just in case of trouble.

17

More Fun in English

I'm not trying to sugarcoat my time in Mrs. N.'s ninth grade English class, but, to be fair, it was a blast. Yes, we had to work, and we had nightly homework. And some of it was monotonous, as well. It was all about writing responses to questions regarding reading assignments, writing various speeches for upcoming oral presentations, reading literature, etc.; you know how it was. It was a relatively easy course, so I really tried hard not to blow it. High school was officially upon me and I needed every high grade I could get to keep me in the running for a decent college and career someday. That's how I thought back then. I admit to being a bit mercenary because there was justified and silent outrage on the home front because of my prior lackluster scholastic performance in junior high, and pressure from myself to finally prove to everyone that I was indeed a good student. However, algebra was fairly difficult, earth science was a bear, German was so-so, gym was okay, social studies was a pip, orchestra rehearsals were comedic, art was a bore, and, lunch was lunch. It was a mixed bag of goodies, but I was elated and enthusiastic that English was in my wheelhouse for a guaranteed high average. However, I was only partly right. Little did I realize that no matter the friendliness of Mrs. N., we still had to perform to her perceived level of expectations. A low mark in the nineties was the best I could garner in her class, all four quarters. There I was, enjoying the class and mired in the muck of a low A average. Go figure! Mrs. N. would often congratulate me on jobs well done but her idea of a high grade was vastly different from mine. At least I had fun in her class. That was also the course where my piano teacher's daughter took an unexpected liking to me. I was between girls at the time (in my mind only, mind you) and never gave E.M. a second look; and there we were, together performing a Western-dialogued short play in front of the class as per a practiced project. There were five of us "thespians" randomly assigned by Mrs. N. to construct a ten-minute play involving the Old West. To be clear, I would never have selected the impresarios in my group. Two were painfully shy, the others nervous, and they were all girls, except for me! The resulting sheriff-villain themed act (I was the sheriff and E.M. was my deputy) devolved into a comedy because I was involved and had a knack, or bad fortune, to turn any serious proposition into a farce. However, E.M. seemed enamored with my style and sense of humor. During our brief classroom rehearsals, she would stare at me intently and nod approvingly, no matter my bawdy and flippant changes of the lines we were going to utter. I think she genuinely liked me, and I unwittingly appreciated the attention from a female. However, outwardly she was not my type. She was not a blonde with assets, such as Hottie Blondie, my blonde and *built* wife of forty-plus years. Flat-chested, slightly gawky and rail thin, with horn-rimmed glasses and dark curly hair, E.M. had known I existed since kindergarten, and she seemed finally armed with the gumption to go for me. She had a great smile and personality but that's as far as it went. We rehearsed, we acted, and then disbanded, back to our mutual cliques. We got a very good grade and managed to crack up the class with our classless humor and wise retorts to each other. But I didn't know what to do afterwards. Should I have pursued her? Was she waiting for me to make a move? I wasn't sure if I really liked her that much after all. Nevertheless, I think our respective mothers would have heartily approved if I had started to hang out with her. It was all so confusing and short-lived at the time, however. Alas, the alleged romance was over, and English had ended. E.M. and I never hooked up and did not speak again until graduation, when I said a few syllables to her. She just looked at me with a blank stare, as if still pissed-off at an ineffectual male who did not respond in a positive way to

her obviously romantical (shout out to Olive Oyl)
overtures years ago. Okay, so maybe I missed some
primitive and awkward cues; so, what? Perhaps I HAD
"noticed" her correctly and just didn't react according to
her wishes? We were fourteen, old enough to know and old
enough to know better; at least I did.

18

No Spittoon

What was that gurgling sound I heard? And where was it coming from? I looked over to my right at the pupil seated in the adjacent row next to me: nothing unusual, just a poker face and a right hand furiously copying down the algebraic equations from the blackboard. Mrs. J.T. was rapidly lecturing at her usual, quick tempo clip, and students had to keep up. She was good and I finally understood math for the first time since about fifth grade. Algebra made sense to me, maybe not to others, but it did to me. Most of my other *smart* chums were a grade ahead of me in math; they were taking Geometry as ninth graders. I didn't care, Mrs. J.T. was getting through my thick, arithmetic-challenged skull and my math-whiz father's ego was ostensibly assuaged. He finally got off my back! My grades were high and my confidence in the numbers game had returned....What was that confounded noise? It sounded like someone was about to get sick. I think it was coming from behind me. Then, suddenly and without warning, N.S., the tobacco chewing, smoking, drinking, and all around nogoodnik sitting in the seat directly behind me barfed all over my back and the back of my wooden chair. He got some on himself as well. It turns out that he had forgotten to dispose of his big wad of Red Man after lunch and continued to swallow tobacco juice until he puked. There was no spittoon in algebra class, and he most likely felt that the hardwood floor was not a good place to spit on while being watched by others. So, he swallowed and then spat everything out onto my back! It was projectile vomiting at its finest. Too bad there was no award for his momentous and launching achievement. Mrs. J.T. turned toward the commotion and was at first clueless as to what had transpired. After being informed by a female snitch in the front row, she made a grossed out face and told N.S. and me to go to the nurse's station at once to get new clothing as she dialed up the janitor's office from the classroom phone. N.S. stared sheepishly at me as I sighed and forgave him as we both sullenly trudged down the stairs to the first floor to visit Mrs. D., the huge, portly nurse. I mean what the hell? What was the point of getting angry? Plus, he was much bigger than me, a freshman idiot in a man's body. He was known as a boneheaded student who was just going to leave school sooner than later. However, I was wrong, for he graduated on time with the rest of us "scholars." Who knew THAT would happen? But for now we were changing into ill-fitting spare shirts as custodians wiped up his mess in the math room. As we headed back to class Principal *Shag* appeared out of nowhere and demanded to know what we were doing in the first floor hallway in the middle of a period. And he meant business; you couldn't bullshit him. He had a nasty reputation as a volatile and vindictive administrator and relished straightening out wayward academicians. I could tell he was quizzically eyeballing me and probably wondered why I was standing next to one of his favorite "whipping boys." However, before he could ask any more questions, N.S. spoke up and told the truth. *Shag* laughed and did not punish him and gave me a consoling pat on the back. I was merely a victim of circumstance. As we sat down again in the newly scrubbed room, Mrs. J.T. kept asking N.S. if he was feeling okay and periodically glanced in our direction, as if disbelieving that such a juvenile and yucky transgression had occurred in her class. This was algebra, not some hoedown barbecue filled with drunk townies munching on gobs of Copenhagen and Skoal snuff. But this was still "Redneckville," so shit like that was bound to happen.

19

Glo-Flop

I swear I laughed when I heard it mentioned as his new derogatory nickname. Mr. A.G., my Earth Science teacher in ninth grade, now had a funny moniker! Ha, ha. Well, I and a bunch of other science nerds had him for Regents Earth Science, but it was basically the same as the watered-down regular course. And I mean it. Mr. A.G. was a newbie for our year in the fall of 1973 and certainly "acted" the part. Part hippie, with shoulder length hair, and part science teacher, he had a penchant for deliberately teaching over our heads and then demanding understanding and knowledge from us country bumpkins. Maybe he would have been alright for a private prep school, such as Albany Academy, but he was way too much for most of the simpleton minds in my rural mudhole-of-a school. Sure, he taught a Regents class which I was a part of, and that alone should have given him solace and vindication for his tough-love teaching methods. But, alas, even we "smart ones" didn't know what the hell he was lecturing about on most given days. Whether he tried to impress the administration with his brainpower or tried to control us *schleps* with endless stories of his superior education, I do not know. What I do know is that we scarcely learned anything of value, while ruminating on and supposedly studying meteorology, geography, geology, plate tectonics, measurement methods, etc. Our lab sessions were often humiliatingly complicated and difficult to execute; near the end of the year there was a nearly unanimous mutiny in his classroom! However, he would periodically sarcastically mollify us by stating that any ungrateful saps could always abdicate to the regular earth science sections if they wanted to. Where could you go when the year was almost over?! Give me a break! And I heard that the non-Regents course was just as hard as ours was. WTF? Then, things got worse…. Most of us dummies were sporting low B averages when Mr. A.G. had us buy the *Barron's* review books to help us prepare for the state Regents exam. He told us emphatically that the books would be aids only, kind of like a review outline and synopsis for a course well taught. We had a few months of schoolin' left, plenty of time to bone up on cumulo-nimbus clouds, the positions of retreating ice shelves and deep ocean trenches. You know, the backbones of esoteric earth science that nobody needed to know, at least none of the young village idiots and progeny of local buffoons. Well, some of us were the offspring of the "intelligent" college professors in town, but, still, after rubbing shoulders with the local redneck rebels' kids since kindergarten, we ended up essentially homogenized into one indifferent mass of clodhoppers with maybe a smattering of high I.Q. gray matter between us. We cracked open the *Barron's* bibles in class and quickly became shocked at all the questions that we could not answer. Mr. A.G. looked visibly ill, our Regents class followed suit, but we were sick and tired of feeling stupid and having learned so little from that long-haired galoot. However, we did not panic, although I did, but this definitely was the right time for it. With a few weeks to go, all my fellow pupils and I had no choice but to study that review book inside and out to quickly memorize salient factoids about the earth that we had failed to imbibe from Mr. A.G. We had other subjects to contend with and here I was nightly cramming earthly science stuff into my already stuffed cerebral cortex, all because of an ineffectual and arrogant teacher. I was pissed but doggedly kept at it, nonetheless. The exam came and went off on schedule; it had NOT been stolen by downstate dumbbell students like many other New York State Regents tests were in '74. And guess what, I scored a 90 on it; one of the highest marks in the class. It was a tough test, with multiple questions that had buffaloed me. But an A was an A. I felt relieved, suddenly liked Mr. A.G., and had a sense of accomplishment. I also learned something about myself. I could memorize large quantities of material in a short amount of time and recall most of it as needed. That personality trait or genetic predisposition or Mrs. G.'s special speed-reading course in sixth grade stood me well in pharmacy college and then dental school, years later. Oh, by the way, Glo was a contraction of Mr. A.G.'s last name with an appropriately added suffix – Flop!

20

Dorcus Giganticus

Okay, so we were a misbehaving bunch of unruly monkeys when Mr. L., the student teacher, opened up his pie hole to begin his spiel that day. Mrs. G.S., the regular Afro-Asian Studies lecturer, sat in the back of the room taking notes as the very tall, very disheveled looking, dark haired man stood in front of us not knowing quite what to do. We were expecting a deep baritone voice and a commanding performance from someone that tall and stern. What we got instead was a mealy-mouthed wuss. Was he anxious and suffering from a bit of the jitters or stage fright? Perhaps he was not confident in his knowledge of the material he was going to present? Were we too boisterous and disrespectful of a grown man starting his foray into teaching, which took him off his game? All of the above? Whatever, but he just couldn't cut it with us. And then he began to lisp and stammer causing us *boyz* to crack up even more. However, we kept looking around at the benevolent dictator, Mrs. G.S., to see how much we could get away with. She seemed stoic and tight-lipped as if to test Mr. L. and see if he had what it took to control us and pound some social studies sense into our bone heads. It appeared as if he had mastered neither skill, but he persevered, nevertheless. Well, this went on for weeks with him dribbling incoherent sentences out of his thin-lipped mouth and Mrs. G.S. glumly sitting cross-legged and shaking her head back and forth. She never reprimanded us, even when my buds G.P. and J. Logg stuffed leftover lunch sandwiches behind the bookcase under the large windows, and even when G.P and V.F. had a minor dustup in the back of class over something or other. It was weird to see boys mentally checked out in that class, especially since we had been relatively engaged whenever Mrs. G.S. ran the roost. The big show was finally over as Mr. L. left us to supposedly graduate himself. Mrs. G.S. took the helm once more and not a word was spoken about the recent fiasco in her class. Our male buffoonery instantly abated, and we got back to the business of studying about Kenya's first president Jomo Kenyatta and his Kikuyu tribal background as well as learning about the generic Moslems (not Muslims) in all "those" turban clad countries with a "stan" ending. We were not taught about the different sects of Islam or even how England had artificially partitioned that part of the world into sovereign "countries" upon its leaving. We learned about the ancient intellectual Egyptians and the pyramids, the majestic Mesopotamian cradle of civilization, and how the "naughty" ensuing

Ottoman Empire devoured the known world; and then how "modern" Arabs got their comeuppance as backwards thinking religious Bedouins espousing theocracies instead of copying the "civilized and enlightened" western democracies. By the way, Confucius (Kong Fuzi) got his duck from Peking and not Beijing and, the Great Wall of China was a dubious wonder and a waste of bricks; the Mongol hordes got around it at will. That's how and what we were taught; an obviously biased, racist and skewed view of Africa and Asia. Their existence was merely a historical geography lesson for us with no real importance attached to actual people living there. They were there for our colorful amusement and jaundiced education. I'm sure we learned plenty, but our lectures were highly tinged with a colonial attitude that emanated from our textbook and from the state-sponsored gospel spouting out of Mrs. G.S. But, hey, the most powerful and influential country on earth wrote our history books so....

21

Making the Tennis Team

It was a foregone and anticlimactic conclusion that I
would make the varsity tennis team as a freshman peon. As
previously stated, I had the right coaching, the right
strokes, a decent serve, and had competed in many
arranged matches at my age level as an adolescent. I was all
set to saunter into that first tennis meeting arranged by
Coach P., take my rightful spot and automatically assume
the number one position on the varsity team. Wrong. I
walked into the athletic room next to the gym, sat down
and looked over the ten or so perennially losing tennis
schlubs who sat there glumly, staring at the floor. Recently
hired Coach P., who also doubled as the seventh grade
reading teacher, introduced me as the next best thing since
sliced Wonder Bread, but no one even looked up; some
senior players even snickered out loud. I was the youngest
player at that meeting and even though most of the
upperclassmen there had heard of me from the tennis
circles in town, none came forward to ingratiate themselves
to me, or to even congratulate me for trying out. Coach P.
then proceeded to tell us about the ladder system,
challenge matches and formats of playing each other. I

didn't realize that I had to play and win many matches among my own team members just to get a coveted spot on the roster. What the heck? He knew how good I was, he had seen me blast the ball from both wings and he knew about my winning percentage among the village players. All these infantile team machinations were below me I thought. I admit it; I was an arrogant prick and thought the top spot would be handed to me with no questions asked. It didn't happen. Seniority played a BIG part on the team. Let me explain. Besides starting rigorous physical workouts in the remaining foot deep snow by late March, we players also had to frequently shovel off the four, shitty, gritty, steel-netted, gravel courts with metal shovels given to us by laughing bus garage mechanics. And after a few days of primitive drills in the cold weather, we started to challenge each other in sanctioned matches to determine the pecking order and lineup of the team. I immediately challenged last year's number one, senior captain J.M., and proceeded to knock him around the court and led 4-3 before Coach P. uncharacteristically stopped play. I claimed victory, but Coach P. said I had not won by two games, so it was inconclusive. What? I felt screwed. The next day I challenged J.P., a junior and the number two guy, and was leading 5-4 when Coach P. suddenly ran onto the court waving his arms and hands to stop the match. Result?

Inconclusive. I was getting hot under the collar. The third day I challenged my best friend F.'s older brother, senior R.F., and was ahead 5-0 when Coach P. maddeningly charged the court and intervened to halt the carnage. I hadn't won 6-0 so the result was again, inconclusive. So, technically I had not beaten the top three players. I complained to him and he cavalierly said that upperclassmen, and especially twelfth graders, ruled! What? I thought he wanted to win. So, what position would I play? He assigned me the number four slot on the six-man singles team but that infuriated the two seniors that were demoted to play number five and six. "Why is a freshman douche bag ahead of me?" I heard R.S. announce angrily. Now, R.S. was the star and starting quarterback of our varsity football team as well as the starting point guard on the varsity basketball team, and here was a no-account frosh stealing his tennis thunder. He later apologized to me after I had soundly whipped him and J.H. (the sixth man) multiple times to retain my number four ranking. I was much better than they, what can I say? I believe that since R.S.'s father and my pop shared an office together at our village college, words were exchanged among the parental professors which prompted R.S. to back off being such a *jockstrap* and to stop openly harassing me. Anyway, I should have been the number one seed, but was ostensibly relegated to number four to appease the senior captain and seniority structure of our team. And every time I challenged up to usurp the status quo, there was always some kind of conflict or excuse used for not letting me play those losers at the top. And they WERE losers, losing most of the season's matches. It wasn't fair but at least I had made the team. My best friend F. was also on the team, but only as a backup doubles player. He rarely saw any action but sporadically practiced with me and, played as needed. I finished the short spring season with a 7-2 singles record, losing two hard fought matches to stacked players from Cobleskill and Newark Valley, respectively. Stacked? That's when the opposing coach has his number one player play down a few spots to get a guaranteed win. I was the sucker that ended up playing those excellent respective senior guys on two rainy and windy occasions. I shouldn't have lost to either but raindrops on my glasses obscured my vision and slipping through puddles of water with smooth-soled Jack Purcell sneakers was a bitch. My coach also stacked me a few times, and I became part of winning schemes on his part. It was all part of the gamesmanship of high school varsity tennis; accumulating the best possible win-loss record, and I very much appreciated that. As a very competitive netman, I always wanted to win, period. "I cannot bear to lose," I would often sarcastically say to teammates within earshot. The season ended in early June, just as the snow around our mountainous high school started to melt. Then Sectionals came up and I faltered as a frosh, losing a close singles match to a clever ball-striking senior from Windsor in the fourth round. I should have won but choked during some easy points near the end of our battle. Oh, well. The completed season was thankfully over, with our team mired deep in the losing column. The oft-bewildered coach had a furtive and gut-wrenching final exit pep talk with us just before we disbanded but it was my turn to smirk as I left the building in a huff. As summer began, I restarted practices again with my old man while loudly and profanely ridiculing my high school coach and his stupid senior rules. I mean, I had beaten him personally many times as a freshman and he still denied me my rightful place on the team. I disliked him. My pop just laughed and uncharacteristically told me to be patient and to keep honing my forehand. He had had another winning season as the local college tennis coach that spring and was in good spirits at the start of summer vacation. Maybe he would stop being such a *nudge* and actually teach me some additional skills in the next three months? I had high hopes and it happened. My tennis acumen improved greatly, and I was determined to be a better singles player, and TEAM player, come next spring.

Take a break!

SOPHOMORE YEAR

It's time to really get serious

$$22$$

Summer Tennis Mavens

The summer of '74 turned into fall and the start of my
sophomore year, yet my tennis playing continued. My
professor father was my coach, hitting partner, mentor and,
worst critic; you know how it goes. However, during the
summers a few very talented, mid-thirties, net men from
the New York City area regularly rented a local house
together to party and play tennis. They not only befriended
my old man on the free college courts, but actively sought
him out to hit against. Pop was good, probably the best
player in our village at the time, regardless of his middle
age. Being the local college tennis coach resharpened his
vaunted skills every spring during the collegiate season and
blasting balls with me kept his stamina and acumen going
through the fall. K.K. was a dentist, M.G. was a lawyer and
N.D. was also a dentist; all hailed from the Rotten Apple
and they loved to come to our small community on
weekends for the mountain air, the wild self-organized
parties and for the tennis. Sometimes they brought their
wives and sometimes they did not, yet always had "fun." I
heard the scuttlebutt, you know. The trio stated many
times that it was their good fortune to find someone so

athletically accomplished as my old man this far north in the boonies. They weren't being rude, just honest. I started out as the glorified ball boy and tag-a-along grunt but gradually wormed my way into doubles matches if one of them was not there. Oftentimes, K.K. would frantically phone my home expressly asking my mom if dad and I could fill in for missing partners of his. I could just barely keep up with them on court and appreciated their patience with my steadily improving game. But that was the limit of the homegrown skill-set that we possessed in our puny settlement: Pop, me and maybe the other standout tennis family in our town, whose members were young and not always available to play. One fall day, just before K.K. and his crew departed for the winter season, N.D. took me aside and laughingly said, "You know, Izzy, I like you, your game, and personality. If you ever become a dentist someday, look me up." I just stared at him, nodded and shrugged. I was currently having trouble in geometry, forget about dentistry! Jumping ahead to 1986, I was at Lutheran Hospital in Brooklyn, about to be interviewed for a general dental residency position by none other than N.D., who was the director of dentistry there. When he saw me, he nearly fell over backwards and instantly recalled the conversation he had with me back in the '70s. He enthusiastically asked about my mom and dad, and if I was

still swinging a racquet. He stated that he and his buddies
had stopped their "country" weekend vacations years ago
but had fond memories of the good times they had
together in the "hills." However, he further said that he
had opened dental practices in Cooperstown, Oneonta,
Cherry Valley, and even in my hometown, right across the
street from the high school. Instead of leisurely vacationing
in the mountains, he now practically lived there, zooming
from practice to practice, collecting money from the
associate minion dentists he had working for him, and
running a fulltime dental residency program in New York
City as well. He wore many hats and appeared tired. He
reviewed my stellar dental school grades and soon showed
me the door, quietly saying that his residency program was
subpar, and that I deserved to go to a better place. I already
knew that but had decided earlier to surprise him with a
visit anyway. It had been a short subway ride on the F train
and great fun to have popped in on him, even though he
had known I was coming. He just didn't equate my name
to my face when I had applied. I ended up doing a three-
year prosthodontic dental residency at the Manhattan VA
hospital, the top program in the country at the time, and
received my MSD (Master of Science in Dentistry)
certificate in prosthodontics. Fast forward a few more years
and, in addition to my own growing practice, I found

myself working Thursday's in N.D.'s Cooperstown location as a prosthodontist. Is that foreshadowing or what? Now as a semiretired dentist in the waning stages of life, I recently reconnected with K.K., who still sounded very bullish and full of bluster, at least over the phone. He bragged that he was a fulltime dentist and ready to take me on in tennis. He was shocked at the turn of events in my life as I was shocked that he was still sticking his fingers in patients' mouths five days a week, and at his very advanced dotage! Anyhow, he was elated to hear that I was a fellow member of the "dental club." He then, once again, threatened to beat me in tennis. I think not, Ken, but thanks for the heads up.

23

Angularly Protracting

It had been an uncommonly good feeling coming off a stellar year in algebra, whence I had understood mathematics for the first time since maybe fifth grade. The concepts had been reasonable, the excellent teacher had been reasonably reasonable, and my previously numerically challenged gray matter had finally gotten its act together! Therefore, I vainly thought that my arithmetical woes were way behind me. Ha. Wrong. Enter, geometry, that voluminous course full of volumetric problem solving, angular dissections and determining the radii and diameters of disparate objects such as cylinders and spheres. And then there were the proofs, those equanimous equations that sought to reconcile the reckoning of the geometric deductions that we deduced on paper while using protractors, rulers and compasses. What? What the flip-flop? Whereas most of my smarty-pants pals were taking eleventh grade trigonometry, I was in the "demoted" tenth grade math section, and now I knew why. Regents geometry was not intuitively rational to me, unlike Mrs. T. had professed it was. She told us to let her "obvious" teachings flow effortlessly into our heads but somehow that form of passive transduction bypassed my thick skull and instead entered an unmentionable orifice down below. Her "new age" *yogic* mathematical mantras never got to my pea brain, it seemed. I was a real *case* in that course, but Mrs. T. was a *case*, too. She had that phony smile on her pale face and elocuted sarcastic rejoinders about the eloquence and sublime easiness of geometry. And always with that reddened and peeling nose of hers, sniffling and dabbing at it throughout each class period. Did she have a perpetual cold? Was she allergic to something? Was she allergic to student stupidity? I won't qualify that with an answer. She was an otherwise middle-aged, decent looking redhead, and had a professor husband who taught math at the local college in town. Wow, two "numbers people" married to one another. I had facetiously hoped that their offspring became English majors in college someday. Anyway, I was dejectedly mired in the muck of an excruciatingly boring class, sitting near the back while half-heartedly listening to the high-pitched whining going on at the front. Day after day, week after week; I couldn't shake myself out of my doldrums when seated in that dreaded classroom. I sort of understood the practical material but not the proofs. They were supposed to simplistically explain the geometric situations; however, they were frequently confusing and left me frustrated. I didn't get "it." On most days I was ready to bolt as soon as the bell rang. On top of that, it just so happened that our class was full of smart, advanced ninth graders, one of which was A.F. He seemed to not only readily grasp the quizzical concepts with aplomb but had the temerity to argue with Mrs. T. about the finer points of geometry that HE thought were salient to our discussions, much to her delighted surprise. He and she would go at it for a few minutes while the rest of us barely functioning dummies just sat there, dumbfounded and wondering what the fuck they were talking about. Now, we all knew that A.F., the son of an unpopular, long-tenured fourth grade teacher and the "crazy" appliance store owner on Main Street, was a smart shit, but he purposely took it to extremes, relishing the fact that he was brighter than the rest of us. Like father and mother, like son, I suppose. Nevertheless, A.F. motivated me to start trying harder. How could an underclassman show me up? I mean, really! So, I bore down harder in class, not to the point of defecating, but almost. And I diligently reviewed the textbook on a regular basis for a change. And I started doing the homework problems with a messianic zeal and determination. A.F. was not going to win at geometry! My third quarter grade was a ninety-six, the highest in the class and higher than A.F.'s. So there, I proved that I was capable of scoring highly while "learning" something that I really did not like or comprehend. But I had mixed emotions about my "victory." As a natural-born competitor, it made complete sense that I had achieved my goal, however, I still did not know math! I let off the accelerator in the fourth quarter and it showed, with my grade dipping into the low eighties again. My New York State Regents mark was an abysmal 71 and that also showed me something. I was a numerical numbskull at heart and knew it, as did fellow classmates and Mrs. T. My old man was pissed as usual at my scholastic shortcoming and now belittled my wondrous algebraic effort from the previous year as an aberration and an unprecedented streak of good luck. As a brilliant civil engineering professor, he was always on my back academically, especially in math, which he found extremely easy and profoundly logical. Oh, boy, and then I thought about the following year....there would be more problems to solve in trigonometry in eleventh grade with that "hard-marking" male teacher, Mr. J.O. Great, just freakin' great.

24

T.B.

Hey, it was the start of tenth grade when T.B. showed up. Not tuberculosis, but a transfer student, new to our class. I spied him in the lunchroom one day, sitting by himself, eating a homemade sandwich. My immediate buds and I seized upon the opportunity to tease this newbie in our school and maybe get a rise out of him. I approached him with a swagger to my step and proceeded to humorously upbraid him; well, it was funny to my pals, who were rolling with laughter at my insults and insinuations. However, T.B., with his thick, dark brown mop of hair, glasses and slender build, just sat their expressionless and kept right on chewing throughout my alleged demonstration of levity. Man, I thought, this nut is hard to crack. Not a smile, not a whimper, nothing. We left and left him alone. As my pals and I sat down together to eat, we replayed my comedic outburst and laughed anew, at T.B.'s expense. Then I noticed him in my Regents level biology class a few days later when he got all the questions right that Mr. L.H. had hurled at him. Then I saw him industriously studying in the library during study hall while my chums and I were busy fooling around, as usual.

And there he was in my European Cultures history course, always attentive and ready to engage Miss M. in studious discourse. Who was this *smart* guy and why was he here, in our hayseed haven, trying to ruin our grade point averages with his brainy brain? I could tell he wasn't a farm boy by his dress, language skills and adroit demeanor. Nor was he a budding jock. Maybe he was the progeny of a college professor, like F., N.K., P.M., and me? Hmmm, he was beginning to become somewhat of a mystery. So, the next time I witnessed him munching at that same lunch table by himself, I literally ran over and officially introduced myself. My "crew" wasn't around me; it was he and I, face to face, sandwich to sandwich, as we began to chitchat. After a few minutes, it dawned on me that I had "known" this *cool cat* for ages it seemed. Our banter was casual yet full of like-minded humor, similar stories and goodwill. It turned out that we had a lot in common, even personality-wise. We started that day as strangers but by the end of chow time were fast friends. Of course, my questioning revealed many things about him, and I in turn divulged my own baggage. I had nothing to hide though and neither did he. T.B. lived just outside of town with his family. They had moved to our dusty settlement from a place called Hartwick, N.Y. because his pop got a better job offer. We didn't exactly discuss what his old man did, but it didn't matter anyway. The next few days saw our "gang" grow by one new member; now there were nine in our bunch. And not only was T.B. instantly initiated into our band of *smarty-pants* comics, he actually fit right in, as if he had always been amongst us. And although soft-spoken, he proved to be very intelligent and quickly mastered our often zany and offbeat, theatrical Monty Python-esque approach to sketch comedy. He got us, right from the get-go. And we reciprocated by quickly including him in virtually all our present and future comedic overtures and audacious antics in school. I recently spoke to him by phone and he seemed the same as I remembered. He was now an engineer and successful in his field, which I never doubted would happen. Thanks, T.B., for letting us befriend you all those years ago.

25

Getting Ahead?

Were extra classes outside of school really necessary for me? I had a respectable low A high school average yet was not pleasing the old man at home. But what else was new? The next thing I knew my mom had somehow signed me up for an evening course called Introduction to Basic Zoology, at our town's junior college. It was held in the manure-stinking building outside the village, on the college farm that taught agriculture majors the basics of animal husbandry, farming, milking techniques, and how to win at a tractor pulling contest. Pop thought it would be great for me, since I so sincerely professed to love naturalistic sciences and all. Plus, I was already taking biology with my fave Mr. L.H. as a tenth grader. However, I'm still not sure how my parents managed to enroll me. Only later did I find out that the program was a purposely watered-down course and part of a 4-H initiative; besides admitted collegians, it was also open to townspeople who wanted to learn some basic zoological principles. Pop dropped me off and I took a seat, with puzzled older college kids staring at me. Didn't they get the memo? I was allowed to be there, honest. The class slowly filled up and I quickly noticed that

I was the only under aged doofus present, as my face started to grow red in self-consciousness. However, who should then stroll in? Why, P.M., one of my "gang" members and fellow science buff. She was absolutely beaming as she took the empty seat next to me and wouldn't stop yakking. She went on and on about how *special* we both were to join with older students and learn "their" stuff. She repeatedly told me that since both of our fathers were faculty members, we were entitled and justified to be there. Oh, boy. I had to calm her down in a goddamn hurry so she would not keep embarrassing us. After she quit squawking, I exhaled and sat there quietly, while clutching a Parker pen, and absorbed the collegiate vibe. The class started and ended a few months later. Did I learn anything from that "pre-veterinary" introductory curriculum? Yes, but the subject matter was below the tenth-grade level and I felt that I had wasted my time. P.M. disagreed. She said that now we had bragging rights. To what, and, so what? We both pulled easy A's, but did we really get ahead of the curve? Were we now more educated than our high school classmates? I think not. Fast forwarding a little to the fall of my senior year found my pop still fretting about my lack of mathematical proficiency. His professorial and civil engineering standards were calculus and differential equations, which he was a whiz at. For me, just having passed the trigonometry

Regents as a junior was an accomplishment. Crap, now he went and pulled some strings to have me take Pre-Calculus with one of his pals at the college. Great. I was all signed up for advanced algebra at the high school with Mr. O. and now had to take that dang college-level course as well. Two tasty treats at once. A double dose of math and a double whammy for my numbers challenged brain! It wasn't fair but I did it anyway. Perhaps it was for my own good? Most of my smarty-pants chums were mathematically ahead of me so maybe this was my chance to catch up slightly? Maybe it was an ego trip for my dad to mollify his disgust at my numerical shortcomings and prove to himself once and for all that I could actually calculate something at the "college" level? Perhaps. It was the early fall of '76 when I started that class, before high school even began. It met twice weekly at three thirty in the afternoon, so I had plenty of time to hoof it down one hill and up another to make it in time for Professor H.'s spiel. And glory be, I miraculously understood the obtuse concepts and got an easy A. However, that Pre-Calculus class had nothing whatsoever to do with the math I was taking in twelfth grade and was sort of another waste of time. And it counted for squat. I couldn't transfer the three credits anywhere and my perfect attendance of the twenty-one hours was admirable; but, so what? Nevertheless, my dad was proud of my A, I had rubbed shoulders with some college kids, Professor H. had spoken highly of me and my arithmetically troubled gray matter recovered its mojo, somewhat. And you know, I also understood and aced freshman calculus 1 and 2 at pharmacy college a year later. It seemed as though higher mathematics made sense to me, whereas high school geometry, trigonometry, advanced algebra and analytic geometry had just been nonsensical "filler" subjects that I swallowed whole, regurgitated during test time, and then happily moved on from. However, I still hate math.

26

Fire and Ice

The title could have just as well been good cop, bad cop, or yin and yang, or oil and water. Whichever. It was nevertheless an accurate description of our high school hierarchy, namely the high school principal and district principal. The word superintendent was not in vogue back then. In previous books I have alluded to the fact that our junior high and high school principal was an untethered pit bull, masquerading as a crew cut-coiffed, former gym teacher-turned-administrator, tasked with the day to day running of the *reform* school he was dealt. However, *Shag* was more than up to the task, meting out suspensions, punishments and evil glances as necessary to keep us boneheads in line. It was the seventies and he had seen it all, from Woodstock inspired long hair to Vietnam War protest marches; from dope to disco. I'm sure he had his own personal peccadilloes yet rose to the occasion time and again to squelch liberal dissent while under the guise of encouraging freedom and individualism. Now, contrast that style of policing with Mr. Z, the large, slightly soft, bland-looking, and largely banal district principal. His style was quiet, serene and cerebral; at least that's what it appeared to be. We students had very little interaction with him but the few times that some of us did, things always turned out sublime. I recall speaking with him on a number of occasions outside his office on the main floor and got the sense that he knew me personally and wanted only the best for me. None of we students quite knew what his overall job description was because our centralized school system was so small. I guessed that he had to visit the teeny elementary school in our boondock region as well as keep the flagship grammar and high school in town running smoothly. Now, for all I know, he was a "velvet harpoon" and a tyrant behind the scenes and, even bullied *Shag* around, though I doubt it. And for all I know he hated me and only smiled and nodded because it was the wise, politically correct thing to do. Who knows? He may have been an astute "politician" and in the perfect job, deftly managing the board, school brass, teachers, and pupils alike. However, no one complained or said a nasty word about him in any of my years there, which were many. To recap, one was an obvious petty dictator, the other, a nice guy. Let's keep it at that, unless I hear otherwise.

27

A Civics Lesson

American Lit I was taught by Mrs. G.H., whose husband
Pat played tennis with my pop and I in a loose
confederation of local players that gravitated to the college
courts to hit with "the coach," my dad. My professor father
was the college men's team coach and I was his apparent
protégé, and most of the would-be competition had to go
through me before he would grace them with a match. Red
haired, blue-eyed and fiery, Pat H. used his wiry athleticism
and a great court coverage strategy which duly impressed
me. He never beat me but came close a few times. He and
his bride were relatively new in town and perhaps he took
it easy on a tenth grader because his wife was my English
teacher that year. However, I vouched for his game and my
pop agreed to play him a few times. Whereas Pat H. was a
thin, live wire, Mrs. G.H. was a full figured, demure, long
dark haired beauty, with a saintly approach to teaching but
with a demonic streak when it came to grading our
mixed-year class of dunces. Her idea of fairness was to
downgrade, not upgrade, any work handed in. For
instance, many classmates, including me, received marks
such as a 79 or 89, instead of rounded up grades of 80 or

90. She was a stickler for perfection and reveled in giving most of us bovine peasants the "business," at every turn. I have to admit I struggled at times in that class although it was basically reading, writing and regurgitation on exams. We read noted American novels and short stories, talked about them in class and then had to write a composition on the material as a test. If a student agreed whole-heartedly with Mrs. G.H.'s opinion, he/she received a high mark as a "reward" but even the slightest deviation from "her norm" resulted in a lousy mark and much red ink on the exam paper. It was her way or the highway. I had a *feminazi* teacher in seventh grade English and this one came close a few times. Although she did not foist any feminist dogma upon us, she nonetheless angrily lectured us "rednecks" about our lack of decorum and sense of civics. That's right, civics. With the Vietnam War over, she was often appalled at our class's continued lackadaisical approach to "everything," including mistrusting the still-opaque government. Our seeming lack of enthusiasm, school spirit and patriotism irked her. A quick glance around our room showcased the post war malaise, with long haired hippie-type *boyz* slouched absentmindedly in their chairs, the crew cut jocks cluelessly staring into space, and the *home gurls* mentally checked out. Mrs. G.H. would lash out at us during those often lethargic, boring and trying times in her class. Storytellers like John Steinbeck

and his *Red Pony* didn't elicit the giddy-up she sought from
we dullards and that further infuriated her. So, in between
a soporific subject matter and her pontification on
American ideals, an easy A eluded me and instead turned
into a low B average. It was hard to get a top-notch grade
with her in charge, darn it. I continually complained to her
husband on the tennis court and he merely shrugged.
Although a lowly sophomore even I could tell that the
older guys in that class had had enough and wanted to
rebel. But how? Tattle on her to the principal? Stay after
class and complain to her that she was too tough to take?
Make snide and rude remarks during class only to possibly
get suspended? Ha, no. I heard the roughneck good-old
boys in that class were planning a stunt that would clearly
send their message of disgust right to her ride. What? I
happened to be walking by the side parking lot after school
one fall day when I witnessed six burly farm boys quietly
pick up her brand new Honda Civic and reposition it
diagonally in the parking spot, making it impossible to get
into or drive away. The tiny two door car weighed a measly
1,700 pounds and was relatively easy to move for such
strapping lads. Strategically placed eyewitnesses told us that
she reportedly went haywire upon trying to leave after
school. But I'm not sure if she equated the classroom
dissatisfaction among the "ruffians" with the Honda

"civics" lesson they gave her in return. Unfortunately, her classroom theatrics continued unabated as did the parking lot debacles until she finally got the message. Finding her flimsy Japanese auto completely turned sideways in an already tight spot did the trick. No one was ever caught or punished, and her car magically managed to stay straight, but not before her classroom atmosphere changed into a legitimate English discourse, devoid of perpetual sidebar lectures on deportment and civility. She ended up keeping her Civic in line and her civics arguments in check. I believe both teacher and students appreciated the tenuous truce. She still graded us harshly, however, no matter how much I complained to her husband about books such as Steinbeck's *Cannery Row*, etc. Oh, well. I kept my head down because I had her scheduled for the next semester in a composition class as well as in eleventh grade next year for American Literature II. Damn, I thought I knew how to read, think and write. I guess not because the quarterly grades she gave me were in the low 80s, but it was not for lack of trying on my part. I conscientiously loved reading literature and enjoyed interpreting the author's thematic intentions. I also liked to express myself on paper, longhand, with a Parker ballpoint pen. So why was it that Mrs. G.H. and I did not meld in a literary sense? Perhaps it was because I refused to be her parrot, thought original deep thoughts and wrote in my own unique style on exams? Evidently. The same thing happened to me in freshmen English while in pharmacy college, a few years in the future; if you didn't suck up to the professor and write just like her, you were doomed and relegated to the dust bin in the class and labeled a "mediocre student." I hated that conceited bitch Dr. D. and still do. But for now I did the best I could and stopped whining to Mrs. G.H.'s soon to be ex-husband, who soon disappeared from the local tennis scene as well. He left, she stayed; life wasn't always fair.

28

All Along the Clock Tower

My insincere apologies for ripping off and adulterating Robert Allen Zimmerman's (Bob Dylan) seminal song title and the heading of Jimi Hendrix's famous cover. I'm sure you all know to what popular tune I am obliquely referring. But I had to do it because it fits this story perfectly. It was the prank of all pranks; a seemingly seamless and foolproof high school practical joke/crime that was never satisfactorily solved. Here is what allegedly happened: My sister and I walked to school together on that Monday morning in late October of '74 like we nearly always did (on rainy or snowy days we took bus 57), said goodbye to one another, parted company, and went in different directions once inside the building. She walked down to the elementary wing and I stayed in the front foyer to meet up with some friends. However, on this morn, there was administrative staff running hither and tither in that lobby, huddling in small groups and talking in hushed tones. Did someone die? What was going on? We students milled around for a bit and then had to get to our lockers and then to homeroom. Nothing was told to us that day, either from the daily announcements or from our teachers. But by the next day EVERYONE had heard the grim news: one of the four giant clocks in our high school's cupola was missing and presumed stolen! It was the clock facing away from the main entrance. I just had to see for myself, so after school on Tuesday my sister and I climbed up the walkway toward our old grammar school building on the hill, turned around and saw the gaping hole for ourselves. We had to laugh out loud. The audacity of the scoundrels; now THAT was some gag. Nothing like the shit I did or said. I had to hand it to whoever pulled off that stunt. It was that good! We stared at the round vacancy and remarked that it looked as though someone from space had neatly plucked out the large timepiece without damaging the surrounding white housing or slate roof. Maybe it was carried off from the inside? My sister and I speculated about it all the way home and excitedly told our bemused parents about the incident. I thought about the lyrics from that 1967 Dylan song *All Along the Watchtower*, whose title I mangled and misappropriated above. The first line goes, "There must be some kind of way out of here, said the joker to the thief." I surmised that there must have been at least one joker/thief, perhaps a group of them? Well, after a few days, the destroyed six-foot-wide and 150 lb. clock was found in the Little Delaware River at Thomson's Crossroad Bridge, in a miniscule hamlet outside our town. A school custodian reported that someone had broken the door leading into the attic and lowered the clock over the roof. Our crack, or cracked, village police team investigated and then things quickly went silent. To my knowledge no arrests were made, nor anyone admonished or punished. How many people were involved in the larceny? Was there an intentional cover-up? Was a deal struck to quietly punish the miscreant or miscreants without word leaking out to us lowly gossipmongers? Was the hallowed varsity basketball team the guilty party? I hesitate to speculate because I really don't know where to start. And I'm just not that curious to begin investigating on my own. However, I'm sure people in the know do know who did it and are laughing about it to this day. Anyway, a new clock was purchased, installed and continues to tick away. I saw it last summer; it looks nice.

29

Meiosis or Mitosis

For those of you that have never taken biology, or purposely forgotten the two basic tenets of cell division, here is a very brief and simplistic explanation of meiosis and mitosis. Meiosis is when a mature SEX cell divides, resulting in two identical cells, each containing half the chromosomes of the original cell. When one of the "half-cells" mates with another one, which also has half of the genetic material, a whole cell is produced, which then further divides and multiplies, resulting in a multicellular organism. Mitosis occurs when a mature REGULAR cell divides, such as a skin cell, and reproduces two copies of itself, each with a full complement of genes, to keep the lifeform alive. So, meiosis is half, mitosis is whole. Mr. L.H., the big, garrulous, bespectacled middle-aged teacher, was a no-nonsense, crew cut-wearing lecturer. After taking attendance, with only his head protruding from behind a high lab bench which masked his size, he would begin the lecture by calling on nearly everyone in turn to answer biological questions. Poor S.O., she frequently got nailed with queries to which she just could not remember the answers. For the whole time we were studying histology (cells), Mr. L.H. would teasingly pose a question that required her to answer – meiosis or mitosis. And she ALWAYS got them mixed up, every time! After a few weeks, it became somewhat comical but not for her. It got to the point where everyone started to help her out; after all, her father would be our math teacher in the near future. Any Brownie points would help, and we sincerely hoped she would remember those who aided her and tell her old man! However, besides a brief moment of levity at S.O.'s expense, the rest of the class period was spent listening, furiously note taking and learning. Mr. L.H. would extricate himself from behind his black marbled desk, hike up his slick polyester slacks, front and back, give our class one last stare-down and then launch into his spiel. Starting at the very tippy-top left-hand corner of the blackboard, the next forty minutes or so would be filled with his intentionally speedy and miniscule printing on the black chalkboard interspersed with explanations, grunts and groans. The grunts and groans were from the pupils! He took no prisoners. You had to be ready and quick in his class. He would finish up on one board and slide it violently aside as he began on the next one. It was all so hurried, and biology can get complicated, you know. But Mr. L.H. was an excellent teacher, at least I thought so. I LOVED biology and couldn't get enough of it. I can't say the same for my other classmates, who often had puzzled looks on their faces and got writer's cramps keeping up with his frenetic pace. I was in the Regents course, and that further made our particular class hard. But I thrived; even the arduous dissecting lab experiments were a pleasure for me to handle. Mr. L.H. knew I was enjoying his course and made no bones about complimenting me numerous times in his droll and understated dry way. The exams were difficult, filled with convoluted multiple-choice questions bound into a thick, stapled, stack of papers that Mr. L.H. personally plopped on each student's desk during test time. But I aced many of them because I enthusiastically studied my notes, voraciously read the textbook, and seemed to easily recall that torpid material when needed. And near the end of the scholastic year, after doggedly perusing the obligatory *Barron's Biology Regents* review book, the entire class appeared ready for the state exam, even S.O.! I received the highest mark on it, a 97, to many congratulations from Mr. L.H. I was damn proud of myself and thanked him, both verbally to his face and silently with my own mental gratitude. He had almost single-handedly validated all my childhood biologic/ naturalistic proclivities, a time period when I used to capture and collect butterflies, insects, salamanders, and mudpuppies in earnest, while self-teaching myself about nature. Although he is no longer with us, I still fondly remember his teachings, his demeanor and subtle sense of humor. I dedicated this book to him. Thank you, Mr. L.H., you were more than alright!

30

Volare

Although he did not write it, the famous Italian balladeer Sergio Franchi helped popularize that simply titled love song with the catchy lyrics; not to be confused with that piece of shit automobile – the '70s Plymouth Volare. Anyhow, it was an Italian piece, written by two Italians and originally recorded by the co-writer. It became an international hit and was subsequently covered by just about every modern-day crooner, including Franchi. It became his signature song and he included it in most of his musical sets when on his numerous and exhaustive world tours in the sixties and seventies. And one of his stops at the time was our high school. But how and why? In hindsight it was probably about his lack of money, but at the time, our school officials probably didn't care and were most likely just giddy to be hosting such a performing legend. And he was good looking and wholesome, too; he had appeared numerous times on the *Ed Sullivan Show* for God's sake! The school brass didn't go after KISS, Deep Purple, Jefferson Airplane, or Lynyrd Skynyrd, you know. They couldn't have gotten them anyway, even though we cretins were actively pumping their acerbic vibes into our skulls back then. But for a few *shekels*, they got a G-rated, genuine Perry Como/Frank Sinatra knockoff. Score! So, what was the big deal? Here's what transpired: On the day of the locally ballyhooed concert, our school's only full size, black, banged-up, grand piano was set up on a raised wooden platform in the gymnasium. Curious students, including me, milled around the locked gym doors between classes all morning, catching glimpses of the goings on through the tempered glass panes. We watched in amazement as our dour and smelly gym was converted into a professional stage, complete with a trucked-in lighting/sound system and extra metal folding chairs that were carefully put in rows for the village hoi polloi to sit on. It was a masterpiece of quickly assembled materials for that evening's gala musical performance. However, during the afternoon, as I checked on the progress between periods, I found that the main gym door was slightly ajar, with no one inside. Now, in that fleeting moment I'm not sure what came over me, but I quickly bolted inside, climbed up to the keyboard and excitedly tickled the ivories, playing a few quick numbers in a noiseless and empty gym. In my mind I pretended to be Elton John, or Billy Joel. It was thrilling to play a properly tuned piano on a big stage; however, my exaltation turned sour before I could run to my next class. Mr. B., the ever-watchful band director caught me red-handed stroking that Steinway and hollered at me to get off that piano stool at once. And he meant it. Red-faced and angry, he berated me for my foolishness and spat out that the keyboard was painstakingly tuned for Sergio, and NOT for some flash-in-the-pan, greenhorn impresario and sophomore *shyster*, like me. Yet there I was, fingering it without a care in the world and flaunting my alleged prowess. What a bonehead I was. Stunned and deeply embarrassed, I silently and hurriedly stalked off the grandstand; for it was not in my character to so obviously flout school rules. Mr. B. and I were seemingly both shocked at my hubris. But why had I done it? I had performed for crowds at shows and numerous piano recitals before. I wasn't lacking in musical exposure. Was it the grandiose staging that had gotten to me? Was that my only chance at "real" stardom, albeit in a beat-up and dingy gym with no adulating fans in attendance? Was I just showboating my limited skills, hoping for an adoring audience of onlookers? I still don't know why I had that moment of weakness come over me all those years ago. Anyhow, other Peeping Tom pupils heard of the commotion and peered into the gym, watching Mr. B. loudly yelling at me. Rats. Now the whole school would know of my willful misbehavior. Luckily, instead of getting into major trouble, Mr. B. let me go as I

impressed upon him that I was already late for my eighth
period class. I came home that night chagrined and in a
depressed mood; I was mad at myself. I also told my
parents and sister that I was not going to the show that
evening. They were in disbelief because it was assumed that
a musical extravaganza was right up my alley. Well, it
wasn't, I emphatically told them, and we didn't go. In
truth, it's not that I was exactly chafing at the bit,
anxiously waiting to hear Franchi's pipes; however, I would
have gone anyway had it not been for my perceived earlier
debacle. I didn't want to catch any flack from anyone that
evening about my previous deviancy, even in a joking way.
Anyway, my folks never found out and my close friends
effectively squelched any remaining school scuttlebutt
about my misadventure. And as for Mr. B., he and I would
lock horns again in the future, in good and bad ways. And
as for "Volare," I never want to hear that song again. Of
course, why would I, since I continue to listen to old rock
staples such as AC/DC, Led Zeppelin and Black Sabbath;
even some Ozzy, now and then.

31

Historical Histrionics

Tenth grade European Cultures was "taught" by Miss M., a youngish, wild-haired women with a perpetual scowl on her puss. She wasn't bad looking; she just presented herself rather blandly and matter-of-factly which minimized her decent appearance. And she minimally psychologically interacted with students, which further distanced us from her. She often seemed harried and troubled, and had difficulty getting the dry material across to the class. Sure, she covered all the obligatory wars of the "old country," the political intrigues and kingdoms involved, and succinctly lectured on the historical significance of it all. And yet, the course was not that interesting, although it should have been. Besides uttering a bundle of facts, her lecturing style was stilted and abrupt, with little "feeling" for the subject matter. She just didn't engage us. Oh, well, "Maybe Miss M. needs a boyfriend?" my chums and I would laughingly lament in private. And that's when Mr. B., the newly hired shop teacher, stepped forward, or did he? Perhaps it was only juicy school gossip or manufactured innuendo, however, the rumors of her dating the *fresh blood* were all the rage within our tenth grade class. Was she or wasn't she shacking up with him? Inquiring minds desperately wanted to know. There was no hookup culture back in 1974-75; however, "shagging and bragging" was always in vogue. But she never let on if the allegations were true or not, at least not to us lowly bottom feeders. And stout and proud Mr. B. was not about to let us in on the secret either, if there was one. Nonetheless, nothing inside the classroom improved or changed, not her demeanor, not her approach to pupils and not her looks. Same old, same old. For all we knew, nothing transpired between the two parties, although there was a consistent low-level school buzz about them that continued to intrigue me. Anyway, I was pulling a boring high B average when it came time to do the annual project for her class. And what a dolt I was. I had plenty of time to plan and then execute an artsy composition. But did I? No! My feelings for her and for that course were in the "cellar" and I arrogantly procrastinated until the eleventh hour before getting off my high horse to do something creative. I had one day left to craft a craft and, to my utter dismay, saw fantastically created works brought in by seemingly artistically challenged kids, renderings that Miss M. carefully displayed all around the room. Holy shit, I had to dig deep to beat that load of bootlickers and their goodly goods. It was crunch time. However, I still felt uninspired. I cut out some pieces of thin cardboard and then glued, pasted, whittled, molded and painted. And the result was a miniature, cheap-ass replica of a castle, with turrets, a working drawbridge, and a water-filled moat with a tiny plastic toy alligator in it. My dad saw it and laughed hysterically. "You could have done much better than that," he callously and dismissively stated. It was obvious that I had spent the bare minimum of time on it and deserved to be academically punished. I walked into the classroom with my wobbling monstrosity and placed it on her desktop on the last day that all term projects were due. And guess what, I got a tepid compliment from her and a high B for my exceedingly paltry efforts. Whew, I had dodged a C. The year was dwindling down and now our class started to hear more reliable scuttlebutt about Miss M. and Mr. B. I guess they had been a couple after all, while "teasing" us with unsubstantiated stories of a breakup. The nerve of them, letting us think one thing and then doing another. The year ended uneventfully, and I lost touch with a few ongoing school dramas that were none of my business, such as Miss M.'s love life. It was just as well as I took my 89 final average and got ready to lose my hearing in the following year's American history class with that always blustery, Mr. T.

32

Sharpen Those Blades

Just past the hospital and high school, along a stretch of
Route 28 leaving our sleepy town and down a steep
embankment with a dirt road access lies a large shallow
pool of water. I believe it is legally named Smith Pond;
however, we never called it that. As youngsters, most of us
could only get to it if our parental units drove us there
intentionally. It wasn't really hidden, just in an awkward
and overgrown place for summer recreation. Although it
was free for the public to visit and enjoy, few people
actually ventured there to find adventure. But in the
wintertime, it came alive! A small, austere, but heated
wooden building next to it served as a warming shack,
complete with rows of benches to sit upon when lacing up
ice skates. That's right, in the summer months the pond
was friendless but during the long snow season it sparkled
with life with the sounds of metal edges cutting into its
gleaming surface. Lightweight tractors continually plowed
off the fallen snow to reveal a large and beautiful disk for
the village people to skate on. My pal G.P.'s older brother
R.P. was the frequent monitor at the shack and served to
keep things running smoothly as well as to pour hot

chocolate for "frozen dainties" after they came off the ice, especially during the bitterly cold evening sessions. By sophomore year, most of my buds and I had become somewhat accomplished skaters, we could even go backwards if necessary. And, being boys and bored with merely going in circles, hockey seemed like the obvious next step. Plus, watching older kids already playing made it easy for us to jump into their fray. Impromptu games would start and stop depending on the number of willing participants present. Since there were oodles of room, we would commandeer and partition a rectangular portion of the slick round surface and then boys of all ages and differing levels of athleticism would begin hacking at that little black orb. Girls didn't play back then. They would glide around on the periphery ensconced in their pompom outfitted figure skates while testosterone-fueled jerks like me attempted to push that hard rubber disk up and down our play area while wearing black, Bauer hockey skates, attached to our sore feet. However, since we had no school team, or even someone in our tiny settlement that had played at a competitive level and could teach us properly, it was an amateurish display of flailing sticks and frequent falls on our parts. Although we knew how to play from watching the NHL on TV, brandishing our wooden Sherwood sticks to score while keeping our balance often proved tricky. Our brand of hockey was so primitive it was laughable, but so much fun at the same time. The rules were that we couldn't shoot the puck above knee level, couldn't push and shove each other, and the goal mouths were delineated by two rocks at each end. The goaltenders wore no pads and had regular sticks. None of us wore helmets or protective mouth guards and only a few possessed genuine padded hockey gloves. At least my trusty stick, with custom applied black tape on the curved blade, had a plastic tip on the end as if that would protect a would-be adversary's mouth and teeth from my blunderous game. Ha, ha. Luckily for us, no one was good enough to hurt anyone else with hard shots or rough play. It's funny that there are hundreds of official and very competitive "pond hockey" leagues across the nation; we played on a frozen body of water because it was the only rink we had. What did we know? I often thought about the varsity high school team sports that I would have loved to play as a young adult: hockey, volleyball, soccer….none of which were available at our football, baseball and basketball obsessed school. I would have excelled at all three of the former. Oh, well. Tennis was my life sport at the time, and I stuck to it. Anyway, my sister and I grew up at that wondrous pond during our winter youth and were grateful to our parents for driving us there on many weekends and evenings to partake in some wintry exercise. They would frequently join us on the ice, as well. Mom showed off her vintage white figure skates while pop would whiz along on his ancient Canadian Tire Mastercraft hockey "shoes." And although the hot chocolate was a welcome treat on frosty nights under the lights, it frequently made me ill upon coming home. Perhaps I was not used to such decadent sweetness because mom always underused sugar in all her cooking. I think it was just me and my nervous stomach; all that hard skating really churned things up, you know.

33

A Bad Break

Mr. K., the tall-challenged, red-haired, athletic alumnus whom I had for gym class since grammar school was my PE teacher in tenth grade, as well. He was my bigoted nemesis; there was no fondness between us. He was a WASP, I was a dark-skinned, funny surnamed "foreigner" who frequently "interfered" in the orderly pecking order of male wannabe sports stars in our Section IV, Class B school. I often outperformed his budding junior jocks in many sporty endeavors and further frustrated him by NOT joining the varsity gridiron team as a speedy running back, much to his football coaching disdain and ongoing ire. (By the way, he begged me to join every fall, including my senior year, to no avail.) Anyway, by tenth grade, he and I started to bury the proverbial hatchet, and not in either of our heads! We came to a truce of sorts; he knew that I played that elitist game tennis at a high athletic level, which undoubtedly helped me to outshine his minor league protégé's on the running track and inside the gymnasium. However, he could not coerce me to carry a pigskin no matter how hard he tried. He reluctantly gave me grades in the high nineties but rarely spoke to me, only grunting or farting in my general direction after a victory or sporty accomplishment on my part. He had been unceremoniously reamed out by my mother in elementary school for willfully ignoring my growing athleticism, and that most likely also contributed to the elevated grades I now received. He probably didn't want any more dust-ups with my small-statured Ma, who stood eye to eye with him. Unfortunately, I was used to a biased paradigm against my family and I from most of the small-minded folks in my tiny settlement, PE teachers included. All the same, I was confident in my physical abilities and appreciated the marks I got from him. It was a stalemate of sorts with no progression of teacher/student friendship as I continued through school and his classes, but I shrugged it off and moved on. Until that one day while playing intramural volleyball in gym: Besides excelling at tennis, table tennis, and soccer, my father had also been an excellent semi-pro indoor volleyball player in an ethnic Estonian volleyball league in western New York and, I seemed to have followed his genetic blueprint of volleyball sportiness. Mr. K. nodded his approval at my spiking, hitting, setting, and serving abilities while simultaneously ridiculing the students who missed the ball badly. I even got a rare accolade from him upon outjumping and defensively stuffing J.P. across the net during a frenzied point. J.P. was the popular basketball superstar (now a local yokel farmer in the dell off of Elk Creek Road) in my class who, as a senior, would become the first player in our high school's history to dunk a basketball during a live home game. And I was there in the back row of the bleachers to see it firsthand. Anyway, J.P. was embarrassed but wasn't overly surprised at my volleyball smarts and just grinned at me. But then it happened. A routine "dig" of a blasted ball resulted in a sharp pain in the base of my right thumb. Either it was a break or severely jammed. Mr. K. knew something was wrong, stopped the game and looked genuinely concerned at my distress. He muttered something like, "Hey Mayputz, run down to the nurse and put some ice on it; we'll save you a spot in the game when you get back." I stared at him in disbelief, still clutching my right hand while heading out to the nurse's station with my gym attire still on. Did Mr. K. suddenly like me or something? Was I dreaming? Mrs. D., the overly portly nurse in her usual muumuu dress, wrapped an Ace bandage with a few ice cubes in it around my swollen thumb, wrote me up as "injured" on my individual medical index card, and sent me back to gym class. After a few minutes of ice time, I unwrapped the primitive bandage and was ready to rejoin the competition, and played out the rest of the period. The months went by and the thumb injury healed as did the relationship between Mr. K. and me. He seemed to finally soften his stance toward me and I toward him. I can honestly say that he started to look at me in a different light after that injury. Perhaps he liked my spirit, or my toughness while playing through pain. Whatever it was, I was grateful. And although he cajoled me yearly to join the varsity football squad, he did so in a defeatist and non arrogant way, knowing full well I would say no. I would like to say that by junior year he and I had fully made up, and perhaps we did. As an aside, that one stupid and needless fluky volleyball related injury has continually dogged me in dentistry. After holding a dental handpiece (the drill) for an extended period of time while carving and whittling away enamel, my right thumb still gets very sore and I need to take a short break in the action before continuing. Who knew that such a non life-threatening accident would forever hurt me in my dental career? Oh well, semi-retirement is a blessing and a balm for that fateful ball/thumb altercation that happened over four decades ago.

34

Lights Out

After my successful junior high run as a "thespian" in two successive operettas, I was done with actual rehearsals and all that song and dance bullcrap. Sure, I enjoyed the theatre, the makeup, and the camaraderie but did not wish to actively participate in any more extravagant productions. Nevertheless, starting in ninth grade, instead of musical numbers, actual plays were performed by members of the high school drama club and talented walk-ons. Because of my junior high experience, I was asked many times to join the casts and to perform in that year's production. No, no, no. However, I did wish to be involved, although in a reduced role. And since I was a keen observer of previous student stagehands and their shoddy work, I volunteered to run the "lights" from backstage as well the spotlights from the balcony section. I was convinced I could do a much better job at the controls than those prior "amateurs" had done. And I was right. But I needed a partner. I know, my best friend F., the pal who also fancied himself behind the curtain instead of headlong in front of the footlights; at least for now, however. Both of us felt confident that we could parlay our limited know-how into tenth grade and be the go-to guys when it came to the choreographed lighting of any future operetta or dramatic performance. But why did we do it in the first place? We weren't AV nerds, nor were we that enamored with the rinky-dink acting or directing of our respective fellow students and teachers. We did it for salient reasons; namely, we wanted quality time to talk after school, time to fool around, plot our next mirthful classroom overtures, and to get geared up to someday star in our own stage-worthy sketch-comedy send-ups. We each had a brief taste of stage presence and kind of wanted to hang around the big top while waiting for our break, so to speak. So, with only a bit of humor and scant experience under our belts, F. and I got the jobs as lighting specialists for all upcoming stage productions, big or small, at our hayseed high school for the duration of our prison time there. Well, we did have supporting help from interested pupils in our grade such as D.F. and D.L., and a few underclass ladies during extravagant feats but we largely handled all the duties ourselves. For those of you that were also involved in aiming the hot and heavy projectors to shine beams of photons onto the stage in the correct order and color schemes as well as working the predigital age levers and analog buttons on a huge upright motherboard backstage, congratulations on a tough job well done. We did likewise, numerous times and, loved every minute of it. However, as stated previously, it was the horseplay between F. and I that we really enjoyed. Did we ever make mistakes? Yes. Did we blow some fuses and fry a few circuits? Absolutely. Were we ever chewed out by the head honchos running the shows for gross negligence and wanton misbehavior? Never, although we came close a few times. The lighting chores were easy for us; the times spent discussing future capers and planning our own comedies, priceless.

35

Orchestral Misfirings

While sawing on that screechy stringed instrument since seventh grade, F. and I had developed a deep and kindred friendship, as well as a love/hate relationship with the wooden fiddle, the glue that had seemed to initially bind us together. We had been inexorably paired by happenstance in seventh grade, as second violin players in the high school orchestra. Our frequently bedeviled and manic teacher/conductor, Mr. Daye, had unwittingly set in motion two male jokesters who would bond tightly and then exert their unique brand of unexpected buffoonery over the entire high school along with their group of likeminded "gang" members. And our monkeyshines were often fomented during those daily periods of music practice. By tenth grade, every able-talented "musician" had been gently coerced to play in the band or orchestra, regardless of the actual skill level demonstrated. Our *homogenized* and *pasteurized* rural school was very small and devoid of "Julliard caliber" performers, so classmates like F. and I made the "team." Although F. had much more "string smarts" than I, my years of rigorous piano training kept me from abysmally failing and I stuck to my school-issued "Stradivarius" until graduation mainly because of F., my erstwhile and willing partner in all things debaucherously funny. He always sat to my right as we cursed at the notes in front of us while yakking and laughing between numbers. Laughter was our common theme, unlike the attitude of most of the "serious" girls that surrounded us. I'm sure we bothered them, and not just because of our frequent comedic outbursts. They most likely also considered us as woefully immature males and not good prospects for current or future dating. Oh, well. There was always time to grow up, plus none of those girls piqued my interest anyway. During sophomore year we were both feeling it scholastically and comically and basically took out our "comedic frustrations" and impromptu improv routines on Mr. Daye and our fellow orchestra laggards. Now, did we wantonly fool around during those practice sessions without a care in the world, regardless of potential punishment and GPA retribution? You betcha! Why? Because a beleaguered Mr. Daye and the perpetually "flat sounding" orchestra desperately needed us, and we knew it. What could he do, fire us? Then he would be down two fiddlers in the first violin section, a patch that already had a shaky sound to begin with. But we knew not to press his buttons too much; in fact we at least occasionally cracked him up with our frantic antics and sarcastic remarks. One day we would be blowing up clouds of rosin (actually baby powder that I had secreted inside my violin case just for the gag) after pretending to get our horsehair bows in order as per Mr. Daye's instruction, and other days we would rig our metal music stand to fall apart halfway through practice, crashing in pieces to the floor. You know, juvenile horseplay that other members of our musical family started looking forward to while pretending to look away in disdainful dismay. Remember, most of the string-strokers were highbrow students near the top of their respective classes, including Mr. Daye's own children. His son was an excellent first cellist and his daughter a fine viola player and neither displayed even the faintest hint of appreciation for our rancorous humor, at least not in front of their disheveled and cranky old man! But when it came time for our individual weekly lessons, recitals and high school orchestral performances, F. and I were all business and did Mr. Daye proud. He was grateful for our long-term participation, and we were grateful for the high grades he continually doled out to us which helped pad our report card markings, quarter after quarter, year after year. It was a mutually beneficial prostitution-like operation going on. Mr. Daye bribed us with very high marks, and we showed up and put out. A definite quid pro quo! However, we had a blast during those orchestral practice sessions; they were always a most welcome break during the day and I greatly looked forward to a bit of fun and *flaying* of the violin (that word is spelled correctly).

36

The Meltdown

No, not mentally but physically! This is the kind of small-town tale that makes perfect sense, if you're from a small town: A rich and popular lawyer's home is broken into by some local "boys" and the wife's gold jewelry is stolen. The group of well-connected native male scions from "good" families tries to smelt the pieces with blowtorches in a garage on Clinton Street. They are caught, local law enforcement becomes involved, and then the whole case gets magically and mysteriously whitewashed with nary a residual rumor to be heard afterwards. Was anyone brought to justice? No. Were there any private payoffs involved? Probably. Was there some political arm twisting that went on? Most likely. Did some villagers know who did it and when and where the homegrown meltdown actually took place? Indubitably. Were the rest of us peasants privy to those potentially salacious and scandalous details? Obviously not. End of story. Hopefully you weren't as disappointed reading this as I was at being denied some juicy town gossip in 1975.

37

Breaking and Not Entering

F., E.G. and I were comparing our new and concealable
squirt guns in the back of the school library, behind the last
row of books, in a darkened corner, and still she found us!
Let me backtrack first: Just like the prior year, the spring of
our sophomore year had its usual water pistol mania, with
many boys involved in the squirting of liquid at each other
during school hours. The ad hoc fad didn't last long, with
confiscations, detentions and warnings issued galore as
soon as the school brass got wind of it. We three were not
protagonists of the waterworks but were packing heat just
in case we had to "defend" our fragile "manly" egos. Tit for
tat; and we were ready. Normally I carried a Greenie
Meanie, but on this day I decided to bring in my brand
new, tiny but fully functional, gun-shaped squirt gun to
show my buddies. As we were comparing our "shootin'
irons," wouldn't you know that Mrs. K., the head librarian
and wife of the soon-to-be-retired local college president,
would somehow ferret us out and nonchalantly collect our
guns? We were crestfallen as she snickered and cackled
boisterously while clutching our property; she was in a
library dammit and didn't care at the noise SHE made. She

153

had scored a victory that day over a bunch of 15-year-olds and was obviously very elated. We weren't punished though; the loss of our prize "weapons" seemed to be enough for her. Plus, she knew F. and me personally from college faculty/family interactions and didn't seem eager to have us officially admonished. However, it's funny how important those water guns were to us at the time. We knew that we had no right to bear any kind of arms in school, unlike at home, where most of us handled and shot our fathers' real firearms with regularity. But somehow those water guns seemed to be linked to our very essence at that age. Ownership of those cheap, plastic, made in Japan pieces meant so much to us. Their loss and our loss of masculine *swag* were devastating. We just HAD to get them back, but how? Of course, we three started to plot our caper during lunchtimes and had the plans of attack finalized between bites of corned beef on one day and grilled cheese sandwich on another. It was going to be easy, as every criminal assumes. Early in the morning we would go into Mrs. G.S.'s room, who taught us Afro-Asian Cultures the year prior, and then into the book depository. Her classroom was linked to the library through an unlocked door, and if that failed then a frontal assault would be used: We would gain entrance by using a skeleton key on the library's old-fashioned front door lock to open it and enter. It would be very early in the morning, before any other students, teachers or janitorial staff would be present to detect or catch us in the act. We were ready. E.G. did not participate because he could not get to school that early, so F. and I became the chumps about to attempt larceny to get "our" stuff back. It sounds like what O.J. Simpson said when he tried to get his football memorabilia back. It isn't stealing if it rightfully belongs to you, right? Well, we thought along those similar lines back in '75. F. and I got to school at 7:30 a.m., the upstairs hallway was basically deserted as we predicted with only a few idiots milling around their lockers at the far end of the long hallway and they wouldn't be able to see what we were up to. We brazenly ran into Mrs. G.S.'s room, which we knew would be unlocked, and made a beeline for the connecting door to the library. This would be easy. The plan was to quietly run into the unlit library, open the top drawer of the librarian's front desk, where reliable snitches had told us she had stowed our mini-soakers, and retrieve them. But then F. and I stopped smirking as we hit that connecting door and it didn't budge. Damn, it was locked. But why? It was always unlocked, as we had recalled. Crap, time to beat a hasty retreat without being seen. We made it outside and looked at one another in bewilderment, our hearts pounding. Okay, now time for the direct approach. I had preemptively brought a couple of old skeleton keys with me and started to try them on the library's front door lock. The third one I tried had promise and while F. acted as the lookout I slowly started to turn the key. However, the key jammed and I could twist it no further. It became stuck tight in the hole. F. and I were panic-stricken because I could not remove it and soon the hallway would be full of tattletales and our jig would be up. We stood with our backs to the library door, hiding the protruding key, and were desperately thinking out loud of ways to escape from the unfortunate situation we had gotten ourselves into. "Why don't we just run for it," F. finally suggested. Well, students had already started to assemble and obviously had noticed us standing there like two "guilty" stool pigeons. "They would see us running away and then notice the key sticking out of the keyhole," I anxiously replied. "We would be instantly reported by the goody-two-shoe skunks in our school," I added. In addition, it was now 8 o'clock and the head librarian would be arriving soon, darn it. We were in deep trouble. What were we going to do? Then, out of nowhere, E.T., a large, muscular, footballer and basketball player in our class, happened to pass by and asked us if everything was all right? We must have looked pale and distraught for him to empathetically engage us in conversation. We had never spoken to him before even though he was an *original*, from our kindergarten days. Although he was the local sheriff's son and popular, he wasn't our friend; he was a jock, you know. He quickly surmised the situation as we frantically told him the details of our failed covert operation. He told us to stand back as he kicked at the key with his black and white, Converse-sneaker-covered foot, cleanly breaking it off in the lock. "Problem solved," he laughed, and quickly walked away as I picked up the incriminating fractured key handle off the floor. Then F. and I hoofed it as the hall quickly became filled with pupils. As we looked over our shoulders, no one seemed to notice anything amiss and we exhaled. Later in the morning, after homeroom, we heard the buzz that someone had tried to break into the library, which forced the custodial staff to replace the door lock, much to their annoyance. We had failed. We had tried to break in, but never entered. The only thing broken had been the key. And all because of some cheap-ass squirt guns and our wounded pride.

38

Biological Cribbing

The mousy, mealy-mouthed and ineffectual female Biology student-teacher was in command; however, the class was out of control because Mr. L.H., our highly respected instructor, had intentionally abdicated all his teacherly responsibilities for a few days. And you know what they say: when the cat's away, the mice will..... But we rats were downright ratty to that poor, teacher-in-training. We were noisy, boisterous, speaking out of turn, and guffawing at our own stupid jokes. We were a wild bunch for two days running, regardless of her threats that an important exam was coming up. We were poised and primed to fool around without the "big guy" being there. It was a spontaneously giddy time, a pause from the endless barrage of his biological dictums. It was as if someone had finally removed the lid off the pressure cooker and gave us small potatoes inside a breather. For two fun-filled days it was open season on that hapless hack from Oneonta State. Then on the third day, and without Mr. L.H.'s omnipresence, it was test time. I was prepared; however, the rest of the students seemed to take the examination period as a continuation of the party atmosphere that had recently been created in the class. The nervous student-teacher quickly handed out the thick, stapled pieces of dread, and we began. There was a little murmuring, a little light talking but nothing unusual based on what had previously transpired in that large room, which also doubled as a laboratory. Oh, there were some grunts and groans mixed in as well because a lot of the dumber students or, should I say, the non conscientious ones, had not bothered to study, as per usual. They were often content to get their low marks and move on from a particular topic and from that whole damn course in general! However, without Mr. L.H.'s looming company, now was a golden opportunity for certain scoundrels to cheat their way to a decent grade. But how? I'll tell you how. Halfway through the exam, my stacked test packet was suddenly yanked out from under my left hand by my favorite All-American-looking jock, J.M., who sat next to me. He grinned as he furiously began copying down my answers. Then he passed my test backwards to more snickering students as I helplessly sat there spinning my head this way and that trying to locate my easy A. The flustered student-teacher eventually noticed the commotion and realized that I had no test on my desk. Appearing overwhelmed and exasperated, she implored, "Izzy, where is it?" I laughingly remarked that it was probably at the back of the class. And I was right, as she angrily confiscated it from S.O., the female pupil who still could not differentiate between meiosis and mitosis. After securing and returning the papers to me, she loudly acknowledged my biological acumen but implored the class to stop cribbing off me. That didn't sit well with that benevolent, blond-haired and blue-eyed "jockstrap" J.M., who continued to steal signs from me for the duration of the period, even after being repeatedly warned not to. I didn't care. He was alright. He and I went back to our kindergarten days together; J.M. knew I was smarter than he and respected me on the playing field as well. I willingly let him see my answers and even facilitated his transgression. That was his chance to significantly boost his lousy GPA and at least finish the year with a gentleman's C. Mr. L.H. returned on the fourth day, reamed out our class for the recent impudence, and glared suspiciously at me as if I had been the unruly ringleader. He then proceeded to rip us apart with a hard dose of Bio, showing off for the student-teacher who timidly and demurely sat in the back, hopefully taking notes on how to teach effectively. Just a note about J.M.: After starring on the varsity football, basketball and track teams, he enrolled in our local junior college and had my professor dad for many engineering courses. And, like with me, pop gave J.M. many breaks and even vouched for his successful transfer to RIT, my old man's alma matter. After marrying a high school classmate (M.E.), J.M. became a highly successful contractor and golf course builder. If you are a supposed "dumb" jock who people are envious of, sometimes it pays to stay humble and likeable; you never know when that attitude will ultimately help you.

39

Musical Fools

The heading suggests more than one person and a plurality of ineptitude. However, only I was the tone-deaf moron and not my best bud F. Although a moderately skilled piano player after years of lessons, NYSSMA adjudications and recitals, I was not born with good pipes, nor could I sing a note unless someone else intoned it first. Nor was I a good violin player. But I had managed to screech out many melodies on the fiddle since the sixth grade, mostly in tune, as I scraped that horse hair bow over four blasted steel strings on a regular basis. Since we were a puny, pint-sized school, any kid with a modicum of talent in the music world was actively recruited to play an instrument and/or vocalize in the choir. Piano was a solitary pursuit and not part of the music department's group mentality. Band and orchestra were the featured dual musical outlets and, as like in the varsity sports scene, there was always a shortage of qualified boys and girls. That's how I got roped into playing the "Stradivarius" and opening up my cake-hole for mistuned sounds to come out. However, the above title actually refers to the incessant tomfoolery that F. and I instigated and willfully engaged in

while performing in the varsity choir and orchestra
rehearsals throughout our high school *schlep*. Basically, it
was an extra chance for F. and I to meet up during and
after school to fool around some more and, to further
foment comedic bullshit which would invariably be foisted
upon our unwary scholastic brethren, teachers included.
Coed varsity choir practice was at least twice weekly, in the
evenings. I couldn't sing a lick yet there I was, rubbing
shoulders with real singers in the bass section, enunciating
the proper words and trying hard to blend in. Nevertheless,
I could hold a note in the proper key and seemed to
contribute, at least somewhat. In the orchestra, F. and I
had risen from second to first violin, second chair, and
enjoyed the paltry accolades of "string" success. We usually
played serious classical pieces seriously; however, it was yet
another chance to talk and to plot our monkeyshines
during those daily rehearsals. Once in a while we would let
go with some snide or sarcastic remarks that got the whole
ensemble tittering. Sometimes our derision was directed at
old Mr. Daye, our funky teacher and conductor, yet even
he laughed at our brazen comments and *chutzpah*.
Nevertheless, our humorous overtures were not limited to
the musical peasantry in our redneck rural outpost in the
Catskills. No, we took our *shtick* on the road, as well.
Every year students from both the choir and orchestra were

"nominated" to be part of the prestigious All County and Area All-State groups, as per the selection committees of the individual schools involved. The musicianship of the elected students would be showcased at a distant high school in front of a large audience of local parental units and the usual parochial pariah. Of course F. and I were always on the bus for those trips, baby! They were usually one-day affairs; you got there, disembarked, practiced with a bunch of other "honored" idiots, and then performed in the evening. But it was the frequent breaks and lunch periods that F. and I looked forward to. And there were lots of them. No one wanted cranky and overworked *maestros*! And during those "rest periods" F. and I did our comically enhanced dirty deeds. We secretly and discretely canvassed the buildings, entered locked and unlocked classrooms, and went places that were expressly forbidden for visiting students to traverse. You know, we did the usual things that were in our adolescent wheelhouse. We sneakily tested the waters, pushed the boundaries of legality but were paranoid enough not to get caught in the act. However, we were never overtly malicious; we never damaged or defaced property, never stole anything or even left a heavy physical footprint of our presence. We liked the adventure, the daring escapades inside darkened hallways and classrooms, and the anticipation of the unexpected. It was all so cloak and dagger and exciting as hell! We did, however, leave our humorous calling cards, namely, rearranging pupils' desks, lightly rifling through teachers' desk drawers, stacking class projects inside waste baskets, and, meticulously writing curse words and preposterous witty sayings on many chalkboards throughout the schools that we had visited. It was juvenile and jesterous stuff, but we loved it. We were never disciplined because no one knew what we had done. This went on throughout our "stellar" musical careers, all through and including senior year. It was great fun and we relished the opportunities to nose around foreign high schools and then laugh about our daredevilry, daring-do later on, as we spilled the beans in confidence to our awe struck "crew" and fellow orchestra mates. I wouldn't recommend our brand of "fun" to anyone, but I'm sure others have also followed our tack, just have not bragged about it, or have been caught and punished. Let's hope not!

40

Waterboys

Why did I repeatedly keep signing up for art classes when I knew they would be more of the same? Namely, Mr. L.'s continued mockery of my supposed talents while rewarding me with decent grades. It was downright bipolar. The same dynamic occurred as predicted in the first two quarters of tenth grade when I took Drawing and Painting with him. I asked for it and I got it! I thought I had an ounce of inherited artistic skills and fought the good fight, demonstrating my perceived-as-feeble oil and acrylic renderings as well as pencil sketches to a tough taskmaster. Mr.-"backwoodsman"-L. turned out to be as demanding as my old man, darn it. I didn't need TWO fathers disparaging my seemingly ineffectual efforts! And I mistakenly thought that high school art was an easy A and my happy place to be. Ha, ha. Mr. L. frequently ridiculed my projects and made me feel incompetent. Maybe he was right. As compared to others in my artsy-fartsy class, perhaps I was more show than tell. Perhaps I was a fraud and only got lucky at times with pieces of work that just happened to tickle his fancy on a given day? Was I only a one trick pony? All these thoughts raced through my head

as I began the third quarter, with the name of the course
called Watercolor Painting. Hopefully I would shine in
that class; hopefully Mr. L. would know shit from Shinola
and reward me with high marks again. Hopefully. But first
we greenhorns had to learn many preparatory steps before
purposely drenching a canvas with colored water. It was a
challenging medium to paint in and had its set of
idiosyncratic rules to follow, including stretching, taping,
drying, etc. What? That's right; those were all necessary
items that had to be addressed before the initial
brushstroke could be stroked. First came the foundation.
Large flat boards measuring at least two feet by two feet
were disbursed to the students along with water-based
masking tape and special white, watercolor paper. The idea
was to stretch and slightly shrink the paper tautly on the
wooden board before drying it so that it would not wrinkle
or warp when water was applied to it. Ok, we all stood in
line in front of the huge sink in the side cubby of the art
room, to take turns soaking our papers thoroughly and
then mounting them onto the boards with the special
masking tape. It was a messy ordeal, with water spilled
everywhere, including on clothing and shoe tops. Woe to
the girls and guys who wore sandals to class. I confess that
I thought our original brand of "water boarding" was
student "torture." Who knew that those two words would

later be appropriated for another type of watery technique used to extract confessions from government enemy combatants? Anyway, after an overnight drying period, the paper/plank combos were ready to be painted on. Mr. L. flamboyantly and smugly began each period with a few master strokes of direction on his personal canvas while we struggling artists watched in awe, silently stroking his behemoth ego at the same time. We had the example in front of us and learned the technique-of-the-day before slowly embarking on our own odysseys into the liquid world of watercolor renderings. I had borrowed my father's expensive Grumbacher brushes and felt prepared to attack my tighty-whitie papyrus using the provided but messed-up school-issued paints and unwashed steel palettes. And, hey, I put out a few gems right from the get-go and must have mildly impressed that impish impresario Mr. L. He also liked the wet images that a few other students splattered on their drenched papers and decided to pair me up with D.T., a fellow sophomore and lukewarm acquaintance, at worst. We had known each other since elementary school yet he kind of faded into the background and languidly embraced the role of an unassuming athlete and pupil. He wasn't dumb or uncoordinated. No, he was just not a go-getter. He was shy and retiring but introspective and insightful about a great many things, as I soon found out. Mr. L. even let a few of our paired teams venture outside our cellblock on sunny days to do our dirty work; first lightly sketching and then slamming colors between the faint lines to try and capture the beautifully shaded landscapes around our alma mater. D.T. would grin broadly as he parted his long, dark hippie hair from out of his eyes before picking up a large bucket of water prior to our outdoor adventure. I did the same. You needed fresh water with which to periodically refill small cups, before dipping the used brushes in them for cleaning and rehydration purposes. We also carried our unwieldy boards and painting supplies as we strolled through the hallways on our way out the front door. Once in a while, *Shag*, our "bulldog" principal, would accost us but let us pass because he knew what we were up to and where we were going. He would grimace and then beam broadly, and I didn't blame him. We resembled two nerdy waterboys, but from the art department and not a sports team. Oh, well, hopefully we provided him with a few moments of amusement. The art that D.T. and I created during that spring was nothing compared to the deep discussions we had. He had a certain gentle and benevolent nature and never seemed worried or hurried, even in his speech. I was relaxed in his company as I continually pushed the boundary of inappropriate comedy that was always bubbling out of me. But our talks did turn serious on many occasions and I was amazed at his deliberate, sensible and sober arguments about many situations regarding politics and life in general. We never socialized outside of that artsy classroom but greatly looked forward to our daily oral dalliances involving psychological and philosophical topics. He came from a large local family, with many brothers and sisters, yet we did not discuss his or my familial strife and resultant stressors. We had bigger problems to ponder; namely, the origin of the universe, the roots of religions, war, liberalism, conservatism, etc. We each spoke about big boy stuff at the tender ages of fifteen. Art ended and we both received stellar grades, by Mr. L.'s exacting and critical standards. Hey, an A was an A. However, the next time I literally bumped into D.T. was at our graduation. We stood and stared at one another with knowing looks on our faces and exchanged a few well-meaning nods. Nothing new needed to be argued or said. And then we parted company for the last time. Sadly, D.T. passed away by middle age. I wished I had reconnected with him, if only to continue our ancient dialogue and perhaps to paint side by side again.

41

Endless Hammering

As already discussed and questioned in my previous books: when does a person decide to quit something that she/he has no realistic potential of getting better at? No matter what the money-grubbing, feel-good and positivity gurus (does Tony Robbins ring a bell?) would have most of us chumps believe, effort and moola spent on a particular endeavor usually yields zilch, or at least results far less than anticipated. Life happens! Of course, there can be various variables at play, including bad genetics, bad luck, lack of outside help, etc., but the bottom line is this: when do you walk away from likely failure? Is it when you are completely broken and destitute or when you see the writing on the wall? Do you dutifully keep plugging along and then wait for and expect a superior outcome while practicing your ass off? Do you listen to the "yes men" in your corner as they convince you to keep giving it the "old college try?" Scholastic achievement often follows this axiomatic curve but at least even a mediocre general education can have lasting benefits. Learning to read, write and tie your shoes is undoubtedly helpful in life. Right? What I'm talking about is sports and the arts. Many little boys aspire to be major league baseball players, many girls want to be professional soccer players, etc. And within both young sexes are also the "labeled" *wunderkinds* who desire to be the next great violinist, pianist, painter, author or actor. Those are all valid and lucid daydreams to have while growing up to keep spirits buoyed and the psyche healthy and enthusiastic. However, when is it time to maturely abandon an infantile and unrealistic ongoing process without psychological damage? I wish I knew an easy answer to that question and only have my examples to go by. Musically speaking, I was born with a bit of talent and piano became my instrument of study, and a significant part of my growing persona. Also at an early age it turned out that I had inherited athletic ability and tennis became my go-to sport. It quickly developed into my primary outlet for exercise, athletic pleasure and competition. By age nine, and with much parental encouragement, it appeared as if I was constantly hammering the keyboard as well as white, fuzzy balls, though with different methods and in disparate venues. Well, there was no tennis playing in the wintertime; table tennis took its place. However, it was virtually the same thing: hitting a round white orb and keeping score, while desperately trying to improve to get to the "next level." Now, I can't blame my folks, or my friends, or even myself for my self-deluded visions of futuristic grandeur. No, I just didn't have what it took to professionally excel in music or sports and, painfully, had to come to grips with that utter reality. I recall endless piano rehearsals, recitals, and successful annual NYSSMA competitions all through elementary school and junior high. And then there were the myriad of concerts that I performed in as part of some type of musical showcase or church services (not Catholic, however). I had reached the dizzying heights of Grade V music and had unlimited determination, but limited talent and ability. After two successive teachers and hundreds of dollars spent, by eleventh grade I was done. I was burnt out and had not developed into the next Liberace. My mom and dad were a little disappointed but all the practice in the world, as well as concentrating and hoping, would not magically turn me into a great pianist. Either you had it, or you didn't. And I didn't. Because my self-identity was so wrapped up with the black and whites, it was hard for me to admit defeat, but I eventually did. I found myself gradually playing less and less and had changed my music from classical to contemporary, to help ease the blow. And I gracefully bowed out of the music scene and haven't played much since. Shameful but true. Tennis also rudely slapped me upside the head. Jimmy Connors was my '70s idol and attaining his level of on-court performance and championship style seemed ludicrously simple. Just practice, practice, practice and think positive thoughts. Ha, ha; bullshit! Although I was a fine high school player with an outstanding win/loss record by the end of tenth grade, I thought I could easily do better. Well, I could not. At the season-end Sectionals, as I was annoyingly losing to a bum in the third round from Section IV, class B, I happened to glance over at the Section IV, class A players, on the court next to me. They were literally slugging the covers off the balls, running from corner to corner and playing like junior pros. I felt disheartened; I didn't possess a game like THAT. I probably would not get a single point off either of them if we had played a match. And to top it off, there I was, losing to an inferior player because I had lost all focus and concentration. It was a terrible feeling. My old man was yelling encouragement from the stands while I was aimlessly and listlessly faltering. He and I had naïvely set unrealistically high tennis standards for me and I failed to live up to them. Whacking balls in the summer only, on windblown, cracked hometown courts with no professional tutelage was not the recipe for future championships. I had been doomed from the start; all that, and with limited skill, too. Björn Borg had won the French Open at seventeen; I was fifteen and couldn't beat a dumpy chump from Bainbridge-Guilford, N.Y. at our local two-bit

Sectionals! What was wrong with me? So, tennis started to fade from my life as a big deal and my father facetiously acknowledged that it was alright to just play for "fun." I really needed to hear that even though he said it to me in a sarcastic tone. My competitive pride had been bruised but was still marginally intact. Well, I finished my high school tennis career after my junior year with an excellent record and actively played against the local college kids and my coach/dad during my senior year and following summer, just not for "wins" anymore. One of my dad's former college standouts visited our home in '77 and my father excitedly asked him how his "professional" tennis career was going. "Well," he began slowly, "I work at a swanky indoor club in New York City, picking up balls all day long while teaching little old ladies how to play." When I heard that, I knew that I had made the right decision in not pursuing or getting too despondent about not being a pro player. Here was one in my own house who seemed discouraged at his overly optimistic career choice of becoming a professional. It was good to hear such honesty and to witness my father's cringing face upon listening to such uninspiring news. Besides humor and smarts, piano and tennis were "my bags" in high school; "special" things that identified me from among the lowlifes in my class. It was an ego boost, something I was good at, perhaps even

to do for a living someday. But alas, neither came to
fruition. Nevertheless, in the many years since those
anguishing times, I have won many amateur tennis
championships in various age groups at the local and
national level, as well as four international snowshoe
sprinting gold medals and a slew of track and javelin first
place awards. Am I still looking to go pro? Is my ego that
fragile that being a dentist, father, husband and writing-
hack is not good enough? Maybe; I just wish there was
money in it for seniors players. I would finally clean up
financially and exorcize those demons of doubt from
yesteryear, at least in racquet sports and on the playing
field. Musically, not so much.

42

Typical Village Living?

This musing (not amusing, although it may be) is a
synopsis of typical village living, at least as seen, heard and
felt by me. Stereotypical labeling of outsiders by many of
my fellow students and townspeople was commonplace.
Thusly, non natives were often unfairly judged based on
the color of their skin, their unpronounceable surnames
and places of birth. It was all part and parcel of purposeful
political incorrectness, prejudices and ingrained biases. But
what did you expect from a stagnant genetic pool? Through
no fault of their own, local yokels unwittingly wallowed in
generational mediocrity. It was a place where only the last
names changed, with the faces of progeny appearing
virtually the same, birth after birth, year after year. Were
small town people really small-minded? It certainly
appeared that way to many outsiders who decided to make
their homes in an outwardly blissful and inviting homey
settlement. My family and I were "foreigners" who plopped
down and stayed amid the redneck brethren, and after
quietly suffering for years, slowly became accepted, but to a
point. We never fit in completely, nor were ever fully
befriended by the village idiots as truly one of their own.

My immigrant parents were college professors and my sister and I, though both born in the U.S., sometimes felt ostracized by the "seemingly" nice folks in town and at school. But we made it, and my mom and dad still live in "that" same dinky village to this day. And there were other crazy examples of stereotypes: nearly every male, including my pop, had legal firearms in the house, and deer hunting season was a sacred ritual. And nearly every home was unlocked during the day and night; however, woe to the potential inebriated college student or uninformed burglar who dared to break into a domicile. They would be shot first and then questioned later. But there were never any reports of gunplay. If you wanted physical relief for your frustrations, you could easily join the local highly ranked gun club (of which my old man was a sharpshooting member), or plink at the plentiful bevy of woodchucks to be found in the many farm fields surrounding our peaceful settlement. If it was spiritual relief that you were after, there were at least a dozen or more houses of worship that dotted our streets and rolling hills. It was a wonder that people got along as well as they did. And you would think that the liberal leaning professors and the conservative farmer-types would not see eye to eye. Well, maybe, but their offspring attended the same rural school system and literally rubbed shoulders with each other in class, on the playground and on the playing fields. There were few, if any, fights due to political ideology. The local high school population was roughly evenly divided between the children of farmers/rural folk, and the offspring of the junior college educators. It was a mixed bag of social customs, intelligence, and cultures, all thrown together in a dusty, one-horse town. The sons and daughters of professors usually left town to attend universities to better themselves whereas the farm boys usually married their high school sweethearts and got busy, eventually filling the town with their whippersnappers and continuing the cliched cycle of "inbreeding." My good friend and fellow "crew" member G.P. had a knack for oration and joined the FFA (Future Farmers of America). He was no farmer, nor barnyard shit shoveler, but was often full of bullshit, nonetheless. However, his speechifying was enough to get him noticed, first locally, then regionally and finally nationally. He is a lawyer today. Sometimes the oddest set of circumstances got you out of the middle of a mudhole. We had one police chief, one sheriff and one jail, being the county seat and all. And that was enough. The Ag and Tech students usually stayed in their dorms on campus while the local troublemakers stayed at home. Since we were a "dry" town up through the late '70s, very few liquor-fueled fights occurred. If you wanted fishing, there were trout in the many tributaries and streams around town. Bullheads? We had them, too. Carp? You know it; that's what the dirty and scummy West Branch of the Delaware River that ran under the wooden covered bridge and then under the steel bridge on Kingston Street was famous for. In other words, if you liked field and stream and huntin' and fishin' you couldn't beat our area. There was no theater and a defunct bowling alley. Nevertheless, there were plentiful no cost tennis courts around at the time, and the college golf course and free town pool provided other avenues of recreation. There was never any hurry to get things done; however, things got done in spite of the perceived lackadaisical prevailing attitude in the air, which was clean and fresh, by the way. I could go on describing the pros and cons of my life growing up in a dinky no-account place. But I will end this rambling report by merely stating the obvious: Regardless of its shortcomings as compared to big city smarts and big city living, I wouldn't trade small town habitation as a youngster for anything. My friends and I grew up as "hicks and hillbillies" and didn't know it, yet most of us managed to have great upbringings in a beautiful setting without undue pollution, crime or strife. Some of us left, some of us stayed. It didn't matter. It was the quality of life that had molded us from an early age and I for one am grateful to this day.

43

The Hoosier Visit

My family and I had already traveled successfully to Florida by automobile twice, as well as journeyed by car numerous times to western New York State to visit relatives. So, what was a measly trek a bit farther westward past our state, Pennsylvania, Ohio, and into Indiana? Nothing. We had been to the Hoosier State a few times when I was in grammar school. But those quick jaunts were considered only perfunctory and introductory forays to meet our filthy rich relatives (my father's female first cousin Aunt M. was married to a travel trailer magnate in Elkhart). However, this upcoming two-week summer vacation junket came with a sinister purpose, only I didn't know it at the time. My Aunt M. (actually my second cousin) and mom arranged the timing of the trip and we packed our bags to depart for the fourteen-hour voyage into the blazing western sun. The car ride was uneventful, save for the intense thunderstorms that we encountered along the way. The flat land magnified the intensity and breadth of the lightning strikes and scared us a little. There was no place to hide, no mountains or hills to act as shields or buffers when inclement weather arose. I finally

181

understood the plight of the local populace whenever a devastating tornado or twister descended out of the heavens and wreaked havoc upon it. I sat in front and listened to our Pace CB Radio crackle with funny, trucker-inspired "driving" comments on channel 19, such as "I'll catch you on the flip flop," or "we got us a convoy going west on I-90." I rarely talked into the mic as the Purple Pansy but when I did, it was cursory stuff, with no agenda or humor. Nonetheless as I sat there watching the endless prairie whiz by, I was struck by the curious things we had brought. Pop made sure I packed my new, Davis II, plastic laminated wooden tennis racquet as well as my Jack Purcell kicks, thick socks and shorts. He also personally stowed my and his Stiga ping pong paddles, sweatbands and white, Halex three-star balls. His attention to my sporting equipment being in his '65 Olds station wagon was disconcerting. Why was he so adamant about my athletic gear? And why did mom take great pains to include my latest learned piano sheet music as part of her luggage? And why was my little sister left out of the mysterious "packing" equation? I would soon have the answers. We landed in the evening, right on time, at their luxurious address on Grady Boulevard. Oh, the "relatives" had a grand house; a huge modified split-level monstrosity with an attached in-law apartment, a fully finished basement (tiled floor, ping pong table, pool table, a Latvian Novus pool table, a full bar, etc.), and a garage housing a late model Cadillac sedan and a sporty BMW roadster. Her and his cars, respectively. There were pictures of a gorgeous Maserati adorning the basement walls, but it was "always in the shop." Uncle L. reportedly pushed it often and hard, too hard. My third cousin, and their only son G., was older than me and had a "cheap" but souped-up, standard shift, Volkswagen Scirocco, which he always drove fast, emulating his father in the MPH department. Police tickets for speeding didn't apply to either Uncle L. or his spoiled, bratty son, because much of the city worked at the plant that he owned. The cops were politically savvy and didn't rock the boat, so to speak. So, enter the woebegone and "unsophisticated" Philistines from Bumfuck, New York, who arrived in an uncouth older model station wagon and without pretense or highfalutin airs. Genetically my father and Aunt M. were related; however that's where the similarity ended. Both had separately immigrated to the U.S. Through marriage to a wily and conniving fellow immigrant (Uncle L.), she and her husband quickly amassed a fortune in the RV business while my dad was still scraping by as an intelligent yet poorly paid college professor back east. And there was one more "relative" to consider: Aunt M.'s electrical engineer brother Uncle A., who, with financial help from her, opened up a successful engineering firm manufacturing gizmos and timers for the food industry. Uncle A. had a daughter my age and two younger sons, the older one being very athletically gifted. And here is where the real story begins. No sooner had we unpacked, kissed each other on the cheeks in customary welcome, and had an evening bite to eat, when Uncle L. ushered the men folk and Uncle A.'s sporty son, who seemed to live there, into the cellar to play some table tennis. Pop was tired after driving all day but managed to squeak out a few victories against the tricky Uncle L., who played regularly in an advanced league in his city. He was pissed as hell for losing a few games to my old man but sarcastically congratulated pop on his winning style. At this point I should have realized that there were more than mere games at stake. There was envy, animosity and familial tensions going back decades. I recalled that on our previous short Florida trips, when we would sporadically visit the already vacationing Uncle L. and his "dynasty" at their luxurious Juno Beach condo complex, pop and he would go at it on the ratty ping pong table that was set up in the basement of the building. That may have been when the seeds of one-upmanship were sown. Hmmm…. Anyway, back to Indiana. Next up was me, to play my third cousin G., the one with the fast car and narcissistic disregard for most fellow humans. I spanked him badly a few times; however, it was expected and only my first test. First test? Yes, this is how related immigrant families sorted out the pecking order among their respective young men: through competition. It no longer mattered what the old alpha males did in life; it was now their progeny that had to man up, live up to expectations and prove which family was superior. Are you kidding me? No wonder pop had carefully socked away all of my sporting equipment before our voyage. He knew what to expect and was hoping I would deliver, big time. No pressure there. And as far as G. losing to me, he was a much better billiard and piano player than I, so we were now even-steven. Then up to the table came Uncle A.'s son and we battled and fought that little plastic white ball into submission, with slams, chops, twists and hard hits. Unfortunately, he bested me every time and I felt more than defeated. Uncle L. was elated as my father just grimaced at me in disgust. It was that important to win. Meanwhile, upstairs, my mom and Aunt M. were casually bantering about nonsense, never discussing the disparate riches of our mutual families or my grandpa Pete, who was Aunt M.'s father's bona fide brother from the old country. My sister just played by herself and was largely left out of anything to do with family honor. I came up the cellar steps sweaty and disappointed as pop roughly grabbed me in the hall and whispered that I just had to do better at tennis the next day. His ego was at stake; these so-called undeserving millionaires had to be shown up and I was the one that HAD to do it. Nevertheless, I was too busy shaking with fear for not measuring up when it counted to grasp the situation. But then I began to understand. All that we poor relations from New York State had was our pride and athletic prowess. This would be our chance to ridicule these nouveau riche peasants and put them in their place, or at least have them show us a little more respect. The next day, a tennis match was arranged by Uncle L. between Uncle A.'s tennis "superstar" son (the same one who had defeated me in ping pong) and me at a local high school court. Now, I had just come off a magnificent spring high school tennis season and felt confident about my game. We drove to a strange high school court and would be playing at night, under the lights. Yikes, I was not ready for that. With my stern-looking father pacing back and forth as well as the crew of male "relatives" looking on and cheering for their "boy," I won the match 6-4, 6-4, in a tight battle of wills and slugging forehands. Pop grinned from ear to ear while Uncle A.'s son angrily chucked his expensive racquet across the court and pouted. Uncle L. couldn't believe what had just occurred. How could a tennis prodigy whose expensive private lessons he paid for lose to a hick from the sticks? How could a country bumpkin like me beat a budding tennis star who practically lived on the courts of the private Elcona Country Club, and whose membership he sponsored? How could his nephew actually lose to ME? It wasn't right, it wasn't fair. We all went home in the same car without a word spoken. My father was proud and later congratulated me on that wild win. The next day there would be a truce with no sports involved. The Eastern European ethos of comparing and contrasting young males from different family clans was suspended for a day. Yay! We were invited to go out to a pricy and popular Japanese steakhouse called Benihana of Tokyo; all fifteen of us, including Uncle L.'s first cousin and business partner Uncle E. and his family, as well as Uncle A., his wife and his other two children. It was going to be a fantastic feast we were told, and Uncle L. would magnanimously pick up the tab. I had trepidations to say the least. All I had heard about Japanese cuisine was that there was raw fish involved. Yuck! Well, it was a hibachi style affair, with only the hoity toity relatives indulging in some sushi and sashimi appetizers to show off their "rich" palettes. We were seated around a huge square table with a hot grill in the middle. And then the show started. My family and I stuck to the main course of rice, greens, and steak, which was expertly doled out to us by the chef who nonchalantly twirled razor-sharp cutting implements in the air while talking and cooking our fare. It was an unexpected display of skill and showmanship and that's why people went there. My family and I were mesmerized as we ate. There was nothing like this in our neck of the redneck woods, that's for sure. Everyone appeared to be having fun. However, unbeknownst to me, Uncle L. and his cousin Uncle E.'s son sat next to each other and were plotting a tennis match whereby M. was sure to beat me. It was all set up and sprung on me the next day. It would be held on the clay courts at the Elcona Country Club, at high noon. Now, I had heard of my opponent's tournament victories, private lessons and physical fitness. Plus, he was a few years older than me and played on his college team. Pop was gung-ho about the situation but not me. I had never played on clay before, hated the heat and had questionable conditioning. We warmed up, a crowd of kibitzing club members started to gather, and I looked over at pop, who just sat there stone-faced, like at an execution. The other male relatives, including the guy I had recently bested in straight sets, were catcalling and encouraging M., but I heard nothing from dear old dad. Maybe even he realized that I was over my head and would be soundly trounced. It didn't happen, however. Sure, M. had beautiful ground strokes and wore nice white shorts, white socks and a white collared shirt, but he didn't have "game." I took it to him 7-5, 6-1 and walked off the unfamiliar kitty litter surface thoroughly exhausted. Unbelievably, the first person who grabbed me in a Russian bear hug was Uncle L., who loudly declared me the unofficial club champion and announced my name to all the gawking onlookers, including my speechless father. Even though Uncle L. had been the perpetrator and arranger of all these athletic bouts, he seemed to embrace my winning attitude and laughed at his thoroughly shamed and inconsolable nephew. And even though we were only related by marriage, Uncle L. suddenly took a shine to me, much to the consternation of his "real" relatives. And then the shit really hit the fan. When M.'s father found out about his only son's loss to a paltry peon, he went nuclear and blew more than a gasket, calling his cousin Uncle L. every name in the book while asking him over and over why he had set up the match in the first place? Was he a moron? What was he thinking? Uncle E. could be really nasty, and even worse when drunk. Uncle L. retorted that he thought it was a good idea at the time, plus he didn't think I would actually win. So, technically it wasn't his fault. I often wonder how badly M. got it that night from his father Uncle E. for not beating me and ultimately embarrassing his "family." However, I was relieved, pop was beaming, and that was the blissful end to all the bullshit of using me as a surrogate sportsman to determine intertribal dominance. And, it felt good to be Uncle L.'s new favorite "nephew." I actually started to like him, too. The rest of the vacation consisted of me playing the piano, reading comic books, continuing to play ping pong, and whiling away the days not doing a whole heck of a lot. Gone was the pressure to perform, and it seemed that the adults around me had calmed down as well. No one argued, no one insinuated anything as relatives came, partied and left. So, what was the fourteen day tally in sportsmanship and in the win/loss column? Well, pop beat everyone in chess and successfully managed to win more ping pong matches against Uncle L. I sucked with a pool cue and at Latvian Novus, however I started to hold my own in table tennis against Uncle A.'s quirky and dorky son. In piano, Uncle L.'s son blew me away; G. was older than me, was more experienced and simply had more talent. But in tennis, instead of capitulating and reinforcing the prevailing wisdom of being a perpetual "loser," I upset the dominant paradigm and emerged undefeated against highly touted foes. It was an unexpected and minor miracle and at first didn't sit well with my indignant "cousins" and their kinfolk. However, it all blew over and we left Indiana still speaking to one

another. So I guess the sports combatants from each side
had won enough to not only save face but to salvage a few
bragging rights as well; until we would all meet up again.
Just a small corollary to this sports story. Although former
aristocrat grandpa Pete and his no-account, freeloader
older brother had independently emigrated to this country
and set up separate lives in distant locations, the eventual
materialistic success of each one's offspring and related
family members could not have become more disparate.
We became the intelligent paupers, first living in western
New York State and then in the sequestered Catskills. By
contrast, the stupid Midwestern "cousins" became
fabulously wealthy and snooty. However, like most ups and
downs in life and in karmic dogma, the reverse is finally
occurring. The riches of the "Hoosiers" have been watered
down and largely squandered through succeeding dumbass
generations while we "insignificant" hillbillies have
prospered. My sister, me and our respective family
members have obtained more advanced educational
degrees than all those western flatlanders put together.
And, through hard work and patience, the trickle of wealth
has finally blessed our "tribe" and turned the tables in our
favor. In a few more years, any competition between our
two "family clans" will be a moot and forgotten point,
even in sports. Amen.

Take a break!

JUNIOR YEAR

It's time to really, really get serious

44

Mom Hits the Books

My indomitable mother: how else can I describe her? She went from being an eighteen-year-old bride, after a rather lackluster high school stint, to a teenage mother and homemaker, and then to a professor of French and Spanish at our local college after garnering a bachelor's and two master's degrees in middle age. But how, and why? Here is the story: After voluntarily leaving a large, cesspool of a city in western New York State, my former immigrant parents were delighted to integrate themselves as best as possible into a tiny, backwater Catskills village with a two-year NJCAA college up on the hill. My dad had secured a professorship at that college teaching civil engineering. He was all set, as was I enrolled in kindergarten at the local elementary school up on the other hill in town. True, there was initial animosity toward me and my family because of our dark looks, dark hair and my folks' accent-laden pronunciations, but we adjusted, took it on the chin and quietly lived our lives in the bucolic settlement we now called home. Then, as expected, my retired, very old-school, immigrant, and paternal grandfather sold his house, traveled across the state and unceremoniously moved in with us. He came in with a bang, like a mean meat cleaver ready to slice and dice our family apart. He arrogantly designated himself the chieftain, the *Hetman* (the old-world Slavic term for a tribal leader), and slowly started to drive my stay-at-home mother bonkers. My father taught all day, I was in school and my baby sister was freshly hatched. Our foursome grew to five people as the two in-laws at our squished rental apartment started seeing red more and more with each passing month. And although we soon had a large, brand-new house built by my pop and grandpa, the familiar infighting continued. Imagine a peasant-bred, muddy, Estonian hamlet in Europe, with ignorant kerchief wearing babushkas needlessly bickering and insulting one another over a fence dividing their respective properties; two old biddies going at it, day after day, year after year. Finally, mom couldn't take it anymore, but didn't know what to do. "Why don't you go to college to get out of the house?" suggested my always logical and most intellectual dad. "I barely finished high school; I'm stupid, remember?" retorted my mother, rather sarcastically. "Plus, where would I go?" she asked him. "Why, right next door," he exclaimed rather smugly. And, so, her odyssey began. Her woeful transcripts from Benjamin Franklin high school in western N.Y. were begotten and sent, a few strings were pulled, and mom became a fulltime freshman at the local Ag and Tech in town, with my father acting as her ad hoc faculty advisor. She enrolled as a general studies major, not really knowing what career to prepare for, or even if this junior college gig would bear any kind of fruit at all. She still had to care for her family at home and now came studying, reading, and learning with a brain that had effectively shut down after her high school graduation, many years earlier. However, pop and I promised to help more around the house and act as her on-call mentors and tutors. Grandpa Pete sneered but clammed up; the possibility of an adult educated woman in the house rankled him some and he had to eat crow, at least for now, unless she failed out, which easily could have happened. But it didn't. Nonetheless, our family dynamic was turned upside down because of her collegiate schedule and new hectic lifestyle. Nevertheless, we were all in it together, even my sourpuss Grandpa Pete, who begrudgingly started to gain new respect for his "doormat" daughter-in-law. Mom started right in, with youngsters half her age sitting all around her and listening to the same professors that she used to socialize with at parties who were now trying to teach her as a bona fide student. Yikes, that must have been awkward at times because they all knew my old man from social and academic meetings, as well. However, that particular paradigm aided my mother enormously. I surreptitiously heard that she was sometimes "helped" along by "friendly faculty," especially in difficult courses like biology and chemistry. In addition, my dad, sister and I all liberally pitched in at home to make sure mom's homework assignments were topnotch as well as book reports that were properly and astutely written. Mom didn't cheat per se, but got more than a leg up from willing accomplices, at least at the beginning when she was just trying to mentally stay afloat in the academic world. However, little by little, with botched biological dissections and catastrophic chemical experiments under her belt, she gained confidence and her previously dormant brain rebooted itself into a scholastic sponge, absorbing all the new knowledge thrown her way. But she had no head for figures or science and gradually gravitated toward linguistics, grammar and English. After two years she finished with an A average and was elected to the junior college's honor society. Then she made a choice to further her studies at the state university close by, via a serpentine roadway and over dual treacherous large mountains, nineteen miles away. Her major would be elementary education with a minor in French. She thought that teaching in our hometown grammar school would be a good fit for her, regardless of a persistent Estonian accent.

At home she still did all the cooking, washing, cleaning, shopping, ironing, etc. It was double duty for her. Even though we had promised her aid, I think my sister and I helped her most by already being grown up and not demanding her time or involvement in our lives. We could tie our shoes, feed ourselves, knew when to come and go, and didn't really need an afterschool "babysitter" any longer. I left for pharmacy college when she embarked on her bachelor's degree and I only heard academic success stories whenever I visited home or phoned her. Much later I was told of the arduous daily commute that she had to do, the multiple fender benders that occurred enroute, and the disastrous winter driving that plagued her. On many occasions she had to enlist the services of her live-in, dreaded father-in-law as a designated driver; he loved to show off his wintry driving skills whenever the snowstorms were too much for her to handle and he loved to lord that ability over her. He was a piece of work, that man. Nevertheless, mom completed the mandatory student teaching assignment in Walton, N.Y., graduated with honors, and was excited to be hired. However, the local school brass whom she personally knew and who had "promised" her a position were now silent. Other close-by municipalities also did not want her. All that work and education seemed wasted, as she depressingly told me one day. She wasn't a local dungaree-clad gal, had a thick European accent, and when push came to shove she got the heave-ho, without even getting started. I was now a senior in pharmacy school and my sister also in college when mom serendipitously lamented her woes to Mrs. H., the very elderly and longtime local college French professor. Because my mom had grown up as a child refugee in Belgium during and after WWII before emigrating to this country, she could speak, read and write fluently in French. Coupled with her B.S. minor in said language, she was a cinch to teach it. Well, one thing led to another and, with a little buttering up of our family friend the new college president, my mother became Mrs. H.'s assistant. Kind of like a teacher's aide in elementary school, but at the collegiate level. It was assumed that she would take over at some point and that's what indeed occurred. However, just as mom was about to assume a professor's gig at our Ag and Tech, the president gently informed her that her position would be part-time at best as the state university higher-ups in Albany N.Y. were seriously thinking of eliminating foreign languages at two-year colleges altogether. What could she do? She met with the president and he came up with an audacious plan. If she got her master's degree in French AND Spanish, then the college MIGHT be justified in hiring her full-time as a dual language professor. But she would have to do all the heavy lifting and get those degrees "Taco Pronto!" I had begun dental school and my younger sister was enrolled in pharmacy college while my pugnacious female parent plugged away again, at the same nearby state university where she had completed her undergraduate degree. So, while smartly ignoring Grandpa Pete's constant grandstanding and his many manufactured familial squabbles, and while teaching part-time, she ground out a French master's degree, as if she really needed one! But she now had the piece of paper to prove she was legit. And too legit to quit! She was hired full-time with the proviso that she would complete a Spanish master's asap. She started teaching French, freshman Study Skills and Basic English and at the same time toiled away in advanced Spanish classes herself. I think Grandpa Pete's car, a '72, rear wheel drive, green, AMC Hornet, had the road (Route 28) memorized at this point because of the hundreds of miles that she had driven it between our village and the city next door, with more miles to go! I was finishing dental school when I heard that mom had gotten her M.S. in Spanish. Yes, Si! Finally. What a time it was, with me about to finish as a dentist, my sister about to graduate as a pharmacist, and my previously dowdy-housewife mother continually buying expensive outfits to look the part of a genuine,

French/Spanish professor. She had more degrees than my father, more brains than my grandfather reluctantly gave her credit for, and a natural gift for teaching. She ultimately forgave the "high school administration" fakes, finks and two-faced phonies who had said they would hire her for our town's grammar school but instead repeatedly employed barely qualified local yokel "milkmaids." Mom ended up fitting in beautifully into the enlightened college community for a twenty-five year stretch of lecturing where her Estonian "accent" became part of the act. We were all proud of her, especially my dad. One year, mom and pop even had a seminal college yearbook dedicated to them, as the "dynamic duo." But if you were to meet her today you would be hard pressed to recognize a gifted lady who can speak five languages fluently (English, Estonian, Russian, French, Spanish) and was once a compelling and energetic college instructress for decades before voluntarily and gracefully leaving at age sixty five, ten years after my dad retired. She continues to be a self-effacing and modest senior citizen and shrugs off her educational and professional accomplishments as effortless conquests. Sure, she once again cooks, washes, cleans, shops, and irons but without a day job to go to. However, that wondrous lengthy interlude in her life got her out from under the dictatorial thumb of Grandpa Pete, made her a good coin, and transformed her into the person she now is. She continues to be an inspirational and perpetual role model for me. If she could do it, anyone can. And that's the truth.

45

The Very Walls Have Ears

Her room was on the first floor at the end of the hall, next to Mr. J.O.'s "famous" math room. It was the second most prestigious location in the unwritten hierarchy of our petty and Podunk place of learning. Mr. J.O.'s room was first, of course. Anyway, Mrs. L.R. was a junior and senior English lecturer and wife of my former eighth grade physical science teacher. She mainly taught courses that involved reading with comprehension and writing with intent. My cunning guidance counselor had figured out that I had a flair for her kind of classes and signed me up, bypassing British Lit. and other related courses that I might have taken instead. I was glad that he had me take her Major Authors I class right out of the gate that fall. I heard she was a good teacher and the subject matter seemed right up my alley. All this anticipatory buildup, and then I met her. She was an old biddy! Now, I knew she was up there in years; previously I had literally run into her a few times on the way to the lunchroom, which was just past her door and at the end of a long hallway. But at closer inspection she was also thin, frail-looking and had that hardened face which suggested that no amount of bullshit could buffalo her. It was obvious that she had been around the block a few times and would not be trifled with. She adjusted her pointy, horn-rimmed glasses, opened her pie hole and set us straight from day one. Wow, she was one tough bird! However, maybe she had to be or was genetically predisposed, or, both? Maybe her withering personality was necessary to keep law and order among the many rednecks in our midst? Maybe? I knew that her two sons, after graduating from our school years ago, both became medical doctors. So perhaps her heavy-handed character and style of teaching produced results not only in the classroom but at her home as well? Probably. She constantly feigned disciplinary action while I constantly sought to do my usual comedic *shtick*. But regardless of our dissimilar ages and approaches to "reading and regurgitation," we bonded at some level. It was "like" at first sight between us. Fast forward a few months and my class was debating that convoluted novel *War and Peace*. What a story! What mumbo jumbo! What complicated Russian names we had to needlessly memorize! I had to liven things up and routinely ridiculed Tolstoy in a teasing way. I had to. Someone had to do it. My GPA was in the mid nineties and I had already proven myself worthy of her by my insightful responses to exacting test questions. And my humorous sidebars and timely rejoinders were slowly gaining traction, too. Sure I could write down some intense prose as needed but I could also tacitly turn into a quirky clown at a moment's notice. However, it appeared that someone had tipped her off about me and my "disrespectful" side. I must have tickled her funny bone in a unique way because she let me slide, time and again, while holding the rest of the class hostage with her acerbic tongue. No one dared question her authority or interpretations of scholarly works of fiction; only I got away with it, but in a joking fashion that she deemed appropriate. My responses to her queries were often filled with preposterous sarcasm or downright hysterical and improbable answers. She laughed, my fellow pupils laughed, and so I continued to seed the room with mirth as the semester (first and second quarters) passed. And many was the time when she would say a few words to me after class, nothing special, just a few syllables in friendship. That's when I started to confide in her, privately of course, before homeroom in the mornings or after school; nothing major and not every day, just a once-in-a-while quick hello and a complaint, here and there. She was always the voice of reason and calmed me down whenever I had gripes against fellow teachers and administration wonks. She also impressed upon me that not everyone in our academic hellhole could be trusted and that I should always choose my words, actions and "battles" carefully, her class notwithstanding. "The very walls have ears," she would often say while putting a finger to her lips to shush me during one of my typical tirades. I took her advice, which only added to my ever-present, hard-wired feelings of suspicion and anxiety. But I greatly appreciated her concern for me just the same. What had started out as a potentially dull and lifeless English class had instead morphed into a daily period filled with wit and comedy, and where I gained the admiration of Mrs. L.R., one joke at a time. She and I parted after the second quarter with mutual respect for one another. For an elderly and seemingly "old-fashioned prude," she turned out to be exceedingly *cool*. I would have her again the following year, not only for two successive semesters (all four quarters) as an educator but as the lead faculty advisor of the yearbook club, which my immediate buddies and I had signed up for. Meanwhile I had to get ready for a third quarter full of s…. I meant more of Mrs. G.H., the same civic-minded, ineffectual instructress I had in American Literature the year prior. Oh, well, at least I had something to look forward to in my senior year.

46

The Blustery Year

Much like the 1968 Disney animated featurette *Winnie the Pooh and the Blustery Day*, our eleventh grade American History course closely followed suit. Mr. T. was a middle-aged, garrulous, stout and bearded teacher with a bombastic bass voice that could literally knock you over. It was always *windy* in his classroom, and the *breeze* blew from his podium and onto us cowering plebes. Was he just full of hot air and a pontificating prick? Not really. He was a well-respected history instructor and the father of a senior tennis player who was on the same varsity team as me. Most of us had HEARD of Mr. T. way before we actually had him as a lecturer. His booming and growling baritone filled the hallways with thunderous historic syllables on a daily basis. And he always kept his classroom door open as if to further foist his resonance onto any interlopers that dared to walk past it. Was he in fact a bully? Nah, just a charismatic and enigmatic teacher in our puny, countrified school. Of course, with that blunderbuss cake-hole of his, most students never misbehaved or dared utter a foul word while in that course as far as I could see, or was so told. Pupils would quickly file in, take their wooden seats and be prepared to get blown away, literally. However, we learned and didn't begrudge him his frequent apoplectic histrionics. But one day my immediate buds and I inadvertently messed with him. Uh, oh. It had been a silly day for my bunch of cohorts; what with reciting the previous television nights' *Hee Haw* jokes and then launching into one-liners from the "new," outrageous *Monty Python's Flying Circus* TV show, we joked our way into Mr. T.'s class. We were still laughing out loud as I took my customary seat on the left-hand side of the room, next to the huge cork board displaying "precious" artifacts and former class projects from "outstanding" bygone history students which Mr. T. reverently displayed and frequently mentioned. I plopped down, opened my notebook and looked up, just in time to see our soft covered, eleventh grade English Lit book come whizzing at my head and the thrower, J. Logg, smirking at his excellent follow through. I ducked at the last second and the book glanced off my left shoulder and struck the flat, clay, Greek God figurine that was affixed to that board right next to me. Rats! The book's blow had irretrievably broken it. Well, J. Logg, being a very conscientious individual, dutifully walked down to the teacher's lounge on the first floor, knocked on the greasy door and asked to speak to Mr. T. to tell him about the fateful faux pas. As J. Logg would tell me later, a teacher cracked open the door and alcohol and cigarette fumes suddenly emanated from the raucous room like a dense fog. J. Logg solemnly admitted his guilt to Mr. T., with no obvious reaction, and then dejectedly shuffled back to the classroom and sat down. He looked rather queasy, as if he had just loudly farted. Mr. T. finally entered our class and like a male lion after battling a would-be rival, put his head back and roared with anger. "Who broke my Greek God?" he bellowed. Now, J. Logg had just told him about two minutes prior that he had done it, and here was Mr. T. prowling around the room and menacingly asking who had mangled the item. Students were paralyzed, no one knew what to say or do. J. Logg sat unmoving, stone faced and tight lipped, but most students had seen him throw the book at me. Nevertheless, no one narked. Somehow, either Mr. T. had disbelieved that J. Logg had done it or promptly forgot. Or, perhaps he misheard and thought J. Logg was merely the messenger and not guilty at all? But he was justified in his madness. Our negligent horseplay had fractured one of his prize possessions and no amount of contrition and apologies could mollify him. We were doomed, or were we? The perpetrator was obviously guilty, but I had a hand in it as well, or at least a shoulder. Mr. T. stared long and hard at the class in general and then relented, as his reddened face turned a normal hue. Although my "posse" and I had high averages in the class, he still could have had us all suspended or punished in some way, if only he had realized that we were involved. But he did not. The next day we "troublemakers" slunk into class and glumly sat down. And there was the porcelain piece, as good as new, hanging to my left! Obviously, Mr. T. had meticulously glued together the fragments of the broken statuette, remounted it on the cork board, and continued teaching history as if nothing had previously happened. Of course, after that nearly disastrous debacle, my comrades and I never fooled around in his class again. But I still wonder why he had not admonished us in some way? Did he really not recall what J. Logg had confessed to him? I don't know. He seemed to chalk it up as an accident and gave us a break. I never would have figured that from him. I guess his heart was as big as his mouth. Thank you, Mr. T.

47

Ditching His Ride

I only witnessed the mock scolding that early afternoon and missed the lead-up to the confrontation between my good buddy J. Logg and Mrs. L.R.: the wispy, elderly, eleventh and twelfth grade English teacher, the one that you either loved or hated. The one married to Mr. I.R., our former klutzy eighth grade physical science teacher: THAT broad. (She would have liked me referring to her like that. She had a wicked sense of humor and in my opinion was an excellent teacher!). She was not only a major writing influence in my young life at the time, but I genuinely liked her. Well, as I rounded the corner from the cafeteria on the first floor, there in the hallway, next to her room stood Mrs. L.R. and J. Logg, face-to-face. My skinny-challenged friend was staring down at the serious looking and spindly teacher, exchanging what sounded like angry syllables. J. Logg was gesturing wildly and looked exasperated. But then a few others and I silently approached the duo and stood there within earshot, but at a safe distance, watching the drama unfold. Suddenly, laughter broke out between the two of them, and then each went their separate ways. I was dumbfounded; I knew the

ending but what was the beginning? I quickly chased down
J. Logg, which was easy to do. He knew what I wanted to
hear and spilled the beans. This is what J. Logg blurted out
to me: He was driving into school and going around the
large circular drive in front of the brick high school
building when he got the urge to check out his brand new
Timex digital watch to see what the time was. Back in
those days, the screen was black, and you had to depress a
button to make it light up. Well, while also trying to light
up a Pall Mall dangling from his mouth and
simultaneously shifting the manual transmission, he took
both hands off the wheel and ended up sliding into a deep
culvert. He wasn't hurt but got stuck, and stuck good. He
could not back out or move his vehicle forward. He spun
the rear wheels frantically over and over, with dirt and
stones flying in all directions, resembling an angry
woodchuck digging a hole in the ground. Meanwhile,
school had begun, and wouldn't you know it; there was a
free and funny show going on right outside the classrooms
facing the deep ditch: It was J. Logg and his half-
submerged and tilted green car. Tons of faces were pressed
up to the windows watching the "humorous ministrations"
unfolding before them. The unplanned comedy lasted a
few hours, what with waiting for the tow truck, getting the
auto extracted, exchanging documents, etc. But it was all

over just after lunchtime. J. Logg finally made it into school only to be accosted by Mrs. L.R., whom he never had as a teacher. How did she even know him, or his name? This is what I heard her say: "How dare you cause a ruckus outside? All my students were watching you instead of listening to me. Your selfish comic routine was not appreciated, Mr. Logg. Why did you go into that ditch? Don't you know how to drive? You wasted my whole morning. What do you have to say for yourself?" J. Logg was stammering and apologized profusely until Mrs. L.R. cracked up and then both started laughing as they parted company. I was in her English class and could vouch for her. She was a good sport and never really meant to seriously chastise him. It was all part of the gag, and he was the momentary patsy. As he related the first part of the story to me, I thought about Mrs. L.R. and her dry sense of levity. She was a staid and long tenured English teacher and not an overt jokester, but I bet she was young once and full of mischief like the rest of us.

48

Nuts to You!

After a wildly successful year in biology, I greatly looked
forward to Regents level chemistry in my junior year. But
you know the old saying: one step forward and two
backwards. And that statement more than aptly applied to
my stretch in chemistry. Now for a quick backtrack: I had
always fancied myself as being a relatively smart and
scientifically oriented young man. Years spent studying,
rearing and hunting for "bugs and slugs" in the outdoors
honed my inquisitive nature and made me a self-taught
amateur naturalist. I loved science and all the concomitant
academic courses that had been forced on me thus far. It
was one of my passions, plus I excelled at it. So, I cavalierly
thought that chemistry would also be a no-brainer;
however, it turned out that I was the one that had no brain
for it. Oh, things started out swimmingly as they always
do, in a class that ended up being a bear instead of a
benign butterfly. You know what I mean. Mr. R.G., the
middle-aged, pipe smoking, thin and harried teacher,
looked like a bespectacled junior Einstein, complete with
an unruly, wild, curly brown hairdo. He was rigid,
sarcastic, and often had a devilish smirk on his muzzle as if

he knew he was only acting sardonically tough to get a rise out of us. But no classroom dissent was allowed so his behavior was often puzzling. It was as if he longed for a verbal melee with a smarty pants student but quickly extinguished any fervent or leading questions from the peanut gallery. Did he want us to interact with him or not? It was hard to tell. After a few weeks, the class fell silent as Mr. R.G. continued to pace around the expansive room and rant and rave at our incompetence while preaching obtuse chemical principles that were hard to grasp. He thought he was doing a masterful job at lecturing yet I was struggling mightily to keep up. Perhaps it was just me? But I thought I was smart, remember? Anyway, during one of those uninspiring and confusing lectures the classroom phone rang right in the middle of his befuddling explanation about balancing chemical equations, the backbone of neophyte inorganic chemistry. Well, the phone was relentlessly buzzing as he wheeled around from the blackboard and angrily threw the chalk stub at the squawk box, shattering the calcium stick into a puff of white slivers. Then he roared, "Nuts to you," at the offending black apparatus hanging innocently on the wall next to the door, as he furiously strode toward it. "Who the hell is on the blower?" he bellowed to no one in particular, as he picked up the receiver. He listened, nodded and then in a very even-toned and jocular voice politely asked S.O. to go to the office where she was immediately wanted for some type of problem. Was he joking? Was he bipolar, whatever that meant at the time? All the students, including me, were stunned to say the least. Nevertheless, he continued with his allegorical spiel as if nothing had happened. Wow, what a *mensch*. His classroom and laboratory antics continued in that manner for the course of the year in addition to sudden outbursts of his maddening and nutty catchphrase. And a ringing class telephone continued to get shellacked by him with chalk, erasers, pens, and his right loafer whenever he felt like it disrespected and disrupted his homily. He and I got along fine and I was consistently pulling a low A average due to lots of frustrating home study and memorization. It wasn't true learning, but it was the best I could do at the time. However, I always had the feeling that you had to tiptoe around him, kind of like being next to a pit bull. You just never knew when he would turn on you and bite. Now, perhaps he was a live wire and the punster of the teacher's lounge and a clown in real life, but in our classroom he was a grave gravedigger and often "put us in the ground." By the end of the year, after diligently digesting the *Barron's Chemistry* review book, I felt ready for the Regents exam. Not. I scored miserably on it, in the low seventies, and almost cried. I ended up with a high B instead of a low A class average thanks to my underperformance on that state test. Most of my smarty friends had done much better than I; I could not understand why I had done so poorly. None of the questions had buffaloed me so what happened? I don't know. My father was beside himself and bitterly ridiculed me for my seemingly arrogant scientific pronouncements which now meant nothing in his book. By his lofty standards, I had failed. The exam had proved it. I painfully guessed that chemistry was definitely not my "bag," whether it was a "science" or not. Fast forward a year and there I was, asking Mr. R.G. to sign my senior yearbook. He had also been my twelfth grade Regents physics teacher, so we knew each other quite well by then (I had done much, much better in physics, by the way.) He was surprised that I asked him for an autograph and happily obliged, quizzically lamenting that few students sought him out for his John Hancock. Really? I wonder why? As he was looking at me, he scrawled "Nuts to you, Izzy," underneath his photo. I had asked for it and he delivered as we both burst out laughing. Fast forward a few years and I was once again sweating bullets while drowning in a sea of chemistry at pharmacy college. Was it me? Most probably. All the different variations of the myriad of chemistries were just not penetrating my cranium like they were with other students. With the exception of advanced Medicinal Chemistry, which I proficiently understood, I was often distraught at the prospect of becoming a charlatan pharmacist because of my faux knowledge of the basic building blocks of drugs. How would I someday be concocting and dispensing pharmaceutical medicaments when I was such a phony chemist? However, there were students doing worse than I in those same pharmacy classes. So, perhaps I was above average after all? I hesitate to give out the answer to that loaded question. And I had "chemical problems" in dental school years later, even though taking some of the same, lame, chemistry courses as in pharmacy college. WTF? Fortunately, there is more to dentistry than chemical equations. I suffered, took my lumps but was rewarded with a summa cum laude finish upon graduation as a dentist. Chemistry had tried to bury me throughout my scholastic career but it didn't work. For years I flaunted my molecular mediocrity in its face, yet the fates were kind to me and let me pass at the time and prosper later in life. But it is embarrassing to this day when I remember all the hardships I had endured due to one stupid type of science that never found a comfortable resting place in my softened brain!

49

Solving that Bird

He was a cross between Clint Eastwood and Gary Cooper, though not as tall. Handsome, middle-aged, fit, blue-eyed, and with a touch of gray at the temples; Mr. O. was a man's man, through and through. He taught Trigonometry, Advanced Algebra, Analytic Geometry and Probabilities as best as he could with what he had to work with: us! Trigonometry began the same way every morning: Mr. O., whose daughter S.O. was in my grade, would sternly watch us sullenly file in, glance at the rectangular watch strapped to the underside of his wrist, take a small sip from the open Styrofoam cup filled with black coffee, adjust his polyester pants upon standing, and would start teaching. However, let's backtrack a little first. His room was considered positioned in the most desirable spot, on the first floor, at the end of the hallway. His long tenure as well as legendary former varsity basketball coach status gave him clout and prestige among students and teachers alike but I wouldn't say people loved him like they did some other beloved teachers; it was more of a begrudging loving respect. He was often gruff and demanding, and because math was considered a grueling and difficult subject, that made him an obvious "villain." But he probably was not. I'm sure his private life was a hoot; however, the only side of his personality that he showed us pupils was that of a tough taskmaster who quickly got annoyed at stupidity in his classroom. And now, back to our morning dose of trig. As I scanned the seated students, you could sense the oppressive anxiety in the air. Palms were sweating, eyes were cast downward, and not a peep could be heard as we methodically went over the previous night's homework together as a class. However, after that, the real nervousness began. Mr. O. would pose problems on the blackboard and called on students to solve them. It was new material and woe to the person who stammered and stuttered without being able to correctly answer him. Mr. O. would often say, "Mr. P. (my close bud G.P.), we can wait all day for you to solve this easy problem, now come on." He would glare with his piercing eyes and he would "sarcastically encourage" but would eventually relent if the student genuinely was about to pass out due to mental ineptitude or embarrassment. While giving me a knowing sneer and pointing to a complex equation on the blackboard, he would say, "Mr. M., why don't you solve that bird for us?" Fortunately, I paid strict attention and almost always got the correct response. But not always. Even I faltered a few times, much to Mr. O's amazement

and consternation. Hey, we all miss some time. After my
family's standard breakfast of oatmeal or farina, my
stomach was curdling and bubbling by nine o'clock in the
morning and there was Mr. O., relentless in his
overbearing berating of us dunces. My intestines were in
turmoil, there were beads of perspiration on my brow, and
I could feel my own heartbeat as well as hear the clock
loudly ticking on the wall. However, through sweat soaked
armpits and damp underwear, we adapted and learned: his
way. No one willingly wanted to disappoint him and get
his dandruff up unnecessarily, but sometimes things just
went awry. Yet no one complained to the administration or
to respective parents. He was our surrogate father away
from home and probably would have gotten approval from
our folks if we had tattled on him. So, we just hunkered
down in his class and took his verbal beatings with a grain
of appreciation. I was pulling a low A average and quietly
gained his tacit approval as the scholastic year chugged
along. And remember, I was the math-challenged
"charlatan" that had "faked" my way through numerology
thus far in high school. Nevertheless, things weren't all bad
in his class and there were intermittent though scant times
of humor. Namely, whenever two tiny slivers of white
chalk would break off the main piece at the same time and
start to meander down the blackboard surface. Mr. O.

would instantly stop what he was doing and bet excitedly on which piece would win the race to the bottom of the board. Everyone knew about this periodic hilarious routine and would exhale, titter, and play along with Mr. O. in hopes of ingratiating ourselves on him, if possible. The course ended, I scored highly on the Regents exam and resigned myself to the fate of having him one last time as a senior, for Advanced Algebra/Analytic Geometry. And, although those future courses (which I miraculously received high A's in) proved to be vastly different and more "problematic" than trigonometry, Mr. O. continued to stay in character. However, he did recognize most of the returning veterans and would usually lay off us, picking mostly on the "smarty" juniors instead. He was one tough-ass and no-nonsense lecturer, but most of us knowingly or unknowingly picked up at least a rudimentary understanding of high school mathematics; the hard way!

50

The Savory Steak

This is a slightly humiliating story but here goes: My mom was and is a great cook and prides herself on her culinary skills and ingenuity. Although a studious college student by day and a "study-wort" by night, she nevertheless donned her proverbial chef's hat every evening, dutifully preparing nutritious and appetizing meals for our family. And she was good, except for when it came to beef and pork selections. My dad loved his meaty grub well done, which should reveal the theme of this story. All steaks and chops at my house were glazed with a thick layer of Heinz tomato ketchup, slammed into the oven and seared to shoe leather consistency. And oftentimes mom would proudly announce the expense of the particular cut before fastidiously trimming it and then subjecting it to a torturous burning. But what did my sister and I know? That's how we ate pork chops, hamburgers and sirloin at my house – very, very well baked. Perhaps a bout of food poisoning in the old country or fear of trichinosis had scared pop into favoring his victuals well cooked. I don't know, he never said. So, imagine my shock and awe when I sampled my first "properly" seasoned and prepared slab of butchered bovine. My best bud F. and I had participated in an all-day orchestral NYSSMA performance (both of us squeaked by on the fiddle) in the state university over the two hills and were to be graciously picked up by F.'s dad. When we came out to meet him in his Dodge Polara he quickly recognized our exhausted countenances (it was tiring playing out of tune for a whole day) and suggested dinner before heading home. We both nodded our heads and I became excited to eat in a bona fide restaurant and not pay for it, either. My old-fashioned folks abhorred dining out, even while on road trips. Fear of "foreign tasting" foodstuffs, fear of disease, and fear of the mandatory tipping may have all played a role in me growing up un-American when it came time to eating outside the home. The high school cafeteria vittles did not count. I mean I had a few burgers, fries and pizza slices here and there, however, never any sit-down meals with my family at a legitimate food emporium, not even at a diner! F.'s father pulled into a Ponderosa Steakhouse on Chestnut Street and I cautiously followed them inside. It was a cafeteria-style all-you-can-eat buffet with meats, poultry and fish that had to be custom ordered. Looking up at the extensive menu made my mouth water. That place had everything, and at cheap prices too. I was fast loading up my plate with veggies, rice, potatoes and a few rolls and

then had to make a momentous decision: what kind of
steak to get. It was a steakhouse after all. I wasn't about to
order chintzy chicken or crappy carp posing as legit fowl
and fish. It was BEEF all the way, baby! F. and his father
each ordered a medium-rare, 10-ounce, boneless rib eye
and I followed suit. Medium-rare: what was that? I hoped
for the best as the pink-colored, weeping and fat-ringed
piece of protein was slapped on my plate. It looked
succulent and had an aroma I had not smelled before. I
was all atwitter as I took that first bite. It was heaven; it
tasted divine, savory and flavorful and many other
adjectives that would basically be inappropriate when
mentioning such a lowly feeding establishment. Even I
knew that Ponderosa was at the bottom end of the food
chain, both in quality and the people it served. But, still….
I quickly devoured the juicy offering in front of me, all the
while exclaiming my joy at eating it. My audible
compliments were amusing to Mr. F., who, as a culinary
arts professor at our local college, most likely thought our
food was barely edible by his knowledgeable standards. It
sufficed for two ravenous boys, however. I probably
embarrassed myself that evening in front of F. as well, but I
had spoken the truth, at least my truth. And later I
enthusiastically confided in my mother about the great
supper that I had but she angrily cut me off in the middle

of my adulatory oratory and flat out stated that she
purposely overcooked the flavorless meats in our home
because that's how both male chieftains (my dad and
paternal grandfather) liked them. Runny and raw was a
nonstarter. I shut my trap and went to bed.

51

Dreams

Not to usurp Fleetwood Mac's blockbuster hit from their 1977 *Rumours* album, but dreams are had by most human beings, including me. Plus, my particular subconscious incarnation was different from Stevie Nick's musical rendition and predated it by a few years. It was a recurring dream of mine in the winter of '75, just before the bicentennial new year and the fateful national election that would result in the incumbent bumbler President Ford's ouster in favor of the Democrat, "Mr. Peanut," Jimmy Carter. For many months during that snowy and cold winter, my dreams consisted of me being fifty years old and having "made it" in life. There were repetitious prologues but no afterlife past that certain age. I happily and vividly recall becoming a wealthy doctor, marrying a vivacious and beautiful blonde and having children. However, fifty was the cut-off point. There was nothing more after that but darkness and emptiness. Was I to abruptly die after attaining that numerical double digit? I was sixteen and a junior, and my dad was late middle-aged and rapidly approaching that "magic" number himself. Was he the reason for my unconscious mind conjuring up some type

of apocalypse? He was relatively comfortable and successful
as a tenured civil engineering professor, so perhaps it was
not HIS subliminal interference with me. Although….And
why was I having those recurrent and nonsensical dreams
for months, it seemed? I don't know. There was no obvious
new turmoil at home and my scholastic achievements were
uninspiring but adequate. So what was it all about? WTF?
I had other "normal" nightly illusions and nightmares,
however, those certain ones kept recurring for a long time.
Nevertheless, the detailed nighttime visions ended soon
enough, and I had largely forgotten about them until
recently. Upon revisiting those turbid thoughts of
yesteryear, and without the help of a psychiatrist or a
regression therapy specialist, it dawned on me that perhaps
those long ago uncontrolled nocturnal cerebral outbursts
were merely snippets of otherworldly foreshadowing or, at
the very least, wishful thinking. I did become a successful
doctor, a dentist to be exact, and I did marry a svelte and
lovely woman, my wife, Hottie Blondie. And I did produce
two children, but I am sixty years young and still kicking.
What gives? Were the fates wrong with the dates? I hope
so, but I will tell you this: I was feeling well physically,
emotionally and mentally up until age fifty, and then a
gradual diminution of all my many abilities ensued. Not
all at once but a slow decline in all aspects of my being.

Granted, although I was still running track, throwing the javelin, winning snowshoe events, playing tennis at a high tournament level, and constantly loving that hot wife of mine, I was noticing a downtick in overall stamina and emotional energy. And by age fifty-eight, all "systems" became even more offline, if you know what I mean. Fortunately, I haven't hit the age of Viagra, but that "department" has suffered as well. Sure, I can still do dentistry at an alarmingly brisk and mistake-free pace but the physical nature of "drillin' for a livin'" has also started to take a toll on me. And multiple knee surgeries, chronic Lyme disease, and battle fatigue (over thirty-four years of mental/dental bullshit) have invariably also contributed to my trickle-down burnout. I realize that normal aging is a bitch and not for the timid, but still, the descent from my version of "normal" has taken me aback somewhat. Nevertheless, was I given a precocious and prescient window into my future during my adolescence? Would things have turned out differently had I actively pursued or squelched those harbingers of thought? It's hard to tell as I mull over my current semi-retirement from dentistry, past athletic endeavors and life in general. Perhaps things developed as they were supposed to without too much preplanned conscious thought on my part? And maybe fifty was the pinnacle of my existence and the rest of this so-called living experience is merely lumpy gravy? I hope so and I'll take it lumps and all because I have competitive pickleball matches scheduled and sincerely trust NOT to be in a grave any time soon, in spite of any morbid concerns caused by novel viruses emanating from CHINA!

52

Upward Mobility?

My father missed his chance at owning a genuine Cadillac after our first landlord passed away and a "long lost" niece suddenly surfaced to abscond with that beautiful car. To dad, it was a symbol of United States meritocracy and upward mobility. However, he had a second chance at the coveted brass ring and he grabbed it, even though it was years later. That first Cadi had been a late sixties sedan; the one that he finally procured in 1976 was a lightly used, '73, limited edition, bronze, nineteen-foot-long, Brougham d'Elegance Sedan Deville with opera lights on the back pillars and a soft alligator roof. It had all the bells and whistles for autos at the time, with a crushed velvet interior, a hydraulic front bumper and automatically closing trunk. It was a dreamboat, alright; it unabashedly screamed opulence and broadcasted the visage of decisively having partaken in the American dream. In his immigrant's mind, pop had finally made it, even on a paltry professor's salary. For an ethnic Estonian, that car represented plenty and seemingly wiped out the miserable and uncertain beginnings of his life in this new country. It was a badge of success and gave him instant bragging rights. However, in homage to the legendary folksy radio personality Paul Harvey's program and catchphrase, here's "The Rest of the Story": My father did not buy the '73 Cadi new, nor did he purchase it from a local dealer. No, it was used, and he had bought it with hard earned cash from my rich, playboy uncle in Indiana, the one that got lucky and was prospering hand over fist in the nascent RV business. Uncle L. had his eye on a new Cadillac and it just so happened that he remembered that pop wanted his old one. But instead of gifting the coveted sedan to my old man, he actually charged him the prevailing *Kelley Blue Book* used car price. What a jerk. He had freely given his wife's many previous cast-off luxury vehicles to non family members yet demanded *gelt* from my dad. Who knows why? Well, somebody knew why, but not me. But we got the auto and had a spacious space waiting for it in our two-car garage. Dad was ecstatic and immediately went to work on it, rust proofed the undercarriage, fine-tuned the engine, and buffed the crap out of the special "fire-mist polymer" paint job it came endowed with. My professor pop was also a virtuoso mechanic and could repair virtually anything mechanical. Cars were definitely in his wheelhouse and posed no problems for him. If he couldn't fix something, he made the part himself and installed it where it belonged. But wait a minute. Now that he had it, where was he going to drive it? Living in "Farm Town, U.S.A.," with one red light, one police officer, one "greasy" diner, and cows peering over barbed wire in our backyard, motoring around in such a magnificent metal steed would be challenging. Our puny village was not big enough to give the Cadi a decent lather. Well, we could have gone on drives outside of town, but then who would see us: bunches of Jerseys and Guernseys who were nonchalantly chewing their cuds and making cow pies? The whole idea was to grandstand a little, to show the homespun locals that a "foreigner" in their midst had a luxury car and they didn't. But alas, our tiny town didn't cooperate. And my father's fellow professors up on the college hill couldn't care less. Most were liberal leaning and driving economical Volkswagen Beetles while here was my dad and his behemoth bronze bombshell. His other car was a "middle class" '65 Oldsmobile station wagon so at least he couldn't be criticized for that. But few people even saw him drive THAT car for he always walked the five minutes to the college. We didn't belong to a country club, or to a local Estonian orthodox church, nor reconnoitered with the well-heeled and well-wheeled. There were no such elements in our dink-hole settlement. So, why did pop get that car again? Was it for his ego and vanity? Mom started to wonder. Maybe it had been a big mistake to buy something

so bourgeois and grandiose while living in noncaring
Peasantville. Nevertheless, we just HAD to start driving it.
It just couldn't sit in the garage with its engine oil seals
drying out, tire rubber cracking, and with dust gathering
on that soft, tan rooftop. Pop finally decided that we
would use the Cadi for long trips, such as our annual
winter break sojourn to Florida. Our quirky and
frequently-in-need-of-repair Olds station wagon would
now get a rest with the addition of a practically new "limo"
to our fleet of cars. My live-in Grandpa Pete still had his
green, American Motors Hornet, you know. But that was
his personal car and we left it alone, except for when it also
needed mending, which was often. It was functional but a
piece of crap. So the Cadi began its second life with our
family, and we enjoyed its bountiful space and luxurious
appointments on many trips to Florida, as well as on
weekend junkets to nearby cities. It was a grand car and
even served as the vehicle that ferried my wife and me from
the Big Moose chapel to our wedding reception in the
extremely remote Adirondacks in the early '80s. I recall
many elderly and bearded mountain men from our
wedding party arguing over who would get the honor of
driving that "land boat" because few had seen or driven
such a prestigious and unique auto before. P.W., a close
friend of my wife's family, won the impromptu wrestling

competition to be the chauffer, slicked back his tousled hair, wiped his bloody lip and smiled a crooked grin at my horrified dad as Hottie Blondie and I slid into the comfy back seats for the ensuing ceremonious ride to the reception at Northwoods Inn, a Fourth Lake hotel/restaurant. P.W. dished out compliment after compliment about the car during the slow, winding ride, never mentioning the recent nuptials, my wife's beauty, or how he had managed to wrangle the Cadi away from my possessive father. And that was the last time it was purposely driven. My father parked it in his garage, and there it sits to this very day. Oh, he promised that he would periodically run the engine and fix a few things here and there, but nothing automotive transpired. Decades went by and that once elegant car became a dried-up old maid. It still looks in mint condition and occupies a majority of the right side of the garage; however, it would now take a fleet of mechanics to properly resurrect it to its former glory days. Pop doesn't want to part with it, however. I believe it is a reminder of his proud past, which just happened to whiz by too quickly. It's his prize, his achievement, and his one gift to himself that assuaged a fragile ego all those years ago. I know for I also own a car like that. Not a Cadi, but a '76 Corvette, which is old like me. Sure, it has had its share of problems because it is an

American automobile and was purposely not made to last, but I love it; I don't want to relinquish it either.

53

German Convention!

Finally the payoff: A Friday off from school to "partee" at a distant New York State high school with other German speaking students at a ballyhooed weekend convention! Yay! I mean that's why my immediate "crew" and I had unanimously signed up for das Deutsch in the first place and doggedly suffered through that difficult foreign *language* since ninth grade, in anticipation of a supposedly "crazy," fun-filled few days during junior year. That and a language sequence were required for a science/math-based Regents diploma. I had patiently waited since freshman year to partake in that linguistic-based field trip and let me tell you – the extravaganza was all that I had heard it would be, and more. It was the Es Sagt's (Empire State Society for the Advancement of German Traditions and Studies) annual and signature happening. Not quite Woodstock, but Woohoo! And the woeful Spanish class didn't have a state sanctioned "party" to go to which further made us German enrollees feel *special*. Maybe we "smart" kids should have taken the much easier Español course, instead of slaving away with our instructress Frau K.? But no, WE could handle it….But perhaps we should have had our

heads examined for gray matter deficiencies that were
supplanted with unjustified oodles of hubris? Maybe,
however it was too late to turn that train around. We select
juniors were all in German III, studying for the rigorous
Regents exam while preparing to "knock them dead" at the
designated festival location for 1976 – W.C. Mepham High
School in North Belmore, Long Island. Bring it on! Long
tenured German teacher Mrs. R.K. was not only a
longtime family confidante but her husband was the local
college's new head man and a good friend of my father.
And her younger daughter N.K. was part of my "posse."
N.K. and I affectionately went way back to our
kindergarten days and that was yet another reason for me
taking her mom's hard class. I had to. What was I going to
do, take the "weak" Spanish curriculum and shame myself?
I think not! Anyway, Long Island was our destination and
we forty or so excited students boarded a long yellow bus
and sarcastically waved goodbye to our alma mater. And
besides a few female chaperones among us, there were
seniors, sophomores and freshmen on that trip as well. WE
had to wait until our junior year, but the rules changed
allowing underclassmen to participate in the convention.
Oh well, the "young kids" were a welcome addition and
most had senses of humor! This was going to be a multiple
day affair while eating, sleeping and staying at people's host

homes while involved in the "Oktoberfest-type" daily
activities. Well, there would be no boozing of Bavarian
beer, but virtually all other aspects of Germanic cultural
life would be indulged in and competed at, such as
traditional folk singing, dancing, soccer, oral declamations,
poetry reading, musical numbers, costume design, games
and stage plays. The bus tour took a while and we were
stoked the entire way. The four-hour ride was filled with
raucous, joking around and tomfoolery from most of the
pupils, even from the usually soporific, silent type, females.
We were stupidly exhausted upon disembarking and
assembled in the large school's designated area specifically
set up for us. We eyeballed German-studying groups of
scholars from across the state, some from gigantic high
schools, some with authentic German exchange students in
their midst. Holy cow, how could we compete against such
stiff competition? We were a dinky and unsophisticated
bunch from Bumfuck, N.Y., darn it. This was going to be
tough. Plus it was our first foray into the world of acting,
gesticulating and athletically proving ourselves in Teutonic
terms. But hold on there *Siegfried*, the German tongue was
hard enough, and now we had to win prizes too? No
pressure there. Nevertheless, strict and staid Mrs. R.K. gave
us a pep talk (in English) on that first afternoon and
calmed everyone down by emphatically stating that our

puny academy had done well in past years regardless of the seemingly high odds stacked against us. Well I quickly gathered my seven (J.Logg was not a German student) peeps and we had our own private powwow, one that saw me set a higher bar than Frau K. had. No more mister nice guy! All those countless official practice sessions were justified, weren't they? Yes, indeed. And those joke-filled private times spent together while memorizing and play-acting weren't wasted either, were they? No, indeed. It was time to lay down the law, our way. It was hammer time! So, unlike the rest of the students from the disparate schools who were awestruck by the fanfare and pageantry of the occasion and gawked reverently at the gay surroundings, we eight "buttnutts" were secretly sharpening our cunning knives and plotting on winning as many events as possible. And it happened. During that first afternoon of competing, we were pleasantly informed that our Podunk school was ahead in points. However, we still had one more important day left to go. F. and I had to take matters into our own hands if we had any realistic chance of staying in front of the pack. I was determined to "get 'er done," and my immediate cohorts enthusiastically agreed. But the first day was over as host families pulled up in their vehicles to whisk us away for the evening. F. and I climbed into Mr. MacDougall's back seat as his son sat up in front with him. The younger MacDougall was also a German student at his host school but was entered in different Germanic events than us. However, as we three teens started an innocuous dialogue in the auto, I suddenly noticed the driver twitching and squirming in his seat. I motioned to F. and we both quieted down as the weird gesturing continued. Did he have to go to the bathroom or something? Was he having a fit of some sort? His son did not react to his old man's epileptic-like bodily movements as F. and I silently started to lose it. We stifled our laughter until we reached our adopted home and then could not stop talking about it. After a stilted dinner, we shared two separate beds in a guest bedroom and could hardly fall asleep in all the excitement. We chuckled and tried to explain Mr. MacDougall's actions and the best we could come up with was to call his strange gyrations the "MacDougall Curse." Yes, he must have been cursed or something to that effect as we laughed ourselves to sleep, but not before planning and scheming on how to best win the dramatic play the next day. It was the event that totaled the most points and could potentially seal an overall convention victory for us. After breakfast Mr. MacDougall drove his son, F. and me to the school, all the while moving hither-tither in his car seat to muffled guffaws from us. I know we were rude, but what the hell? Upon entering the school, F. and I quickly sought out the auditorium to see firsthand how the other short plays were unfolding and to size up the competition. Our own group was slated to go on stage in the afternoon session and had time for last minute rehearsal tweaks. As I sat there in the back row observing other performances, it dawned on me that the elaborate costumes and serious enunciations by many of the featured thespians were top notch; we didn't have a chance unless we tried something completely different. Each play ran about a half hour and we had to make every minute count! So unbeknownst to Mrs. K., F. and I called an emergency early rehearsal for our troupe. Although specifically told not to willfully trespass, F. and I selected a vacant and previously locked classroom on the second floor, hurriedly herded our fellow troubadours into it, and in the darkened space rebooted the entire production. We practiced in the dark. Our suggestions at first shocked most of the actors, even L.P., the senior director, but they trusted our judgment after we impressed upon them the dire straits we would be in if we played it straight. Luckily, my close friend N.K. was not in the play for she obviously would have tattled to her mother that our NEW and "improved" rendition of *Schneewittchen* (Snow White) would NOT be a carefully orchestrated and choreographed montage of dour students stiffly saying their boring lines and shuffling around stage while being summarily judged. No, our German teacher would have fainted if she had known in advance that F. and I had transformed *Snow White* from a dramatic endeavor and into a campy, lighthearted, romping farce. We had added comic dialogue, sound effects, belches and farts to spice things up. To procure "things," F. and I had previously raided the school's locked band chamber and adjacent prop room and "borrowed" drums, tambourines, slappers, a xylophone, and numerous sound-making gadgets; all unbroken items were eventually returned of course. S.S., a gifted singer, musician, comic, and intelligent freshman, was not only the trumpet playing Herold in the skit but delivered big time behind the scenes with all the sound effects as per my tutelage. He and I would team up again in the future for legitimate musical duets (me on the piano and he operatically vocalizing) and acts of comedic debauchery on stage. And hats off to A.H. and E.B., the two pretty, smart and sassy female leads who not only shared secrets and smokes between themselves but also had wicked senses of humor. They were both *cool*. I still loosely communicate with them to this day and sometimes wonder what would have occurred had I dated one of them back in high school? On second thought, no. They were both TOO much for me back then….Anyhow, it was time to perform our "enhanced" *shtick* in front of a packed house. As the outrageously clothed, kindhearted hunter, I led the send-up and the whole cast followed my lead. Frau K. sat in the front row and mouthed encouragement to us as we began our spiel. However, her phony smiling face quickly turned beet red in embarrassment as the judge's mugs turned beet red in apoplectic laughter and their hands began knee-slapping in appreciation. Our interpretation of *Snow White* was not from any familiar fairy tale book unless Benny Hill had written it, and he had not. Frau K. cringed and slumped low in her seat as we delivered punch line after punch line of lowbrow, corny gratuitous parody, complete with perfectly timed slapstick sounds emanating from backstage. Snow White (A.H.) burped (courtesy of S.S.) upon eating the "poisoned apple," snored inappropriately when the prince (S.O.) approached, and struck him 'round the ear hole after he bent down to kiss her. The Wicked Queen (E.B.) loudly passed gas (courtesy of S.S.) at every turn and Doc the Dwarf constantly slapped the other six "dorks" as if channeling The Three Stooges. Yet, much to the consternation and objections by the other schools present, we received the highest score possible as the three judges stood up in unison to clap upon the play's completion. Other schools and their not amused pupils complained that it was supposed to be a sketch, not a sketch comedy. They were right in a way, and the next year a provision was made to include a humorous act as part of the convention. However, for now we basked in the glory of not only winning the coveted lead prize but for putting our puny school into undisputed first place at the gala. Of course other German teachers surrounded the now beaming Mrs. K. and tepidly congratulated her on the audacity and genius of turning a pedestrian play into a show stopping number. She looked over at F. and me from the crowd around her, winked and exhaled deeply. Later that evening at a reserved dinner in a fancy restaurant, Frau K. facetiously lectured our entire group to never pull a stunt like that again, as she reverently clutched "The Play" trophy and grinned. But all was forgiven as we rejoiced in our victory. And she made sure to write in funny material in all ensuing productions which she wrote for upcoming German conventions in future years. Who knew that a little levity would go so far as to win a prestigious state championship, and in German and not football! After staying overnight once again at the "cursed" MacDougall residence, F. and I were praised the next day by our home team for our leadership and *chutzpah* throughout the weekend activities. We took it in stride as usual. We had fun and only left a few classrooms unlocked and slightly pilfered. And after that Sunday morning's remaining few events, the awards ceremony commenced. To thunderous shouting from me and my chums, our school received top awards in almost every Germanic category imaginable, including the coup de grâce, the overall first place finish. I was satiated and satisfied for only a brief instant however, for on the bus ride back home I was already formulating "stuff" for next year's festival, whether F. wanted to hear about it or not!

54

A "Real" Career

I would be starting my senior year in high school in the fall but had nary a logical thought about my future. Medicine and science were the top contenders but nothing specific. Although my parents were both intelligent, their guidance was next to nil. My father wrongly assumed that I would outgrow my "infantile" entomological leanings and become a stoic and dowdy civil engineer, like him. No frills, no thrills, no fun, but a job for "real" men: enough of this foolishness with insects and mudpuppies. My mother, although a major influence on my youthful naturalistic pastime, was mute when it came to MY college and career decisions. It was assumed and implied that I would do the right thing and suddenly choose engineering as a vocation. Just like that. Needless to say, my junior year was overloaded with very stressful undercurrents in my household. My gruff father gave me zero advice, zero talks and zero life plans. I was supposed to magically wake up one day and be an engineer and make everyone happy and proud. Period. No pressure there! For some unknown reasons, neither parent ever bothered to have a serious conversation with me about ANYTHING scholastic as I approached the zenith of my high school tenure. Whenever I mentioned the possibility of medical school or any science–type endeavor I was immediately shot down. "What if you finish undergrad with a B average in Biology, then what will you do?" my father would always say. "You can't get into medical school with a B average. What would be your plan B? And what undergrad college would you go to, anyway?" "We're not connected and you're not brilliant." And that was that. I was a loser from the get-go. No one was helping me so why even try? I might as well apply to Clarkson, become an engineer, and get it over with. That was my destiny, or was it? I was confused and conflicted. I consulted many high school chums; they were useless. I had no real girlfriend to talk to either. However, I did have a best friend and he was determined to apply to pharmacy college! Hmm…. pharmacy college? Science/biology/chemistry equals a job right out of college? Maybe I should consider this? There was a *college night* coming up at my pop's college with a pharmacy school in attendance. I was going to go and see what happens. At least I could get a brochure.

55

College Night

I didn't go by myself, perhaps I should have. My old man went with me. It was held in the large gymnasium at his place of employment. He was an engineering professor and knew many of the visiting college reps. He steered me away from the "obvious" pricey colleges, the "LIBERAL" Ivy League colleges, and rolled his eyes and sighed deeply whenever I even feigned interest in a particular university. My father thought all of this was a gigantic waste of time. He knew better. Until, of course, we chanced upon the engineering college tables. Clarkson, RPI, and RIT (Pop's alma mater) were some of the culprits present. My father personally knew of these institutions and their respective representatives, and instantly started kibitzing with them. Like-minded and self-righteous, those were the blokes to listen to. Unfortunately, while he was busy adulating the choir, I snuck off to the pharmacy college table and gleaned from the reps as much as I could before my dad brusquely showed up. He was not pleased at my disappearance and admonished me for being so rude in front of his buddies. After all, I was going to be an engineer. I tucked the pharmacy college brochure into my coat, and we went home. Nothing was said, as usual. After all, I was going to be an engineer!

56

Schoolin'

My best friend F. had recently turned sixteen and successfully obtained his driving learner's permit. Oh, boy, now it was time for more four-wheeled fun! E.G. already had his early '70s, gorgeous, convertible, blue and white Pontiac Catalina that he gave us rides with, and J. Logg had his dark green, four-barrel carbureted, standard Chevy Chevelle, that we jerks all liked to go fast in. But F. was new to the driving game and didn't have a car. However, his generous old man had a powerful, teal, '68 Dodge Polara 500 that he loaned to him on a regular basis. It was a beautiful, rear wheel drive automobile that drove as smooth as silk. I didn't drive, I was still too young, although I was a constant and content passenger in my friends' vehicles and eternally grateful for constantly being picked up, shown a good time, and then deposited back home, alive. J. Logg must have logged hundreds of miles just driving over to my house to collect me and then take me back. I was included in many outings that I otherwise would have missed had it not been for him. Thank you. Sometimes just cruising around town and up and down our mountainous back roads was a fun thing to do on weekend afternoons. That's what many boys did back then. We weren't looking for trouble, but sometimes the speed limit seemed like a suggestion and not a warning. You know what I mean! It was late May when F. and I teamed up to do a historical term paper/project together in Mr. T.'s class. Any topic even remotely resembling American "history," would be accepted. But as usual, F. dawdled while we "explored" many ideas together as precious time ticked away. Holy mackerel, we only had a few days left to get our shit together, research and write about something, and then present it to the class. Again, we left things for the last minute. Most of the girls had already handed in their "masterpieces" and here we were biting our fingernails at the eleventh hour, well, at least I was. F. was of a different temperament than me. Things like meeting deadlines, endless studying and memorizing useless minutia were not his strong suits. Whether academically, theatrically, musically or personally, his outward lack of worrying or angst always perplexed me. As a close chum, it always seemed like I had to light a giant fire under his ass to get him moving and to get things done. But the end results of our frequent collaborations were often brilliant, or at least commendable. Just a quick aside: F. was actually a brainy fellow, went on to earn a pharmacy B.S. as well as multiple advanced science degrees, and has had a superlative career as a well-known medically oriented research scientist and top leader in his field. My becoming a pharmacist and then a dentist was of no surprise to former classmates, but no one in high school would have predicted such stellar future success for F., including me, and we were best buds at the time! Now back to the story. Well, we had a few days left and suddenly had a great thought. Why not do a project about the dilapidated one-room schoolhouse relics that still dotted our vast rural area? Why not? It was a capital idea, or was it? My family and I had personally driven by a few of them in my youth, but were they *kosher*? I mean were they actual one-room schools from yesteryear? There were no signs on the properties, no neighbors to ask and no Internet to quickly look things up and to verify them. Was it all hearsay from various grandfathered myths and legends at best? However, F. and I still thought it was a hoot of a history project. So we quickly got started. On a Saturday, we met at the Flintlock Free Library on Elm Street, in the middle of town and, within a few minutes of scouring old records of our locale, were rewarded with at least twelve names and locations of ancient schools that formerly pockmarked our lowly village. Most were built before centralized heating, cooling or plumbing, before school buses, and some were constructed before the 1800s! There had been an official, pricey and private academy in town incorporated in 1819 that later morphed into our present-day public school, but at the time it was reserved for the village elite's sons only. If you were a poor farmer on the outskirts of "civilization," in the proverbial boonies, an all-grades grammar school manned by one female teacher is where you would send your progeny in those days. Well, we had the locations, now we needed transport and a camera. F. provided the car and I had the Polaroid. The next day, on a sunny Sunday, F. borrowed his dad's Dodge Polara and I borrowed my dad's Polaroid SX-70 Land Camera, the fold-out, instant photo producing mini machine. Sure, my family had "real" cameras, like pop's expensive Leica and my grandfather's old-fashioned bellows-and-plate Zeiss cameras used for portrait photography and weddings, of which he was formerly involved in years ago as a side hustle. Both male elders in my family considered that new-fangled Polaroid a joke and let me "play" with it. Why we had bought it in the first place was a mystery, however. Our family was not prone to purchasing the latest gadgets; nevertheless, I had the new gizmo looped over my shoulder as I climbed into F.'s car and off we went. There were lap belts on the car seats, but why bother? That was for wussies. F. had his permit, allowing him to drive in the daytime, to and from school only, until he got his official license. This was a school project, so it was kind of related, you know. We knew where our lone, goofy police officer was usually staked out, trying to catch out-of-town speeders, so we avoided that area. With our lunches packed, F. stepped on it and gravel flew from the spinning rear wheels as we tore up and down largely deserted, dusty and hilly, unpaved roads, kind of like "them" Duke boys did in the *General Lee*, their car from Dukes of Hazzard fame. But we were ahead of our time. That TV show didn't air until 1979. Our show was the present, 1976! F. was an excellent driver as he one-handedly maneuvered his sleek, metallic steed around twisty corners and curves. We zipped by endless dairy farms and contented looking, brown skinned, cud chewing bovines, scattered in the green pastures. Using different autos and drivers, we had been on these unsanctioned trips with our buds in the past, so we kind of knew where we were going. I was the navigator, with rudimentary maps and sketches in my lap. I would have F. abruptly stop, wait until the dust settled and snap a shot of what was standing or crumbled before me. Each expensive film cartridge had ten preloaded frames in it, so you didn't want to be wasteful. After much whirring and clicking, the camera magically disgorged the picture and it developed in front of our eyes. The color print was primitive by today's standards as I painted it with a special fixer that was part of the process. However, there was our first evidence of a one-room schoolhouse in our farm infested area in my hand. Hurray! Only five hours, two-food-and-pee breaks later, we were finished. We had ten "good" photos for our portfolio. Some of the pictures showed overgrown decrepit wooden structures, others just piles of rotten lumber; a few of the schools and unkempt adjoining outhouses were shuttered but stood proudly amid the weeds as if ready to once again be graced with barefoot children of all ages. One even had a name and logo on a faded sign in front of it. Wow. We were all set. That night I hand printed the names, places and a brief history of the schools on various colored construction paper, carefully glued one photo per sheet, and stapled the whole darn thing together. It was obviously a homespun and last-second endeavor; no typing, no lined paper, and only eleven pages in length, counting the colorful cover. And it definitely was not a legit term paper, with proper annotations, a bibliography, etc. It was a bunch of Polaroids, hand printed labels, bylines and factoids cobbled together with rubber cement and staples. At least my printing was top notch. We plopped it on Mr. T.'s desk on Monday, the due day, and sat back in our wooden seats, relieved at having had finished it. Well, Mr. T. did not take kindly to our piece of trash on his blotter, was about to ridicule our amateur hour production in front of the whole class, but then stopped mid sentence as he quickly rifled through the pages. He smiled and then snorted hysterically at our *chutzpah* and ingenuity. Only F. and I could have thought of such an innovative and whacky project. Who else? And who would have thought that our local and archaic scholastic history would prove to be more interesting than Lincoln's Gettysburg Address, Nixon's impeachment, the moon landing, and other students' orations. Our classmates sat in stunned silence as F. did the abbreviated oral presentation the next day. He tried and failed to seriously expound on our town's forays into the education realm; it was hard for him to maintain a straight face while Mr. T. sat laughing at his desk throughout the five-minute speech. Of course, we received the top grade in the class for a Sunday afternoon's work. But then again, it was our brilliant and offbeat topic and not weeks of grunt work that had done the trick. Working with F. was usually a pleasure, although typically it was a last-minute, hand wringing, wrenching and heart stopping adventure. If only his pop's car could have talked....

57

The Polara and the PSAT

It was late spring and the time of year for standardized testing. You know, the PSAT exam for all juniors who wished to practice-up before the real McCoy was administered during the following fall and, to see where they currently stood intellectually. Most college bound eleventh graders in my class had signed up for the multiple hour stress test which would be held on a Saturday in a nearby village high school. And unlike my own children who diligently studied and took multiple practice exams for weeks before their PSATs, my friends and I believed our teachers when they said it was basically an unimportant "intelligence test" and consequently we didn't prepare for it, not one iota. It was supposedly "nothing;" the "real" exam was the one to worry about. How naïve we were. Of course there were review books available back then but none of us bothered to purchase any. We were "smart" plus this test supposedly did not count for anything. It was going to be a breeze…. J. Logg, E.G., G.P., T.B., and I piled into F.'s father's Dodge Polara and followed the large bus loaded with other students, out of the school parking lot and onto Route 10 south, and on our way to the testing center. We knew where the PSAT would be held but followed that bus as if tied to it. And then, with G.P. chirping and instigating trouble from the back seat, F. started to drive recklessly. The more G.P. egged him on, the more F. swerved and bump-drafted the bus, getting within a few inches of its back bumper at times. The kids in the back row on the bus were howling with laughter as were we, thinking that we were *cool* tailgaters. F. continued to steer irresponsibly and weaved back and forth with abandon. Then, unexpectedly, the bus abruptly came to a standstill because of a rabid raccoon or rogue rodent which was crossing the road in front of it. That sudden stoppage forced F. to pump the brakes hard, loudly screeching to a halt within a few millimeters of the school bus's emergency door. As usual, we weren't wearing any seat belts, and neither were the kids on the bus. It could have been a horrific accident. G.P.'s goading and rabble rousing had unduly influenced the usually level-headed F. and we almost "bought the farm." We just sat there exhaling deeply after the near miss and took turns yelling at G.P., but things got worse. Out of the stopped bus stepped a red-faced Mr. M., one of the guidance counselors and a chaperone for the trip. Normally a fun-loving and even-tempered fellow, this time he was hollering at the top of his lungs even before F. had cranked down his driver's side window. Mr. M. chewed him out but good, calling him every name in the book and pointed at the rest of us as if we were all a bad bunch of careless assholes. G.P. had a knack for being able to talk his way out of virtually any deleterious situation but not this time. There was nothing he could say to ameliorate our obvious guilt as Mr. M. stormed back to the bus and told the driver to proceed. Also, and luckily for us, there were no cars behind our vehicle that morning when the possible mishap occurred. And, as you can guess, for the few miles remaining on our trek, no one said a word. We pulled into the Warriors' parking lot, stumbled out, tried not to make eye contact with Mr. M., walked to the cafeteria, sat down, blandly listened to the proctors and started penciling in our answer sheets based on the asinine PSAT queries. I for one was not in the mood to sit there for hours, especially after a near death experience. In between obtuse and nonsensical questions, I recalled all the times that we same boys would carelessly go joy riding on weekends in that powerful Polara or in E.G.'s gorgeous blue and white Pontiac Catalina convertible, or in J.Logg's standard shift, Chevy Chevelle. Lying to our respective parents under the guise of going somewhere important and doing something constructive, we raced around rather carelessly on largely deserted unpaved county roads, over our local hilly terrain

while shootin' the shit and enjoying one another's
company. We could have instantly and stupidly died on
multiple occasions and it would have been a tragic waste of
budding manhood. However, maybe that was the wildest
thing that we could have done at the time. We didn't do
illegal drugs, recklessly womanize, drink to excess or smoke
(except J.Logg and his Pall Malls). Perhaps driving around
haphazardly was the least of all existing boyhood evils and
fortunately we emerged from those daredevil romps
unscathed. Oftentimes, we would end up at our gal pal
P.M.'s house in the evening and join up with our other two
home gurls, N.K. and L.B. P.M. had a finished cellar with a
pool table, ping pong table, full bar and with a beer tap
that worked. It was a great place to crash and to relax. Her
old man was a college professor like mine and was *hip* for
that era. He had an older son and daughter and they
turned out okay in spite of all the booze in the basement.
So, he let us drink responsibly and we did not abuse his
trust in us. No one got loaded, no one barfed, etc. It was
all in good fun. By the way, P.M.'s parents became my
dental patients decades later. Anyway, my wandering mind
eventually snapped back to the PSAT and I finally
completed it. My buds and I did poorly on it, not realizing
that the tabulations would be used to determine merit
scholarships and be an integral part of a portfolio when

applying to colleges. No one had told me about its importance, darn it. I vividly and numbly remember looking over my crappy scores while my dad berated me for being so dumb. What else was new? I promised myself that I would studiously do my revision during the upcoming summer break and be super ready for the actual SAT in October of my senior year. And unlike my children, who not only adequately prepared themselves for their SATs and scored insanely high on them (my son got a perfect score), I did not. I didn't really study for it and once again achieved lackluster math and English grades. I was humbly embarrassed and could not believe that I did not do better. Was it the testing methods, the questions themselves, my lack of brainpower and review? Or all four? I don't know. And unlike my Brainiac son, who also "killed" the separate ACT test while enroute to becoming the valedictorian of his prep school class, I hated tests of all kind back in my day. Nevertheless and unfortunately for such an exam hater, I have taken more than my fair share, including very difficult pharmacy and dental state board examinations, both of which I aced. Who knew that I had it in me?

58

Dishonor Society

I just couldn't call it by its real name, especially since I was not a "made" member. I still get justifiably pissed off whenever I recall my mental anguish on that fateful day in 1976. So, what happened? In my high school, every spring saw the induction of at least twelve *special* juniors into the National Honor Society. It was a prestigious and almost religious convocation with the full attendance of high schoolers in the gymnasium. It was a highly sought prize, rewarding the best of the best that our school had to offer. Those few that got in had purportedly and unequivocally shown qualities of leadership, character, school service, and scholarship. In addition, the credo was that they were "reliably" and "accurately" predicted to go far in life and achieve great successes. They supposedly had unlimited "potential." Really? Ha, ha; what a joke. Now, my omission from that group could have been tolerable had all the newly minted members been superior to me in any of the categories mentioned. But that was not the case with that scurvy lot. Not only did my best friend F. and I check all the required boxes with aplomb, we often went above and beyond the norm during our high school lockup. And

later, between his B.S., R.Ph., several science master's
degrees, and a pharmaceutical Ph.D., and my B.S., R.Ph.,
D.D.S. and M.S.D. degrees, I believe we both more than
fulfilled the promise of bright futures. Yet in '76 we were
left off that "magic" list. We both got screwed. I think back
at the "losers" in that tainted bunch and shudder. A few
ended up barely graduating from shitty state colleges.
Anyone off the street with half a brain could have singled
out excellent candidates who actually fit in much better
than many of the ones chosen. True, some did belong in
that coveted society but the others? Absolutely not! Were
those certain bozos selected because they were teachers'
offspring, teacher's pets, were politically connected, or had
favoritism in their favor? It was all hush, hush, you know.
All kinds of rumors circulated after the fact as "concerned"
high school educators and sympathetic parents consoled
my folks and me and promised to get to the bottom of
things, so to speak. However nothing was done or
investigated and that was that. Perhaps I messed things up
for myself because of an unpronounceable surname and a
seemingly immature and snarky sense of humor? I guess I
must have been a real "character" and stymied my own
cause. Maybe I dragged F. down with me, as well? His
older brother got in as did his younger brother years later,
both with lower class averages and with less exemplified

activities than he. My younger sister got in as well, although she did finish second in her class and was much more "serious" than me. Were F. and I victims of circumstance because of a nefarious plot against us? Was it really discrimination, stupidity and cluelessness or cunning cleverness on the part of the selecting teachers and board members? I'll never know but I can never forget or forgive. Both of my children made it onto their respective school honor societies because they most definitely belonged on it; just ask them. I will tell you that I did not make it into the Rho Chi Honor Society at my pharmacy college because there were brighter students with higher GPAs than me who positively earned a spot on it. I understood and didn't squawk a bit. In dental school I finished third in my class and was unanimously elected to the Omicron Kappa Upsilon dental honor society because I squarely deserved it, no ifs, ands, or buts. That's how life was supposed to work, fairly and justly. Right? Although, I must say that my dental school class valedictorian was maliciously denied inclusion into the honor society because of his four years of outspokenness and fighting for students' rights. Perhaps he had rubbed the right people the wrong way as I had, all those years ago? Maybe I am in good company after all?

59

Mate Hunting

I was sixteen, had a decent *Saturday Night Fever* wardrobe for special occasions, had a personal chauffer, my father, and a top of the line automobile to impress the ladies with. Well, my dad owned our '73 Cadi but I was the handsomely accoutered and "available" suitor to be displayed at various ethnic Estonian festivals, to catch the eye of a potential pure blood female consort! At least that was the plan. My mom had the dates and times circled on our kitchen calendar of those few but well attended weekend outdoor shindigs in the Catskills that promoted Estonian culture, customs, costumes, dances, and authentic eats. Many of the WWII immigrants knew each other and hobnobbed while speaking in their native European tongue, including my folks. However, no matter my enjoyment of the surroundings or the good-natured fellowship of the people present, I always felt as if I was intentionally on display. And it didn't help with my mom running around playing matchmaker for me. She was constantly asking my opinion of teenage girls that I was introduced to via their also scheming parents. I wanted to have fun, nosh on Estonian vittles, watch some choreographed dances, and go home. But no, I was paraded around the site like some eligible prince, if only the ladies had cooperated. But they did not, at least not to my knowledge and not in the daylight hours. I had dressed for success and failed. At the end of a long day, there was always a teen dance, held in a large and darkened pavilion with loud American music as the sound of choice. We were still in the U.S. of course and most, if not all, of the youngsters were like me, born and raised here. That is where I could have met and hugged up on a genuine Americanized Estonian gal, but it never happened. My folks panned those late night "boogie" soirees as decadent and unseemly for meeting a "proper" girl. The music was "obnoxious," the girls wore "revealing" attire, and only desperate idiots would hang out with them. Well, I was no idiot, or was I? We would pile into our grand Cadillac sedan and slowly exit the venue after dinnertime, with pop making sure he drove slowly to show off our alleged wealth to onlookers and possible future contacts. So, while the young people were dancing, talking and jiving up a storm at that late-night party, my folks would spend the next hour or two during our car ride home dissecting, ridiculing and condemning yet another failed attempt to fetch me a legitimate bride-to-be. My younger sister and I sat glumly in the spacious velour back seat as mom and dad's puritanical diatribe continued. "Where are all the "good" Estonian ladies?" they would lament out loud. Where, indeed? Maybe in Estonia? There was always some type of Estonian church-sponsored social function coming up in a nearby city as my excited mom started to plan and plot her next moves to get me pre-engaged. It wasn't so much a sporadic religious outing for her as it was a cunning plan to meet and greet eager parents afterwards and shop around her son as a willing commodity. By now I also felt that I was somehow letting down our side. My parents would often suggest that I was being too picky or standoffish or not interested in their "game." While some of that may be true, tell me how easy it is to walk up to someone from the opposite sex and quickly and succinctly begin a conversation that would result in a betrothal? And in broad daylight, with two sets of dour and pushy parental units standing next to us no less? Come on! My immigrant folks had met in western New York State with my mom's older brother (Uncle Tony) being the nuptials broker. He and my pop had played on the same semi-pro Estonian Club soccer team and became good friends over time. One thing led to another and my parents dated, wrote furtive letters to one another for years, and eventually got hitched. In their old-fashioned minds that was the tried and true method to hook up and tie the knot. Why was I so recalcitrant? Mom was busy slinging Cupid's arrows in all female Estonian directions, but I was continually ungrateful and dateless. Of course, my dating life in my village high school also was nil. How dare I even think about going out with a "plain, local farmer's daughter?" God, forbid. I was above all that, or, was I? Plus, I had no car. The junior prom was approaching and, I had already asked a senior, J.D., to be my date. She and I had a hand-holding type of relationship with no heavy petting, kissing or other extracurricular activities. We had known each other for a while and spoke during orchestra practices and at her locker during most mornings. She was a lanky, afro-haired, extremely musically talented, smart lass with big things planned for her future. Her dad was a biology professor at our town's college and our respective parents knew one another. But I was just a casual, nice boy in her book, and I understood that. My folks accepted our basically platonic bond and never sought to squelch my juvenile crush on her. The prom came and went, she graduated, and I remained single, regardless of the myriad of Estonian festivals that we had traveled to in the ensuing summer and early fall. I was just a loser. Fast forwarding a few years found me canoodling with lots of college-aged women. I don't remember a time after the freshman pharmacy college orientation picnic when I was unattached. I always seemed to have female company around me and never lacked for *intimacy* with girlfriends. Maybe I wasn't such a loser after all? And by the end of my third year I had successfully dated and mated with Hottie Blondie, a freshman pharmacy chick who would later become my wife. Although she wasn't a thoroughbred Estonian, well, maybe an inconsequential quarter on her father's side, she was a svelte, blonde and blue-eyed babe with more than an ounce of brain and two years my junior. Hotsy-totsy! Mom and dad were deeply saddened at my seemingly flippant choice of a genealogical mutt for a spouse but eventually acquiesced and reluctantly became her in-laws. So, what would have happened if I had somehow gotten spliced to a pre-approved, Estonian woman of my parents' choosing? Would I have ended up any happier? Would my children be fluent in the mother tongue? Did it really matter? I don't know as I look back on my nearly four decade-long marriage to a smart and sassy, hot blonde. I think I made out alright; and a BIG no thank-you to some dumpy and kerchief-clad Estonian babushka that I might have ended up with, instead.

60

The Junior Prom

I had planned on asking C.V., our grade's relatively recent transfer student and resident hot blonde. However, she may have been a tad dishonest about her appearance. I did hear stories from a reliable source, her best friend N.K. who was one of my oldest female pals, that she highlighted her long golden locks and took hours to put on makeup. Nevertheless, it didn't matter; most of the heterosexual fellows in school and around town still longed for her. And that list included me. Although way below my league scholastically, she was a gorgeous girl and good looks triumphed over brains, as sad as that sounds. Regardless of being an average student, she continually garnered much attention from horny male faculty members and boys alike, and coyly reveled in it. And why not? She was no dummy and instinctively knew how to use her beauty and wiles to "get ahead" in a patriarchal world. Although she did not have a steady boyfriend per se, there were always those "reliable rumors" floating around school that she supposedly and discretely hooked up with males as her hormones dictated. And instead of being slut-shamed, her alleged trysts only made her capital rise in our hopelessly backwater school. However, most of our Oshkosh-wearing *home gurls* despised her, if you know what I mean. Anyway, our respective parents knew each other from being fellow college employees in town and, after prodding from my mom, I got up the gumption to ring her home and asked for her hand to the prom. Her well-spoken mom answered the blower and sadly informed me that she was already spoken for by another boy from my class. I was just too late! Time for plan B. I had been paying attention to and playing infantile handsies with senior J.D. for close to a year and fancied her my "girlfriend," although her interest in me was not wholeheartedly reciprocated. She was an attractive, brown curly-haired, extremely intelligent and musically talented lady with soft curves and a demure disposition. Why we were mildly attracted to each other I do not know. Orchestral practices and recitals had brought us together, which was followed by casual chit chat at her locker during many mornings. The innocent flirtatious beginnings were followed by the obvious human sexual dance of touching one another before succumbing to more ardent behavior. But the former is as far as she would let me go, darn it. A few light kisses and hand holding were the norm between us. It was the best I could do at the time, what can I say? So, with C.V. being unavailable, J.D. was the obvious choice to take to the prom. I wouldn't say she was second best or that she would have gotten mad if I had not asked her, but she was gracious enough to say yes and we were all set. And soon the wheels got in motion, including the zoot suit pressing, the expensive corsage and accoutrement purchases, and limousine rental. Well, almost. Pop, mom and I picked up J.D. in our family's bronze, '73 Cadillac Brougham d'Elegance sedan Deville. It was the biggest and most luxurious car that Cadillac produced at the time, short of a limo, ambulance or hearse. Why rent one when we had one? My dad parked in her driveway as my mom and I exited to meet and greet her family and her. J.D. looked amazing with a slinky homemade dress that clung seductively to her. I awkwardly put on her wrist corsage and tried to make small talk with her chuckling dad, all the while pulling at my starched, tight, white shirt collar. Her younger sister watched the proceedings intently as if memorizing her own future machinations in this "consummating" American high school ritual. My pop then whisked us away to the high school and even opened our back doors as a gesture of fealty because of the special occasion at hand. What a dad. J.D. and I entered, sat at our table, looked around at all the couples, danced and ate the light refreshments served. A local and untuned band droned on and on playing the theme song over and over again: *Color my World*, by

Chicago. It got to the point where we got sick of it, although it was a slow number and gave most of us guys the chance to feel up our dates, over and over again. Bonus! But then, like all good things, the prom ended, pop dropped J.D. off at her house and I was ferried home. And that was it. J.D. and I never discussed it afterward in school and sort of fell out of orbit with each other near the end of the school year. She graduated and reluctantly accepted a small silver necklace from me at her commencement ceremony. I didn't even know what college she was going to; such was our blasé and mostly platonic romance. Sadly, our so-called relationship had never even reached second base…. It always only hung around the first base pad. And you would think that we would justifiably go our separate ways because our time together was finally at an end. But your thinking would be wrong, Bucko! Fast forward to the summer after my freshman year at pharmacy college: The Wooden Nickel was the main local bar on Main Street in our newly "wet" cow-pie town and functioned as a summer repository for we collegians and local rednecks alike. We happily comingled with our former high school classmates that were in colleges and even close chums that had decided to make our town their future homes. Lo and behold, on one such steamy and sultry Friday evening, my former "gang" and I were shooting the shit at the Nickel while shooting pool when who should stroll in, run up to me like a long lost lover, throw her arms around me and plant a big wet one on my unprepared kisser? Holy Toledo, it was J.D., that former feminine ingenue "girlfriend" of mine who acted like a well-practiced vamp, that's who. She had been my lackluster junior prom date, my hesitant and trepidatious high school squeeze and now she wanted some real action? But, why? After not hearing from her for two academic years, there she was all over me like a cheap suit, knowingly massaging my arms and body and impervious to the stares and catcalls of my immediate surrounding buddies. What the hell? My best friend and pharmacy college roommate F. had known about our previous high school dalliance and winced at me, reminding me with his facial contortions about my current college girlfriend: Tumbleweed. My mind was reeling. I fleetingly thought about my steady in college but here was the lovely J.D. forcefully pulling me into the parking lot. Was she drunk, stoned, horny, or all three? I wasn't sure as we took a stroll across the street to the village square and plopped down on a bench. It was late and there was no one around, save for patrons entering and exiting the bar we had just left. So what was her deal, as she crossed her long, bare, silky smooth legs over mine and sat there, flushed and smiling at me? After a few perfunctory utterances on my part, she took over and it quickly became obvious that she had no boyfriend, was in town for the summer and still had the hots for me. Why, and since when? When I protested and rejected her memory of things, she shushed me and started kissing me with abandon. I was tentative, suspicious and taken aback by her actions and sadly never got into it with her as I probably should have. Here was a freebie, and I didn't bite. Perhaps my feelings for my college girlfriend were too strong or maybe J.D. scared me somewhat. I don't know. We fondled each other, talked, laughed, and necked for a few hours on that wood-slatted bench in the center of town, underneath the civil war monument, next to the darkened courthouse and county jail. It felt good to finally express my former feelings to her and to get an appreciative vibe in return. This was going to be a great summer, I hedonistically thought. But it didn't materialize. She dropped me off at my house (I had earlier walked into town) after much foreplay in the front seat of her parent's tan, Pontiac station wagon and I bid her goodnight, anticipating at least more of the same in the very near future. I never saw her again. WTF? Where did she go? None of my peeps seemed to know. I could have easily called her house or even visited there unannounced, but did not. I had naïvely thought that we would see each other in town; maybe she thought I would formally ask her out to start legitimate dating? I don't know what occurred. Perhaps I blew it. Or maybe she had woken up the next day and ashamedly slapped herself after recalling that evening of juvenile and ineffectual fornication that she had initiated? All those questions and no good answers. I still think about J.D. once in awhile and have mentioned my saga with her to my wife, Hottie Blondie. She has no answers for me either but reminds me that carrying a barely flickering torch for someone for over forty years is borderline pathetic and pathologic. Perhaps she is right.

61

Chemical Cornucopia

I had successfully completed my junior year and looked forward to rewarding myself with lots of bug hunting, bike riding and tennis playing. It never materialized, however. My best friend F. had already started his second summer tour of duty at the village drugstore and the grumblings in my home intimated that I had better follow suit and finally get "serious." I just HAD to sort out my heretofore ambiguous career plans at the cost of having fun. I just HAD to. A peck of pressure, beginning in junior high on yours truly, was not only still present but ratcheted up a few notches at the 'ole Estonian immigrant homestead. Darn it. I had to have a plan yesterday and then execute it tomorrow, without any help or guidance in the present. Wow. I wished I had a scholarly blueprint to follow. However, my simultaneously professorial and Old World dad wanted to reap the bragging rights of my future life without sticking his neck out and pointing me in the right direction. I was supposed to magically wake up one day as an engineer or doctor and make everyone happy and proud. But how was I supposed to do that? No one told me, and yet my know-it-all father was in academia, for

God's sake. No wonder I was stressed all the time and continually bit my fingernails. Duh! Nevertheless, my mom had great news for me: Because she had recently enrolled at our local Ag and Tech college to "make something" of herself, she unwittingly befriended a few older females in the same boat as she. One of those "elder" students was married to the owner of a pharmaceutical manufacturing company in the next crummy village over. My mother pleaded my jobless case for me and the next thing I knew I was hired as the chief bottle and glass washer at G. Laboratories for the entire vacation's duration! Perhaps mom had purposely made a clever connection for me? She knew that I had that pharmacy college brochure in my bedroom. Maybe by working in a pharmacy-related work environment would give me some forward momentum as to my future career? Was she smarter than I took her for? Hmm….Nevertheless, deep inside I knew I had to "man up," stop fooling around so much and at least give the illusion of maturity. And because all my friends had jobs, I might as well have one too and only get together with them on weekends like the "working class" did. Plus, and most importantly, maybe I could get my grumpy and harping Grandpa Pete off my back for being such an alleged slacker who wasn't funny and would never amount to much. Anyhow, F. wanted to be a pharmacist

like his maternal grandfather had been. I wanted to be.... I
didn't rightly know but maybe working in a "chemical
plant" would give me some type of positive inspiration?
And it did, sort of. Mom made all the logistical
connections and sweated the details for me, including
setting me up with a daily ride to and from the job as well
as packing me a sandwich lunch. All I had to do was get up
and go to work! Two beautiful babes in a '74 green Chevy
Camaro pulled into our driveway on my first day and,
jeepers, all three were knock-outs! Each woman was in her
late twenties, one worked in the laboratory section where I
would be, while the other was the personal secretary for
the boss, Dr. D.G. I crawled into the tiny rear seat area as
both ladies giggled and lit up Marlboros for the fifteen-
minute trip. At least they had the decency to crack the
windows so I wouldn't suffocate in the back. Next, one of
them slammed in an eight-track tape, the same one we
would listen to every day: Paul Simon's *Still Crazy After All
These Years*. When the song *My Little Town* would play,
both females would loudly sing along and laugh as if to
sarcastically reinforce their stereotypic small-town
existence. I just sat there quietly as the Camaro with its
rear wheel drive and eight-cylinder engine literally zoomed
over the mountainous highway with ease. Upon entering
the defunct former milk producing plant, which was

haphazardly converted to a makeshift tablet production emporium due to fire destroying the previous pill plant in an adjacent puny village, a strong scent of ammonia hit me square in the nose. That unique and pungent stank would forever remind me of G. Laboratories. Anyway, while one girl walked into the quality control room, the other quickly ushered me into Dr. D.G.'s personal office for a quick meet and greet. A middle-aged, short and stout man vigorously shook my hand, explained my duties to me, and had his head scientist collect me as he and his secretary started to titter behind the closed door. As the tall, jocular scientist and I walked to the quality control chamber, he spoke at length about the genius of Dr. D.G.; how he had run away from home to be a trapeze star in his youth, became a navy commander, and had earned multiple degrees including one in nuclear physics, as well as a Ph.D. At that time, G. Laboratories manufactured knock-off generic prescription headache tablets for Boots Pharmaceuticals, a major generic drug company in those days. His lab made other pharmacy products as well, but the former was Dr. D.G.'s patented invention and money maker. So basically we made the round doses which were subsequently sold to Boots, which in turn sold it to pharmacies through a third-party vendor. No wonder drugs cost so much; they did back then, too. But G. Laboratories had to keep strict policies when it came to making drugs to ensure constant bioavailability between batches as well as consistency from tablet to tablet. And that's where I came in. With protective eyewear and special rubber gloves on, I was the guy that washed and cleaned all the beakers, pipettes, Erlenmeyer flasks, etc., either with soap and water or sulfuric acid, before drying them in special ovens. I don't know who did my job before I came onboard, however fellow workers seemed to appreciate my sudden presence. The sterilized equipment was used to test the agents that were made right off the production floor, to make sure each and every light blue pill was perfect. A gas chromatograph checked if the correct ingredients and amounts were used and a hardness tester determined at what poundage the pellet broke apart; and aquariums with body temperature water had rotating tubes filled with stomach acids and intestinal juices that tablets were dropped into, to see how long it took the drug to dissolve. Other sophisticated experiments were also performed, and all the data was collected at intervals and given to the head scientist. He would in turn run out to the production floor in his flowing white lab coat and confront Dr. V.V., an Indian dude who was the chief operating officer in charge of the actual manufacturing process. Between the two of them, they tweaked the formulations as needed to keep the pills *kosher*. Besides those two scientists and Dr. D.G., the rest of the rank and file was mostly local male farmers, male blue-collar rubes and cocky male oddballs, with a few pretty women thrown in here and there. I scrubbed and scoured that glassware from morning till quitting time and never broke a single piece of equipment. It was tedious labor because each performed analysis resulted in more dirty dishes, so to speak. However, once in awhile I was allowed to run a few of the trials by myself and beamed with pride when I handed over my documents to the head honcho in our testing hovel. At ten o'clock every day we had a break. Powdered white, jelly filled donuts and coffee were liberally distributed as all the forty or so factory employees bantered and relaxed for a while. I had my token two donuts and then trudged on back to my sink and sulfuric acid container, the one whose contents made a hole in my left cuff one day without me realizing it. Only after my skin started burning did I notice a smoldering dime-sized hole in my sleeve. Ouch!!!! That acid had eaten through my lab coat and dress shirt in a matter of seconds. Yikes. Oh, well, that was the worst thing that had happened to me and I never told my mom. I threw away that shirt without her ironing it, by the way. The days went by with jokes and jibes within our sequestered little center. However, during every early afternoon there was a palpable silence with all eyes focused on the large clock affixed to the concrete wall. It was the usual time when Dr. D.G. would burst unannounced into our dilapidated quality control quarters, personally chat with the six of us, grab a handful of his own medicine for his "two o'clock daily headaches caused by a certain 'hot' secretary," and then bolt onto the floor to check on his other workers. What a scene it was. As a lowly worker I was paid minimum wage and the summer passed quickly; however, I got to know my fellow riders quite well. Both were fond of playfully bashing their employer but the one "typing" in his personal den wanted to divulge more juicy gossip but always stopped short because of my presence in the car. Damn. The summer ended, I got a heartfelt handshake and college recommendation letter from the head man and my mom bought nice scarves and smokes for the ladies that had picked me up daily for that three-month work experience. Anyhow, G. Laboratories ended up moving back to its former dinky hamlet where Dr. D.G. built a huge facility with all the modern chemical bells and whistles. I heard that for years he grew in success until his sons sold the business to a pharmaceutical giant. I sincerely hope his "headaches" finally went away. I relished those days away from home doing something that I would never have predicted I would do and interacting with "interesting" adults that I would otherwise have avoided. I guess I grew up a little that summer, at least that's what my mother kept saying, as if to mollify my disbelieving father and cynical paternal grandfather. Sure, I still saw my closest buddies, hit more than a few tennis balls, and collected my share of miniscule fauna on weekends and evenings, but gone was my carefree and undisciplined youthful life. And gone were the days of Dr. D.G. making pills in a dank, stinky, refurbished creamery, on a shoestring budget while using misfit grunts like me.

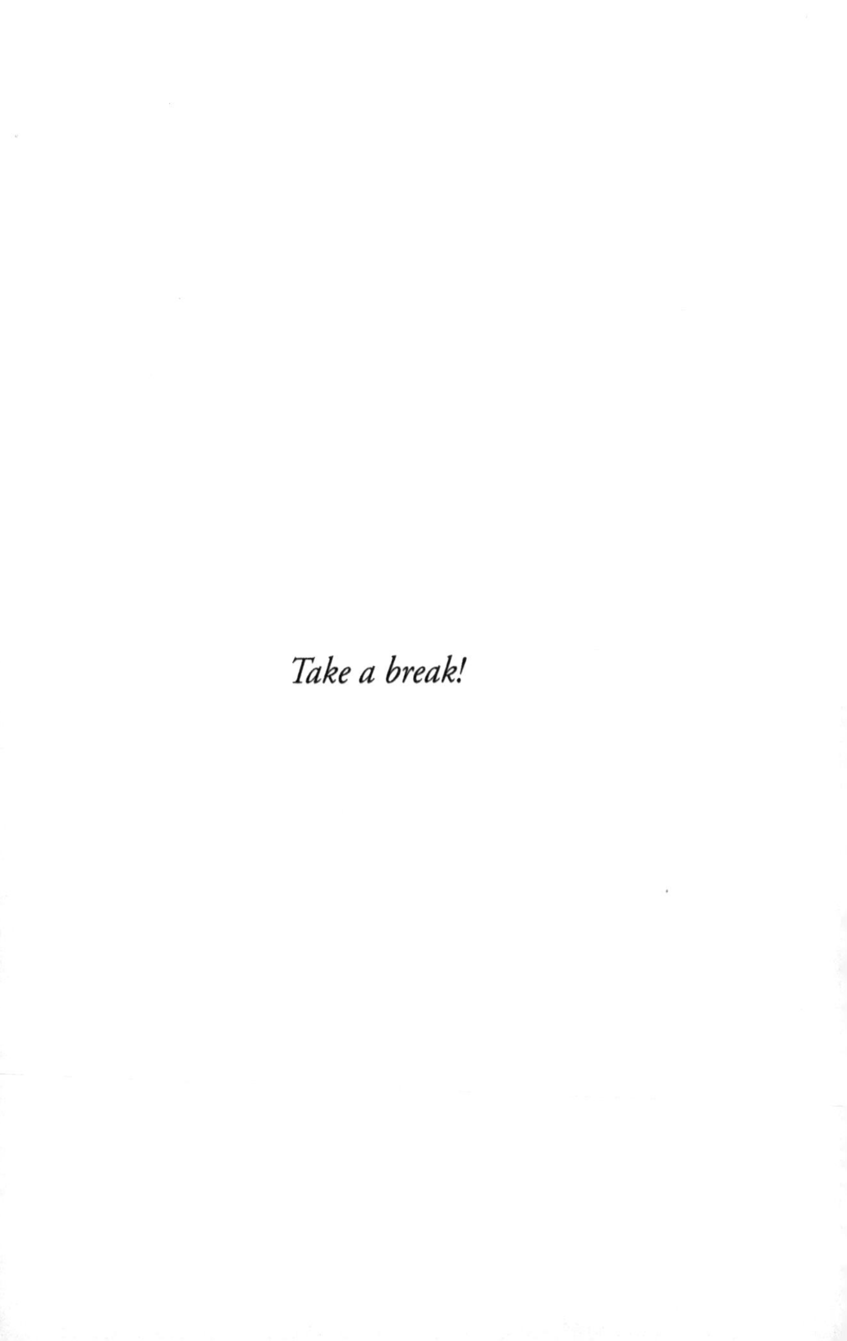

Take a break!

SENIOR YEAR

It's seriously too late to get serious

62

Vegemite and Foster's

Our teensy-weensy, bumbling bastion of learning never failed to attract foreign students as part of the American Field Service program, or AFS for short. Nearly every senior class had a girl or boy from a distant part of the world who studied, lived and dined among the small-minded simpletons of our settlement for a whole academic year. And my class was no exception. My buddies and I knew someone was coming, but who, and from where? Previously we had arrivals from France, Uruguay, Spain, Argentina, etc. I'm sure that in the storied history of our esteemed "reform school," most major countries had sent at least one sucker into our midst, to wallow with us in our fetid cesspool of bigoted idiocy. I wondered what continent the next jerk would be from. Finally, a week before school commenced that fall, my best friend F. privately and seriously confided in me that in fact he and his family were going to host an Australian exchange student named Dave W. for the first half of the year. F.'s family had worked tirelessly all summer long to logistically make it happen. I had known nothing about it and was floored. Normally F. and I kept no secrets from each other, but I understood

295

that this was a different situation, that no one was to know until classes officially began. No one except for me and my immediate bunch, of course. Well, we were sworn to secrecy and waited with bated breath till HE arrived that evening. Besides the F. family welcoming him, we "posse-members" also planned a type of introduction ceremony, complete with two six-packs of imported Australian Foster's Lager beer. We were all set. J. Logg brought the suds and me, while E.G. ferried the rest of the "gang" in his Pontiac Catalina convertible. We bounded into F.'s house and made a beeline onto the back porch, where we could see people standing around and talking. And there he was, the exchange student from down under! He stood about six foot four and looked like a cross between Sasquatch and Peter Frampton. With very long curly auburn locks cascading down from a large head, he resembled a rock god from some infamous hair band of the '70s. With a wide nostril nose, large hands and feet, could he have also been part Aborigine? In fact, that's what he later said he was, but I wasn't sure if he was joshing us or not. Nevertheless, I was impressed with his masculine and imposing physique; I was also piqued by his seemingly disarming and laid-back mannerisms. I mean, he had just traveled thousands of miles to a strange location, with strangers surrounding him, and probably suffered from severe jet lag, yet he stood there politely fielding questions in a relaxed bodily position. This guy was special, he was a *cool* customer. Finally, the F. family gave way to us "gang" members to have at him. And we did. I was probably the most obnoxious of the bunch as usual, and began the teasing process of a potential new recruit. But he didn't flinch. And I'm sure he looked upon me as some short (I was actually 5'10"), egotistical twerp who thought he was a funnyman. I tried to roil him with purposely leading and needling queries, and he just smirked. He was unflappable, thus far. Then J. Logg offered him the Foster's, which he made a face at. What? I thought it was genuine Australian beer and here was Dave only reluctantly accepting a bottle of it. The rest of us cracked some tops and were ready to enjoy the beer. (The drinking age was 18 at the time, even though I was shy by about three months. However, the F. family allowed us to have a few brews on occasion at their house whenever my pals and I visited). Dave spoke up saying that Foster's was considered shit in his nation, comparing it to Genesee or Utica Club in our country. How did he know we felt the same way about those latter two brands? Anyhow, at least he had a backbone and spoke up when it was important, such as when analyzing ales. However, we didn't begrudge him his opinion and quickly quaffed his native beverage; even he swallowed the "swill."

But then he blurted out that he was hungry and asked F. if he could have a Vegemite sandwich. Now, I'm not sure if he said that to be a *pill* or if he really meant it. His smile never wavered as Mrs. F. (F.'s mother) calmly and matter-of-factly informed him that they had Peter Pan crunchy peanut butter and Wonder Bread but were fresh out of Vegemite. She had a sense of humor, too. Dave said that he hated "Peter Butter" and asked where he could get some of that perverse paste from his home country. Wait just a minute. What the hell was Vegemite, anyway? I had never heard of it. Dave explained that Vegemite was a popular, black, Australian food spread made of brewer's yeast extract and vegetable/spice additives and, was loaded with B vitamins. "It is also probably high in cyclamates, nutraceuticals, phytochemicals and hypochondriacs, as well," I said out loud, to much laughter from my pals. Dave grinned. The taste is purportedly bitter, salty and meaty and needs to be eaten in small, thin increments. He went on to say that it was not for wussy Americans. Well, I had eaten schmaltz herring slathered in vinegar and onions, as well as Estonian borscht and chicken gelatin, so what was a little topping-sauce from Aussie-ville? Bring it on…. But, alas, I never got the chance to try it but I'm sure the F. clan procured it for him during his stay with them. The subject of careers came up and Dave said that his folks owned a fifteen-hundred-acre sheep farm in Greenethorpe, New South Wales, kind of a meager setup by Australian standards, but marginally profitable. He expected to take it over some day and continue in the family farming and sheep-shearing business. My buds and I stared at him, not knowing whether to believe him or not. Meager? Was he joking? He wasn't. F. and his parents owned one hundred fifty acres of farmland and it was considered large by our village standards. F.'s father was a college culinary arts/hotel management professor but had inherited "the farm" and maple sugar shack from his dad and continued to run both. Fifteen hundred versus one hundred and fifty were vastly different numbers. But I guess everything in Australia was bigger and more exotic, kind of like "things" in Texas. But was he a typical Aussie male? I didn't know. He was the first one I had ever seen up close and personal. And were they all this huge, charming and mature? Who knew? Wow! So, we met the exciting exchange student, exchanged pleasantries with him and went home, eager to tell our respective parents about Dave and the successful exchange of ideas and humor that we all had indulged in. It was a slight clash of cultures, but he spoke "English" and seemed delighted to be where he was, at least that's what I observed during the two-hour long introduction session. I will mention Dave W. fondly as we go forward during this senior year and there's a very good reason for that. For along with his many outrageous colloquial witticisms and obtuse observations, there had never been a better or more beloved foreign exchange student than he in the recent history of our school. Dave quickly became the tenth member of our whacky group, was the place kicker for the varsity football team, and fulfilled his many speaking obligations, not unlike a Miss America winner. However, those mandatory and tiresome slide shows about his home country did illicit a common refrain from him: "Knackered at eatin' Jell-O with ol' ladies fahkin' bloody oath mate," he would sometimes mutter to me. But he did all that while maintaining a full albeit watered down scholastic schedule, and while being physically and mentally separated from home. He became my physics partner (someone had to get him through that hard course), my good friend, my fellow comedic thespian, a German convention participant (he didn't know a lick of the language nor did he take it in our school), and was an all-around nice guy. He willingly participated in many events, rarely said no to an offer, but was discerning and savvy enough not to get into trouble. As to our nutty "posse," whether his heart was always in it was hard to tell, but he called us *mates* and made the most of his time here and good-naturedly played along with our many spoofs and gags. I don't recall him ever being depressed or dour, just jovial and full of life. We often teased him about the hordes of girls that he would be seducing but that never materialized, to my knowledge. He managed to keep it in his pants and there were absolutely no salacious stories of hanky-panky associated with him during his yearlong stay. He told us that he had a steady girlfriend back home and that was that; he is still married to her to this day. He was universally loved, admired and praised by all who encountered him. Thanks Dave, ya fahkin' cobber, for making my senior year so enjoyable and "interesting!"

63

The Phone Call

I had really enjoyed my summer job at the nearby pharmaceutical plant before my senior year. I was employed as the head bottle washer and cleaner of dirty beakers, glassware, etc. It was a busy place but I never broke a single piece of equipment. But, so what. It was a job. I was grateful for the extra money and experience working with real scientists. I still, however, had enough time during the evenings and weekends to play tennis and catch my fill of butterflies and other critters. Senior year had started and we had to meet with our guidance counselors that September to get our lives figured out. Mr. T. was a former shop and agriculture teacher who was promoted to guidance counselor. We had met many times since ninth grade for course guidance and future plans. So there we were, in his tiny orifice next to the nurse's station, staring at each other, not knowing what to say. The room was full of brochures from local two-year and community colleges – that's where the majority of our "farming community" high schoolers ended up going. You know, to learn about John Deere tractors, animal husbandry, artificial insemination of cattle, herding, treating rashes on cow teats, etc. Useful stuff if you were going to inherit daddy's farm. I blandly looked at those brochures dismissively. "What do you want to do, Izzy?" he remarked, also rather blandly. "Something in biology," I answered. He knew my grades were top notch, especially in all the science classes. But curiously he never mentioned any Ivy League colleges. Perhaps I wasn't that smart after all. And he knew I wasn't connected in any way. Legacy? What was that? Anyway, we bantered about for a while; the subject of engineering came and went. No interest whatsoever. Finally I blurted out near the end of our session that maybe I just might be interested in pharmacy. I still had that pharmacy brochure from last spring's *college night* carefully tucked away in my top dresser drawer in my bedroom. I admit to whipping it out occasionally and musing about being a pharmacist, whatever that was. I mean I had been inside drugstores many times but never really knew exactly what a druggist did besides selling pills. Mr. T. nearly jumped out of his shoe tops when I mentioned the word pharmacy. He told me to stay right where I was; he'd be right back. He quickly vanished into his adjacent inner office and proceeded to call someone on the phone. I could barely make out some muffled laughter, and there was lots of silence. What was he doing in there, on my time? But he had told me to stay. What was up? He

returned just as abruptly and proceeded to shake my hand
vigorously up and down, as if he was milking it. His
Cheshire cat smile never left him as he loudly
congratulated me for getting into pharmacy college.
What??!! No grades were sent, no SAT scores reported, no
teacher recommendations obtained. What??!! Evidently the
two-hour-away pharmacy college had a penchant for
accepting qualified small-town boys and girls. All he had to
do was contact the dean of admissions and plead my case.
And that's exactly what he did, and I got in, over the
phone! The rest of the required documentation and
materials would be formally sent later. His word was good
enough for the dean and I was all set. Really, I was
dumbstruck. He patted me on the back as I left his office,
still smiling about a job well done, on his part. I told some
of my pals; they were in disbelief. I told my best friend
who was going to apply to the same college later in the fall
like normal students did; he was pissed off at me. I had
stolen his thunder. But it wasn't on purpose. I had just
gone in there as required to get some ideas together for
college applications and walked out practically a
pharmacist. I told my parents at dinnertime that evening.
My father just stared at me without speaking. As a
professor, he knew the application process, etc. This just
couldn't be or could it? My mother remarked that I would

make good money and there were plenty of jobs available, or so she heard. My father lightened up and quickly acquiesced to the idea of me being a pharmacist. Now this was a clever plan. Even If I ended up with a B average, I would still be a pharmacist. There was no need for a plan B. This was going to be it. And it was full of SCIENCE, which I professed to love. This could be better than engineering. Blasphemous but brilliant! Of course I still had to go to college and all, and it would be no picnic, as I soon began to realize. And it was a five-year program....

64

The Drive-By

I had just gotten into college; it was time for a fall road trip to check it out. That's what you did back in the late '70s. You got into your trusty station wagon and hit the road. My father knew exactly where the pharmacy college was located. He had made numerous trips to that city for professorial conferences and had passed it on many occasions. It is funny how he never told me about those trips; I had never asked, I guess. Of course, I had never expressed an interest in pharmacy before…. Anyhow, I assumed we would spend some time in the city, look at the college, step inside, and maybe even mingle with some pharmacy students. It was going to be exciting! My sister and mother were also going. The whole damn family piled into our 1965 F-85 Oldsmobile station wagon of course. I had heard that the pharmacy college was small but part of a larger university which was located in a nearby city. I was all hopped-up as I closed the car door. My pop said nothing. I also knew it had no dorms – that turned out to be a problem in the very near future. But today it was time for a quickie two-hour trip, just to get the feel of the drive and to show me the school. It was fun trekking through winding mountainous back roads from our dinky village; over hills and dales, through gullies and gulches. Small talk consumed us during the trip. Two hours later the city appeared. OK, what do we do first? Pop drove straight through downtown as if on a messianic mission, aiming right for the college. No time for eating, drinking, defecating, or sightseeing. No worries, soon the university grounds would appear and we could officially park on "MY" campus. There would be food, water and bathrooms. I eagerly fondled that well-worn pharmacy brochure I still had from *college night* and anticipated buildings and green spaces galore. I grew up in a small college town, where my father was a civil engineering professor, so I kind of knew what a bustling college was supposed to look and "feel" like. We were driving slowly on that Saturday when suddenly my dad abruptly pointed to his right. We all swiveled our heads in unison to look. There it was, a red brick, ivy-covered, lone building resembling a very tiny high school. We drove by, stared and kept going. Good thing I didn't blink. Are you kidding me? That was it? How disappointing. Of course the brochure did not show any "distance" shots, only close-ups of the college. I felt duped. Dad turned the car around and headed back toward it, intending to find some parking. He pulled into the 10-slot college parking lot and turned off the car. There were nine other parking spots available. It was quiet, too quiet. I naïvely bounded for the front door but stopped briefly to read the small, nondescript sign on the teeny-weeny front lawn; it resembled one of those campaign signs you stick in the grass. It said "PP College of Pharmacy." I bolted up the marble steps and found a locked front door and an aged bronze sign that read "Closed on Saturday, Sunday. Open Weekdays from 8 a.m. to 5 p.m." There were no students, no professors, and no life. I swear I heard distant laughter coming from nearby motorists as I futilely tugged at that big brass front door, looking like Dorothy being rebuffed at the entrance to the Emerald City in the *Wizard of Oz*. I was embarrassed. I went back to the car and we headed quickly to the nearest Mobil gas station (that's the brand my father used) for a bathroom break and a Snickers bar apiece. I think we also shared a 7-Up that day. My father then asked me rather enthusiastically if I liked the school. What? What could I say? He was going to pay for it and I was already committed to going. I kind of nodded half-heartedly as we began our trip back home. It was NOT what I had envisioned at all! This was going to be my bleak confinement for five years. Could I take it? I wasn't sure. To my father, it was a place of learning. Beauty and comfort had nothing to do with anything educational in his book. He smiled, I pouted. Our ride home was quiet but I did manage to throw out that damn pharmacy college brochure, out the passenger side window. I littered, so fine me!

65

Not So Horrible

The last word of that title was lifted from a long-running cartoon strip starring a Viking chief and his long-suffering wife, Helga. Well, you can guess the surname of the newly hired instrumental music teacher that replaced our beloved and often bedeviled Mr. Daye. He was a freshly minted music instructor, with Beatle-esque dark bangs, glasses and a huge build. Not muscular, mind you, just a big-framed fellow. He also possessed a thin, raspy voice and frequently grinned, especially during times of stress and student ineptitude, which were plentiful. However, he was the newbie and we were the veterans in our *one-horse* school and like the proverbial substitute teacher he often took the brunt of the many shenanigans pulled on him, especially by yours truly. I mean my buds and I sometimes couldn't help it. He was an easy mark. Mr. H. tried in vain to ingratiate himself on we singers and violinists but instead of showing gratitude we reciprocated by purposely teasing him, often making his teaching life miserable. Our infantile bullshit, phony promises of ardent practice, and regular all-around horseplay during orchestral rehearsals and choir practices incessantly plagued him. He was the perpetual patsy but, nonetheless, a good sport. His oftentimes quizzical smile never wavered however, as he acquiesced to F.'s and my many harebrained schemes and sketch comedy/musical stage productions during senior year. I don't believe he ever admonished my lot of cohorts one bit as we basically ruled the comedy roost at our school. It seemed as though he just didn't know what to do with us at times. Mr. H., thank you for letting us run musically and comically rampant in our "esteemed" school. Your immediate predecessor, Mr. Daye., also had his hands full with a few of us but begrudgingly did not squelch our levity either. Your loose reins and sense of humor were much appreciated and allowed my friends and I to grow as students and comics during that anxious and trying time called twelfth grade.

66

The Last of P.E.

I had stoically withstood Mr. K., that fiery Phys Ed teacher, since the latter days of elementary school. He and I had clashed for years but our mutual animosity toward each other seemed to have cooled off by the completion of my junior year. And the last few years of gym classes saw me receive top grades and a few rare compliments from him as well. So I was athletically confident going into my senior year with a "new" P.E. instructor, Mr. G.M. Although the polar opposite in personality, looks and temper, as compared to his diminutive redheaded counterpart, Mr. G.M. was also an outstanding athlete and probably could have bested Mr. K. in some of the same sports they formerly played themselves when they were in high school. Mr. K. was a local product and had the "coach" swag going on whereas Mr. G.M. seemed like a humble teacher from *nowheresville*. All we boys liked him immediately and the girls swooned whenever they encountered him. He was a young, handsome man; what can I say? But that's where my arrogant smugness almost got me in foul trouble. After that long stint with Mr. K., I thought that my sporty accomplishments in tennis and the besting of most of the "jocks" in gym would entitle me to a free ride and high grades while riding off into the senior sunset. Wrong. Didn't Mr. G.M. get the memo? Why was I getting B's from him when that biased bastard Mr. K. had given me A pluses? What the hell was going on? Although I greatly enjoyed the class, and his blasphemous inclusion of heretofore "unheard" of sports such as soccer and badminton, he was a hard and seemingly aloof marker. He rarely talked to us, unless showing off a particular skill that we needed to learn. It was hard to get an A in his gym! We were deeply mired in soccer when I decided to start taking things seriously. I bought a pair of soccer spikes from the Montgomery Ward store on Main Street (actually, my mom did), laced them up, and started to outplay just about everyone on the playing field. That act alone impressed Mr. G.M. and his demeanor toward me changed immediately. My grades rose and we started up a casual sports-minded banter. By the time spring arrived I was blasting homeruns right and left playing softball and kept my GPA hovering in the A range. I finished the scholastic year with an even ninety average. The takeaway from this story is that while I had my beefs with that prejudiced Mr. K., he ultimately gave me most excellent grades. And while I probably had unanticipated fun and learned more about physical fitness and European sports from Mr. G.M., I suffered in the report card department. Go figure. I had already been accepted to college and didn't need to boost my GPA during twelfth grade; however, it was the principle of the thing that bothered me. The kicker is: I should have aced Phys Ed my senior year and I did not. In hindsight, I wished I had had Mr. K., instead. There, I said it. But don't tell him because he might look me up and make me do a somersault or twenty squat-thrusts, just like old times.

67

Billy and Boston

F. and I were over at N.K.'s house on Clinton Street, my former stomping ground as a child. I used to practically live on her porch in the middle to late sixties; she was a close friend of mine back then, and, continued to be so throughout our high school tenure. So it was of no surprise that my best bud F. and I converged at her place, talking bullshit, but mainly trying to figure out a logistic pattern of work for the yearbook club which we and a bunch of like-minded fellow seniors had joined. Of course, most of those "other" seniors gave way to me and my immediate nine cohorts because it was the logical thing to do. We had the brains and the bravado and had successfully buffaloed our faculty advisor, English teacher extraordinaire Mrs. L.R., into giving us the reins to put together the yearbook. What could she do? I know she liked us, however, she was in no position to argue as we basically took on the project ourselves with barely her blessing. Anyway, I found myself sitting on the floor in N.K.'s living room as her mom, my former German teacher Frau K., approvingly acknowledged our presence and left us alone. N.K.'s dad, the local college president, looked in on us, lit his pipe, said a few predictably humorous and sarcastic syllables, and then retreated to his front room library. Suddenly, another female appeared unannounced in our midst: it was N.K.'s older sister, home from college on a visit. I knew her well and perked up as she excitedly told us the latest "news." You know, "news" from a coed collegian was to be taken as gospel. She was older than us, "wiser," and had the *in* and *cool* info about all "happening" things. You know what I mean. Well we were all ears as she laid it on us: Billy Joel had performed at her campus and she was in love with him and his music. She went on and on about his mastery of the keyboard and his sexy bruised tenor vocalizations as she metaphorically floated around the room alleging total musical fealty to him. Wow. "I want to be a groupie," she said dreamily as I, dumbfounded, stared at her. Was she serious? After quitting Beethoven and Bach, who my previous dogmatic piano teacher had baroquely enforced, I meandered into Elton John, and to Billy Joel, whom my new teacher had introduced me to. I subsequently also quit formal lessons with her but continued plinking out modern tunes on the piano. I was familiar with Joel's offerings and agreed that he was a gifted composer, musician and singer. But was he good enough to justify having groupies, or "band-aids?" I didn't know. Maybe it was a female thing? Then an LP was slapped onto the

'70s-era Hi-Fi turntable in the room's corner and Joel's 1974 offering, *Streetlife Serenade*, came alive. I had heard a few selections from it already but here was a chance to listen to the album in its entirety. F., N.K. and I stopped our scheming small talk and relaxed to the tunes of Billy as did N.K.'s older sister H., who unceremoniously foisted her idol upon us. I didn't complain and instead closed my eyes and took in the beautiful toned notes. Because you know at my house, all "modern" music was derogatorily associated with the failed "Hippie Beatnik" movement, the "uncouth, haircut challenged Beatles," and Abbie Hoffman's left-wing liberal agenda. In spite of the fact that my father was a local college professor, my folks were very conservative and old school; I was surprised they let me play pop songs in the house at all! Opera selections and classical musicians were the soup-de-jour in our limited record collection. Now, whether my parents were actually diehard aficionados of that tight-ass tripe or merely pretended to indulge in highbrow music because of some misguided theory of pretentious middleclass upward mobility, I don't know. But I strongly suspect the latter. Nevertheless, and at every chance, I listened to the "new" tunes that were belted out here and there on AM radio and slowly started to fall in love with progressive and hard rock: King Crimson, The Moody Blues, Jethro Tull, The Guess

Who, and that brand new band called Boston, baby! Blasphemy! While lying back on the tan shag carpet and politely listening to Billy Joel sing his last song, I uncharacteristically and whimsically said out loud that I wished I could hear Boston. N.K.'s sister quickly obliged, whisked off the Long Island Jewish crooner's disc and put the needle on Boston's first and only vinyl orb to date, which proved to be a mega platinum work of hard-core genius in 1976. She had the record all along and although I was slightly familiar with *Foreplay/Long Time*, I didn't know the rest of the tracks. So I listened.... and I was blown away. It was sublime; perfectly instrumented by Tom Scholz (the original LP was produced by him and he played virtually all the instruments in the studio recording) and sung by Bradley Delp. I was in heaven. It was love at first hear. Forget about Billy Joel. I mean, he was very good, but Boston was the bomb! The wailing guitars, the high tenor notes hit by Delp; it was musical magic. And I wasn't the only one mesmerized by them. Nationally their record hit number one, etc., etc. I never told my parents about my gradual distaste for all things condescendingly classical and my growing appetite for lowbrow fare when it came to music. They didn't have to know. And to this day, even after the untimely passing of the original lead singer, the old Boston songs remain in my brain and I cherish them. As a constantly evolving group, they are still performing, with only one original geriatric band member and founding father (Tom Scholz) remaining. However, I really don't care to hear them live. I bought and own their first two records only, when their unique breakthrough sound was pure and captivated my soul with legendary musicality; a format and formula that they can no longer reproduce. I've heard some songs off of succeeding LPs and their new rock does not roll for me. Sometimes it's hard to get over a first love: *More Than a Feeling*, the first cut off Boston's debut album was more than a feeling for me then, and still is. *The First Cut is the Deepest*, as penned and sung by Yusaf Islam (Cat Stevens) in '67 sums it up.

68

They Got Me

Although as the frequently acerbic personality behind many kooky capers that transpired in my high school, I often elected to stay "hidden" and witness the comedic carnage from a distance, and with a poker face on, if possible. I preferred the role of instigator or provocateur and did not relish being the center of attention for possible retribution. I immensely enjoyed the company of my friends but never got "lit up" and was never the "life of the party," either. Sure I could mingle with strangers and say witty things if necessary; however, I was not a huge fan of idle small talk, unless plotting some incendiary tomfoolery. In addition, I prided myself for my observational skills and being "in the know." I "heard" and "noticed" things and remembered them…. I always had my ear to the ground plus fellow students often confided in me, knowing that their gossipy secrets were safe. It was hard to punk me with a revelation that I had not already known about. So, it is with great chagrin that I share this story: I uneventfully came home from school on the Monday of my seventeenth birthday on that October afternoon and fully expected some type of usual family display of affection and remembrance such as presents, a cake and congratulatory speeches on growing a year older. My younger sister gave me her artistically inspired handmade card; mom and pop grinned while giving me a brand new, authentic, leather, black-and-white soccer ball; and my normally garrulous grandpa Pete jokingly pulled upwards on my ears as per an annual, old-world, superstitious tradition to induce growth in male heirs. Nevertheless, the party proceedings seemed rushed and my haul of gifts scant. A lousy soccer ball? What the heck? I was slightly suspicious but blew out the candles on my mom's homemade chocolate log cake, ate a large slice of it and excused myself to go to my room and study. My mother intercepted me in the hall and emphatically told me to take a shower. A shower? "Why?" I quizzically asked her. "Well, because your friend F.'s mother phoned earlier and invited you over to his house for a birthday party," she continued. Oh, so that was why our own dinner and the cake routine were over so quickly. As I toweled off in the bathroom, it occurred to me that my best bud had not mentioned anything about a get-together at his home on the twenty-fourth, and we shared just about everything. And Dave W., his live-in Australian exchange student and my good friend and physics partner, said nary a word to me all day. Well, he did drop the Aussie slang phrase that I might *suss it out*, but I didn't know what he meant and let it slide. But wait a minute, as a matter of fact none of my pals had engaged me linguistically that day. Hmm….Oh, well, I would be ready for a small, ad hoc "sit-down" with the whole F. clan, which I knew very well. Pop dropped me off at F.'s house just outside of town on Route 10N and I bounded into the red, ranch-style domicile, expecting to see his two brothers, his parents and Dave W. But, no, a loud chorus of voices piped up and threw me backwards. I was stunned. How, why, when? There were tons of people present, all laughing at my expense, taking Polaroid photos of my bewilderment, and contentedly guffawing at my red-faced astonishment and unease. All my close friends were there, as were many others in my comedic orbit. I was utterly speechless, which was a rare occurrence. Everyone was in on the gag, except yours truly. The nerve of them! They got me, but good. It was an evening of utmost revelry, ping pong, beer, cake, and ice cream, with Mr. and Mrs. F. beaming and talking about my humiliating surprise. Then N.S. and S.S., two underclass brothers, German students, choir and music participants and fellow "comedians," presented me with an intricately molded and fired clay figurine in my likeness, complete with a Viking helmet and shield, a Groucho Marx face, a tennis racquet in the right hand, and mounted on a wooden base. And I received a bevy of presents from all present. I was deeply touched and got misty-eyed. I was uncomfortable with all the adulation and was in awe at the effort mustered by all involved to put on such a lavish shindig for little old me. I could be harsh and definitely obnoxious and yet there were smiling faces all around making me feel good inside. I could also be a real *pill* at times often bedeviling friends with my sarcasm and caustic wit, yet they stood by me and even had me eat cake! I still have that porcelain statuette of me which rests on top of the book shelf in my writing room; it survived countless jostling moves around the state intact and I revere it as a testimony to the many friendships I willingly and unwittingly forged while in high school. I'm glad "they" got me that day and "got me" in general, without any explanations necessary regarding my oftentimes perverse and quirky sense of humor. Thank you.

69

Contraband

We were cocky seniors and that alone should help explain the title. It was Halloween night; F., J. Logg and I had finished making the rounds to our mutual friends' homes and then scooted up to the high school in F.'s father's '68 Dodge Polara for the obligatory "dance." I had announced that annual fall spectacle over the PA system on that very morn as part of the "Viking" (a nod to the Monty Python gang) morning announcement team. We weren't celebrities, but, hey, we were SENIORS, dammit! Anyhow, the Polara was parked, and we went into the fray; not to dance, mind you, but to socialize and schmooze. Only the girls danced in that darkened gym, the straight guys just looked on boorishly and thought sexy thoughts, as usual. Remember? Suddenly my close bud J. Logg accosted me just inside the gymnasium door opening and told me that the *fuzz* was looking for F. What? Sure enough Dave C., the newly minted local patrolman, whose knee I used to sit on as a child while he mowed old widows' lawns on Clinton Street with his John Deere tractor, approached and "professionally" asked me where my friend F. was. What? What was going on? At least his gun was still holstered!

Whew! I anxiously replied, "Hi Dave, how's it going?" He instantly recognized me, didn't say a word, and responded by taking out a notepad and pencil. Oh, no. Everything that I would further say could be held against me from that moment on. Somehow he knew that F. and I were close buds and he put the mental squeeze on me. "Well, where is F.?" he flatly asked for a second time in a cop's trained, monotone voice. "I don't know," I stammered. "Go and get F. out of the gym, WE have some questions for him," he added. We? It turned out that Dave C. had a partner, Officer W., which I hadn't accounted for. He nervously stood off to the side as if anticipating a flash mob brawl or murder. He had his hand on his service revolver and looked agitated. Great, just great. I literally ran into the hot and sweat-stinking (only from the dancing gals, you know) gym, collared F. and dragged him out into the foyer while quickly telling him the gist of the situation. He looked panic-stricken, as did I. We were supposed to be "good" boys, not the local louts that the cops were always dealing with. We were the "good guys," or were we? Officer Dave C. grabbed F. by the arm and told him point blank that he had "contraband" in his car and needed to explain himself. F. looked at him in puzzlement. What the hell did that word even mean in that context? Officer Dave C. proceeded to escort him outside and into the parking area, with J. Logg and me close behind. Other kids watched the proceedings with confused stares. This really couldn't be happening, or could it? We looked at the cars in the lot and saw the green Polara covered with shaving cream and standing out like a sore thumb. Someone or a bunch of "enemies" had jokingly plastered his car with white, fluffy slime which obviously invited a visit from the nosy police, who were surreptitiously policing the event. However, upon further scrutiny of the vehicle with a brightly lit flashlight, Officer Dave C. determined that he had seen firecrackers on top of the dashboard in the auto. And it was true; Mr. Logg had bought the blasting bonanza down south a few months prior and his son J. Logg had in turn shared some of the "stuff" with F. But he had stupidly left the unexploded members in the car, in plain view. Well, after J. Logg's heartfelt explanation of actual ownership and my pleading rejoinders, Dave C. decided to confiscate the booty without so much as a citation, ticket or arrest. J. Logg got a stern lecture but nothing further occurred. F. was free to go, as were his "accomplices." What happened to those fireworks is anybody's guess, but J. Logg reported that he heard "bangs" going off the following summer from Officer W.'s home, which was across the river from his house. Cops, you know how they are….Anyhow, after that near disastrous debacle, we three pals went back to the dance but left shortly thereafter. We just weren't in the mood anymore. Officer W. eventually quit the police department and left town altogether to supposedly pursue opportunities elsewhere. Officer Dave C. quit the one-horse force as well and became a long-tenured postman, delivering mail to former jailbirds, arrestees and humdrum villagers, including my folks. But I often wonder whatever became of his official-looking notepad which had F.'s, J. Logg's and my incriminating or exculpatory scribblings on it? Perhaps it had been used by Officer W. to light fuses with?

70

Calling Mr. L.

My usual "gang" of fellow conspirators, and others, had finally wrapped up another late-night session of tedious yearbook work with our advisor Mrs. L.R. in her English classroom at the high school. Our fall mission was to photograph, lay out content, write copy and bylines, arrange the pictures, and solicit monetary contributions from townspeople and businesses. Mrs. L.R. expertly guided us because she had done this with every prior class for as long as anyone could remember. We appreciated her because no matter how much we argued, she always brought out the best of our ideas yet gently condemned the foolish and impractical ones. She had a knack for assuaging egotistical students full of themselves, including me. As we left the school, and before piling into E.G.'s Pontiac Catalina and J. Logg's Chevy Chevelle, one of my bright female compadres had the bright idea that before going home maybe we should goof on the school's typing/business teacher, just for fun. Mostly business students, like J. Logg, took typing from him as part of the Business Regents curriculum. But I had him, too. I was a senior and currently enrolled in his mixed grade Typing 101 class because my mother thought it would be a good idea for me to learn typing before I started college. She turned out to be correct, darn it. Anyway we were all in on the ruse and drove to his house in Sherwoods, which was comprised of a small section of homes on the outskirts of our dinky village, right before the bridge over the West Branch of the Delaware River. We stopped at the street end of his short driveway, got out, stopped laughing, picked up a few small rocks and tossed them hard onto his roof. G.P. quickly ran onto his stoop and rang the doorbell at the same time. Interestingly, L.B., P.M. and N.K., our usually stalwart gal pal partners in crime, sat in the Catalina coupe just watching we male "hoodlums" do our dastardly deeds. Sure they were part of our jestful "posse," but were "missing in action" when it counted that night. Anyway, as the cars kicked up dirt during our quick getaways, I turned my head in the passenger seat of the Chevelle in time to see the lights go on in the house. We four kept cracking up as J. Logg steered back into town, with E.G. and the rest of our "crew" following close behind. But before we could be dropped off at our respective domiciles, T.B. shouted from the back seat that he had Mr. L.'s phone number. Now why would he have memorized THAT particular number? But T.B. was like that; although book smart, coming up with great hijinks was also one of his strong suits. And even though a studious and pious-looking transfer student, no wonder he fit in so beautifully with we bunch of *characters*. "Perhaps we should call him?" T.B. questioned out loud in a most understated and droll voice, which made J.Logg, F. and me burst out laughing anew. J.Logg parked his ride on Main Street, in front of the lone, see-through glass telephone booth which was adjacent to the party-line phone company, as E.G. slowed his convertible blue cruiser and eased in behind us. All headlights were doused as yakking boys and girls tried to cram into that claustrophobic rectangular call box, the one with a hanging black pay phone bolted to one of the clear walls. However, three of us had to go in first. T.B. had the number and loose change, and F. and I had the humorous *chops* as the illicit fun began. One more aside: Mr. C.L. was an elderly, slightly effeminate "confirmed bachelor" in town, at least that's how certain men without spouses or kids were referred to back in those unenlightened days. Of course, he could have been a flaming gay pride activist at heart, and surreptitiously entertained dubious sexual partners at his inconspicuous abode for years. But living and working in a quaint and conservative rural village was just not the right place to reveal any personal LGBTQ leanings. However, for all we knew he truly was a single heterosexual man, without a wife and children. T.B. tossed a dime into the slot and dialed up ol' Mr. L. He picked up the phone at his end and that's when F. and I launched into our quick-witted routines. "Did y'all find out who troo dem cinder blocks at yo damn roof?" I queried him in a fake southern/creole drawl. "Hey, man, was that you running around naked in your house?" mocked F. in a Tommy Chong-inspired stoner voice. Before Mr. L. could answer those two questions, I taunted him some more with a politically incorrect Chinese accent. And then we freelanced, peppering him with insane, inane and sometimes *dirty* inquests. We three initial jokers were howling as my other pals were busy jostling for position inside that tight booth and taking turns putting the receiver to their ear holes and listening to his bemused responses. Mr. L. would hear out our funny questioning salvos, then reply as if part of the gag. He didn't sound mad or bewildered at all. Had this in fact happened to him before? Had previous students done "things" to him also? Were we part of some prewritten twilight zone script, only we didn't know it? Was he taping us? Did he somehow figure out who we were and acted coyly on purpose? The levitous fiasco ended rather abruptly because T.B. ran out of small coins. But as we finished our laughter, I mentioned those above concerns to my buds. My comrades stared at me rather annoyingly. "Leave it to Mayputz to ruin a perfectly good tease session of a pervert," I heard each of them say in their minds. No one was chuckling as we got back in the cars and were respectively driven home by J. Logg and E.G. I thought I was the funny one, the instigator, the politically incorrect hack. Perhaps yes, but also a slightly paranoid and empathetic human as well. My "gang" still liked me, I sincerely hoped.

71

Physics Foibles

That title is not quite accurate, I'm afraid. I was acing the lecture portion but had a somewhat difficult time in the laboratory part of the course. Perhaps it was just me, but I doubted it. Maybe my ineffectual partner was partly to blame? Bingo! But wait, he was my friend, fellow "gang" member and Australian exchange student, Dave W. You know, the lovable lug from down under that had the entire school under his charming and disarming spell. Yes, THAT guy. Yet even though he had graduated from high school in his home country, that didn't make him a whiz at Regents physics or any other academic subject. I assumed he had taken it before; it should have been a no-brainer for him to excel at it the second time around. However, it wasn't. He said he had learned it the hard way, whatever that meant. After our second disastrous laboratory session, and in a thick Aussie accent, he exasperatingly said, "Izzy me boy, you take over because you seem to be on the knocker while I'm up a gum tree and ready to go walkabout." What? Come again? Loosely translated, I guess it meant that he was clueless about the proceedings and ready to quit while I seemed to quickly grasp the difficult concepts. Fair enough, at least he was honest about his scholastic shortcomings and I begrudgingly appreciated it. Mr. R.G., the often cranky and no-nonsense teacher adroitly noticed Dave's ineptitude but gave us a break, at least in the early rounds of physics lab. Thank you, Mr. R.G. for not immediately flunking us. I convinced Dave to stay on and cleverly enlisted the help of T.B., the recent transfer student and brainchild of our "band." He was the one that I had cribbed chemistry lab notes from the year before to get A's. Hopefully, he would be willing to cooperate again, this time to save Dave's and my ass from certain failure. He worked on the black marble table next to us in the lab and agreed to help out as needed. What a pal, what a pal! Well, the year progressed with Dave and I muddling through rigorous experiments while covertly checking our data and observations with T.B. next door. Mr. R.G. never caught on or if he did he kept it to himself. And in spite of Dave's many audacious Australian witticisms and unique phrases, which frequently made me burst out in nervous laughter, we managed to keep it together during those strenuous lab periods and came out with A's in that section of physics. How Dave did in the class as a whole, I do not know. I received an overall A, thanks to T.B., my dubious scientific brain power, and personal perseverance with that torpid topic. With my anxious disposition and frantic desire to get top grades, putting up with Dave had been an anguishing experience, and he knew it. It bit the bag, big-time. Nevertheless, I had kept my cool in that lab because that big Aussie bloke had assured me numerous times that he was not an Aboriginal defect (as he put it) and repeatedly said to me, "No worries mate, don't be a Sheila; she'll be right." And he was right, after all.

72

No Exchange

By midyear, Dave W., the fully settled in and likable Australian exchange student, was happily living with my best friend F. and his family. However, as per the decree of the American Field Service (AFS), he had to move in with another boy and host family as soon as possible to finish out the scholastic year. Unfortunately, that rule was known to us from the beginning. It was done so that if a foreign exchange student was having a miserable time in his present "foster" home, at least the year would not be a total loss as he/she now had the opportunity for a change of venue and "family" members. Well, Dave W. wouldn't have it. He didn't want to go. Although a friendly and polite Aussie, he dug in his heels and refused to budge from his circle of friends, domicile and familial support. D.L., the other student excitingly waiting for him, was furious. That was not supposed to happen. Of course, D.L. was an AV nerd and not exactly popular in our school. No one paid him much attention. At least Dave W. had fit in beautifully with my "gang" of goofballs and he much appreciated our sense of humor and scholastic dominance; we were involved in *everything* it seemed. D.L. was not. Also, D.L.

and his family seemed to practice a dubious and conservative Christian religion and that alone may have been off-putting to Dave. He loved his current host family and us wisenheimers, and did not move. And then he was given an official last-minute reprieve and could stay where he was. Hooray! We felt badly for D.L., for he had trumpeted the imminent arrival of a popular exchange student to his house. But it was not meant to be. Most students in our class knew what had transpired and congratulated Dave W. on a job well done, much to the chagrin and ire of D.L. Our festive mood included an impromptu "mob meeting" at P.M.'s house on a select Friday evening. We ten friends celebrated by hoisting up more than a few cold ones at her home; she was the "gang" member who had the finished basement, full bar, pool table, ping pong table, and lenient and reasonable mom and dad. We partied hardy that evening while I'm sure D.L. dejectedly sulked at his residence. He had not been invited; duh! We stayed away from him the rest of the year, but I think Dave W. had made the right decision. D.L. was not part of our group and never would be. It would have been psychologically awkward for Dave W. to uproot himself just to have a new "brother" after so thoroughly bonding with F., his folks and my bawdy band of bushwhackers.

73

Time to Wake Up

High school Health was a half-year course for me commencing in January of '77, my senior year. Students could take it at any time, as long as they were in grades nine through twelve. Using similar out-of-date textbooks as our previous junior high bout with Health, this version was also chock full of the same inane, old-fashioned lectures given by the same, inane and maybe slightly insane teacher, Mrs. R.G. But you really couldn't completely blame her for the spectacle because we were the same dull, uninspired and recycled students, just older but no wiser. So there we sat, day after day, listening to but not quite hearing her boring soliloquy; she droned on about this and that, and mentioned more of the same old…. Some of it we had heard of before, some of the stuff we had personally experienced, and other material we didn't give a damn about. Hey, it was Health class, an easy A if you half-heartedly paid attention and pretended to take notes. It was a soporific no-brainer. However, one day I had a brainstorm in that demented gray matter of mine. Why not liven things up a bit? Right? I enlisted the help of two underclass female friends of mine who agreed to participate

in a "wake-up call" for Mrs. R.G. I surreptitiously hid a
metal wind-up alarm clock inside the unlocked wooden
teacher's desk upon entering the class as the feminine duo
climbed into the always unused coat closet right next to
the door, in the front of the room. We were all set as the
frequently frazzled Mrs. R.G. finally blew into the
classroom. The whole class was in on the gag as the clock
loudly ticked away and the jack-in-the-box ladies
expectantly waited, to spring out when the alarm sounded.
As usual, Mrs. R.G. unintentionally, or maybe
intentionally, attempted to put us all to sleep, although on
this day everyone was anxiously awaiting the joke to burst
forward. And it finally did, though it was not as funny as
we all thought it would be. The clock alarm went off, the
two gals popped out of the cloak closet and ran to their
seats, and the class erupted in loud laughter. However,
Mrs. R.G., whom we expected to either get mad,
embarrassed or laugh, did none of those things. She just
stoically stood there, staring into space, as if it was just
another normal day in this hellhole of a high school with
its putridly, peasant-minded pupils. She seemed to have set
the bar very low and we did not disappoint. And instead of
admonishing us she started teaching again as if expecting
this kind of outrageous and school-suspension-worthy
behavior. Really? Boy, I was terribly disappointed. No

anger, no outrage, not even a stifled chuckle. I looked over at my Health class gal-pal and fellow fun loving senior S.G., who sat next to me in the adjacent row. We were both puzzled. Mrs. R.G. was tough to break. Perhaps she was as sick and tired of teaching that course as we were sick and tired of trying to absorb it? Maybe she was basically numb while pandering healthy education to us numbskulls? It was hard to say; her lack of a positive response of any kind spoke volumes, however. The class ended as a small group of us instigators closed ranks and discussed what went wrong. Mrs. R.G. blandly but knowingly glanced in our direction, turned on her high heel and left the room as we tittered about our dismal failure, and HER state of mind. Hey, we tried.

74

Quits for Tennis

I was the heir apparent, the next in line, the kingpin....
But, alas, it did not happen. I didn't go through with the
anointing process and abruptly quit the varsity men's tennis
team just prior to the mandatory spring meeting with
Coach P. and the rest of the players. I was supposed to be
the undisputed number one player yet abdicated my
obvious and rightful place after fighting for it since ninth
grade. But why? I was the team's only senior, was ranked
first in Section IV, Class B, had compiled an impressive
34-4 win/loss record in three prior varsity seasons, and was
poised once again to do some serious damage to the
competition, this time as an experienced twelfth grader. In
addition, my insincere coach was salivating at the prospect
of me finally winning the singles championship at
Sectionals for 1977. Previous years had seen me
uncharacteristically falter during Sectional play; this was
purportedly THE year of triumph for me, the team, the
school, and especially the underhanded skipper. However,
none of it materialized. After my successful junior year I
soured on the team, and coach P. in particular. However,
there was more to the story. I was still very bitter about not

getting inducted into the national honor society where I should have been a shoo-in, plus I was now actively practicing with my old man and his college players on a daily basis. I didn't need any more asinine and purposely orchestrated tennis drama like in past years. Coach P. and his "so-called" team could take a hike up some fire tower in the Adirondacks for all I cared. I had spied his tall and gangly physique in the hallway one day in early March, marched right up to him and brutally blurted out that I was done playing. Period! He was stunned and mortified yet said nothing conciliatory. His lengthy "psychological warfare" campaign to somehow inspire and motivate me had been futile and backfired badly. It only made me quit. Even the returning underclass net-men could not convince me to further swing a racquet for my alma mater. I was finished with high school tennis. Years later I lamented the fact that I had never tried out for the varsity track team instead that spring. My very good friend E.G. (who had won the *Weasar Award*, named in honor of '73 graduate G.S.D., for being the hardest hitting linebacker on our football team) was on it running the 880, and I would have fit in beautifully in the 110 and 220 yard dash events. However, small-statured track coach Mr. K. (my former gym teacher/nemesis and local yokel) never really took a shine to me over the years and only reluctantly gave "that dark-skinned 'Russky' " high PE grades in grades 7-11 because I frequently outshone his best jocks in gym class. And he demonstrably hated that. As a senior, I felt that my presence on the track team would just antagonize him more, regardless of my sprinting abilities. Anyway, fast forward more than a few decades….USTA tennis is not the only lifetime sport where I continued to pick up winning hardware as an oldster in various age groups. I had missed the boat to be a varsity high school track star but ironically have accumulated numerous first place medals while sprinting in adult, USATF-sanctioned, short-distance races. I also picked up and continue to excel at the javelin throw, even now as a grizzled senior citizen. Go figure. To ruefully recap: my high school varsity tennis team had lost me as a player and sucked mightily during the short spring season of my senior year. Good, they got what they deserved, as I did. But I should have gone out for track.

75

Driver's Ed

Okay, it was another class besides Typing that my mother strongly suggested I take as a senior. And she was right about this one as well, I reluctantly have to admit. Most of my male buds already had their limited learner's permits supplanted by driver's licenses and there I was, enrolled in a class full of freshmen and sophomores. I guess I could have pushed the envelope earlier and demanded my American rights as a young driver, but I lived in town. In addition, J. Logg was my usual ride and my folks were leery of giving me driving "freedom." So I begged for rides from my friends and was always happy to see J. Logg swing his dark green Chevy Chevelle into my stoned driveway to whisk me away for some "fun." However, at the start of twelfth grade, mom and I both knew that I wanted to start driving soon, or I would start driving her bananas with my belligerence. Dad was clueless as to my plight; he wanted to keep me Amish. What? No, he was just his typical absent-minded professorial self, continually thinking that I would never grow up, get old and move away someday. Time always seemed to slip away from him, but I was physically there to remind him that I was indeed old enough to drive him crazy. Mom promised me that if I took Driver's Ed, then I could drive, period. Therefore, with mom's prodding, I sheepishly sat down amidst the younger students for a spring semester's worth of driving instruction in Driver's Ed (third and fourth quarter). Mr. J.K., who also doubled as the assistant coach for a myriad of varsity sports teams at our school, was a stout and recalcitrant teacher. There were days of boring classroom theory and days of repetitive road work, where four students plus Mr. J.K., would pile into the donated (courtesy of Lewis's Buick Dealership) four-door, teal Buick Century, with an extra brake pedal on the passenger side, and ply the largely deserted county roads around our village during school hours. Each student took his/her turn behind the power steering wheel as Mr. J.K. barked out orders and corrections as to our technique and roadworthiness. Parallel parking was a bitch for most students except me. I had learned to park my pedal pusher fire truck as a three-year-old, maneuvering it backwards and forwards between cones during the summer months. Imagine Mr. J.K.'s surprise and displeasure when I nonchalantly, and one-handedly, put on a parking display with that Buick while violating all the rules. He muttered swear words under his breath and then accused me of taking Driver's Ed merely to get an easy A because he wrongly assumed that I already knew how to drive. When I told him the story of my toy fire engine and daily practice sessions he winced and didn't know what to say. His anger at me abated and I kept on driving him batty. However, there was one distressing episode where that extra braking foot pedal on his side saved the car. I was parking in front of the tennis courts and somehow messed up. I still don't know how it happened but suddenly the car violently lurched forward as Mr. J.K. forcefully applied the brakes to stop it. I sat there shocked and bewildered looking, not because he had just saved us from crashing into the curb and then the tennis fence but out of embarrassment for screwing up. I mean, the other dolts in my car routinely almost got us killed every time we drove together, but I was supposed to be good; a senior and all. Oh, well, nothing happened but I still remember that episode to this day, every time I park my damn car! The course ended and I received the highest average in the class as well as the Driver's Ed award at graduation. It was a silly "reward" to give to a senior and most of my pals laughed at me as I rose to receive it. But, hey, I could now drive with the best of them. Then I borrowed my Grandpa Pete's '72 AMC Hornet and passed the road test on my first try, no matter how many times the instructor from Walton, N.Y. tried to coerce me into turning the wrong way onto one-way streets. He tried to snooker me a second time by making me do a three point turn on a one-way street, so that I would end up facing the wrong way against traffic. Knowing he was trying to hook me I kept my cool, refusing to drive forward while smiling at him. He ruefully snickered back at me and knew the jig was up. And then I managed to execute a perfect parallel parking job as well, furiously and two-handedly turning that stiff manual steering wheel while looking out the narrow rear window, glimpsing my nervous and quaking pop in the back seat. I received the official state envelope in the mail after a few anticipatory days and congratulated myself on a job well done. Now I was all set. At long last I finally had that coveted driver's license in my wallet at the start of summer vacation. It was a warm evening as J. Logg dutifully pulled into my driveway to pick me up as usual; some things just didn't change.

76

The Drug Talk

We were in the home stretch, the final quarter of school, the end of the line. And NOW our frequently discombobulated health teacher decided to teach us about the dangers of "drug" use? We were almost ready to fly the coop and there she was, wildly lecturing and pontificating about legal and illegal substances that could harm our health. I guess it was better late than never. Perhaps we needed such a talk to set us straight before hitting the skids out there in the cold, cruel world? Maybe. However, most of us dopes were already familiar with alcohol, as well as cigarettes, dope, and "pills." However, her daily teachings were not of a "scared straight" variety. Instead, she carefully reviewed the scientific facts about illicit substances and then imputed her moral standards onto us as a teacher and a mother. She really did not judge us; she only wanted to impart her commonsense wisdom on any remaining fools in her midst that could be headed into addiction and worse. Oh, there were plenty of snickers and eye rolls from "those" seemingly *mature* senior students that had been more than experimenting with naughty vices since junior high, such as premarital sex, smoking weed, popping

bennys and dexies (both are amphetamines), sucking on
Red Man chewing tobacco, lighting up Winstons in the
girls/boys lavatories, hitting the whiskey bottle before 8
a.m. and polishing off six packs of Pabst Blue Ribbon beer
with friends while hiding near "the wall" during lunch
periods. You know, normal stuff from the "bad element,"
so to speak. However, even those students weren't really
"bad," perhaps a bit misguided and willful against school
authority, but those were heady times back then. Mrs. R.G.
continued lecturing while some clucking chuckleheads
chuckled at her. Nevertheless, we all managed to at least
learn something. At least I did. Then one fine spring day it
was time to revisit the horrors of common cigarette
smoking and its consequences on pulse rate and blood
pressure. After outlining the additional cancer risk,
yellowed teeth and bad breath that could occur when
sparking a cig, she asked if there was a volunteer in our
class to demonstrate the ill effects that nicotine had on the
body. Now, purchasing smokes or other tobacco products
was illegal for persons under eighteen; however, enjoying a
cancer stick was allowed, just not on public school
property. J.F., a lukewarm friend of mine, casually raised
his hand and proceeded to put a coffin nail between his lips
while reaching for his trusty metal Zippo lighter. Mrs.
R.G. was delighted but gazed anxiously at the windowed

class door for fear of reprisal from a passing teacher or administrator. She hurriedly attached a blood pressure cuff around J.F.'s arm and using a stethoscope proved to us that his pressure and heart rate did indeed skyrocket while he sat there impassively drawing in and then exhaling the hazy white vapors from his nose and mouth. He was a seasoned pro at this. Plus he looked *cool* doing it, regardless of being part of a tacky and controversial class project. I had always secretly admired J.F. for his wit, easy intelligence and nose thumbing attitude toward all scholastic activities. Learnin' came naturally to him and studying was for nerds, so he often said. Well, we gave J.F. a congratulatory clap after the conclusion of the trial and he nodded to us in return. Just an aside: J.F. had been a recalcitrant and frequently truant transfer student, had some domestic issues going on, and managed to graduate under the radar. No one had expected much from him. I found out only later in life that he became an accomplished bio-statistician for a large pharmaceutical company while also raking in big bucks and accolades. It turned out that he had accumulated multiple powerful degrees, including a Ph.D., and became somewhat of a superstar in his particular field. I wonder if he still puffs away on Benson and Hedges, or did he move on to unfiltered Camels? Perhaps he quit and is now a paragon of smokeless virtue in his dotage? Anyhow, thanks to J.F. and Mrs. R.G. I learned firsthand about the folly of smoking and never picked up that tar-filled habit; other damning vices of natural and unnatural origins, I cannot comment about. Suffice it to say that my future undergraduate college years would see me curiously explore and participate in a wide world of "sordid adventures" that a formerly naïve high school student typically experiences. J.F. would have been proud of me, I think.

77

Showtime!

It wasn't good enough to merely be known as an alleged funnyman. No, my levity-tinged personality sought out ever larger audiences to showcase my humor as my co-conspirators and I progressed through the dull *rural reformatory* we called high school. So, what better way than to grandstand on our grandest school stand; the stately auditorium! My best bud F. and I had been planning and subconsciously practicing sketch-comedy routines for years, and we finally decided to be brave and possibly execute some versions of them before a live audience. We did have violin, orchestral and choir recitals under our belts and I had scholastically performed in junior high operettas and on the manual keyboard numerous times in NYSSMA competitions, as well as at many disparate holiday and piano-teacher-organized soirees. We both felt ready to go to the next level and entertain the troops, so to speak. But how were we going to break into "high school show business?" Neither of us even belonged to the school's Drama Club, and being the leaders of the lighting crew did not count. We needed a break; someone who could vouch for us. Someone who could say that we were worthy of a shot at the "big time;" that our horseplay and my classroom silliness could translate into a novel theatrical act that was actually funny, and not just corny *corn-pone* that people would fart at. The annual and hoopla-laden AFS (American Field Service) Show, honoring that year's foreign exchange student, was just around the corner (March 25) and since the Aussie Dave W. lived with F., that was our "in." All we had to do was convince at least one adult in charge that we wanted to do something extraordinary, something comedic that had never been done before. But who would that sucker be? Enter Mr. R.H., the newly hired music teacher that had replaced the lifer, Mr. Daye. Mr. R.H. desperately wanted to fit in and tried hard to ingratiate himself upon his string-playing students, including seniors F. and me. He was the perfect patsy to hit up. So far, so good. Now, sophisticated singing, dancing and oratorical programs were already lined up for the show; we had to get our shit together quickly if we were to have a non embarrassing slot in the lineup. First, we pleaded our nonexistent case in front of the gullible Mr. R.H. and then lied that Dave W. had heartily approved our send-up. Since honoree Dave W. was nominally in charge of the whole damn extravaganza, we got our spot secured. Mr. R.H. spoke to a few other fellow teachers involved including the good-natured British Lit teacher, Mr. N., as well as to Reverend S., the master of ceremonies and whose two boys would appear in my act. We received the final nod of approval to proceed and got our act in gear. Great! Now all we had to do was write and practice our non entity! We decided to go with a musical themed burlesque-type ditty, involving barbershop quartet-like singing with some debauchery and slapstick mayhem mixed in. You know, the Marx Brothers and The Three Stooges meet the Monty Python brigade and Benny Hill. And that's how the plan for the Barbarino Singers was born, or hatched, I should say. The usual group of suspects was rounded up by me, similarly to how Mr. Phelps (Peter Graves) assembled his *Mission Impossible* force for a clandestine caper on that seminal late sixties and early seventies TV show. None of my *home gurls* or J. Logg were involved, just E.G., F., G.P., T.B., plus Dave W. and two extra underclass brothers that could perform AND sing on key. Actually, the younger of the two, S.S., had an operatic, perfectly pitched voice and appeared with me in last year's German convention's main dramatic skit. I basically had those two blokes lead the vocalizations while the rest of the players kind of sang along while doing their best stand-up routines; they stood up next to one another in a row while I played the role of conductor/maestro. With politically incorrect, phony Italian accents, we practiced our singing/hoofing and

joke-filled routine, smartly employed a curtailed version
for the dress rehearsal so as not to get canned, and were all
set to run rampant on the unsuspecting saps in attendance.
Finally, our turn in the actual show came and we delivered.
I had previously and discretely seated myself in the
audience next to that pseudo-athlete and insufferable
pompous poser N.Z., who surprisingly did not give away
my identity. With my hair wildly curled and in a fanciful
costume, I purposely kept a low profile. As my other group
members gathered in fake confusion on stage after
introductions, I suddenly popped out of my seat and
dashed for the stage, apologizing profusely to my cohorts
for "falling asleep and being late." But wait. Where was
Frisbini? With lots of banging and door slamming, out
from the back of the auditorium came running F., with a
huge flailing overcoat and yellow wig on and with me
intercepting and admonishing him in the center aisle, right
in front of a laughing Mr. Z., the district principal. F.
temporarily sat on his lap to "hide" from me, but I grabbed
him by the lapel and started yelling as I bum-rushed him
to the side steps of the stage. But then, as preplanned, he
tripped and did a somersault over the railings, fell flat on
his face and finally stumbled onto the wood flooring and
got in line with the rest of the Barbarino Singers. As I
quickly looked offstage, I could see Mr. R.H. (our faculty

music director) laughing his ass off but at the same time
frantically thumbing through our handwritten script and
not finding any of the parts he was witnessing us perform!
That was funny in itself. Many more manic actions
transpired with us warming up out of tune, with me losing
my baggy pants, and F.'s toupee being stepped on by G.P.
and "killed" because T.B. and E.G. thought it was a blonde
spider. The packed house was losing it and loving it, but we
had one more trick up our sleeves. We suddenly turned
serious and sang a wonderful song which was in the script
and did it perfectly. People gasped as our faux
incompetence turned into a stirring and heartfelt ending,
bringing to a close our twenty-minute japery. We had
brought the house down and loved it. The AFS show
concluded, my troupe and I were roundly congratulated at
our unprecedented presentation, and we moved on.
Although I felt a little down after so many weeks of intense
planning, next up was the high school play, and we were
ready to be the warm-up act. A warm-up act? There had
never been such a thing in the history of our school.
However it was time to strike while the iron was hot, so to
speak. And now that the higher ups and facultative
anaerobes (teachers) had gotten a whiff of our comedic
prowess, it was just a matter of presenting our next debacle
to Mr. N., the head of the play production called *Egad,*

What A Cad. But we had a defector in our midst. Of all people, my best bud and comedic sounding board F. abdicated from his "responsibilities" to our group and decided to try out for the actual play! The nerve of him! Just kidding. He was a born performer and easily got the part he sought. We were the ones that lost out, darn it. I enlisted the help of Aussie Dave W. and that loquacious and funny junior S.S., whom I had worked well with as part of the Barbarino Singers in the AFS show. I wrote out a "magic show" format with me starring as The Great Zach-Fu, a bumbling, stumbling yet perseverant magician surrounded by inconceivably inept assistants. Think of Tim Conway in the role of a derelict showman, trying to do failing magic tricks. We were billed as a *Stupendous Display of Prestidigitation.* A "stupid display" would have been more apropos! I had my curly-haired-do and was attired in red knee socks and bright green velour snowshoe pants while "impatiently" waiting for the action to start. Dave W., dressed only in pink shorts and a long blue cape, methodically maneuvered a large cardboard box onto the stage in front of the maroon, floor-to-ceiling valance. He was my reluctant and touched-in-the-head sidekick, my assistant, my truth-telling foil. His name was Yur-ass, which I emphatically enunciated. Of course, it had been a linguistic setup because later in the show when Dave W.

incomprehensibly laid down for a rest I angrily shouted, "Get up, get up. Up, Yur-ass!" Moaning, speaking gibberish and literally climbing the curtain, he "ruined" my every attempt at "magic," such as pulling off a loosely basted sleeve from my coat resulting in ping pong balls and cards falling onto the ground right after I loudly announced that there was nothing up my sleeve. Meanwhile, E.G. was hidden from view inside the box, frustrating yours truly by handing me inappropriate and unasked for stuff through the hole on top and through a hole in the wide, black magician's hat strategically positioned over it. Tennis racquets, a stuffed toy rabbit, ice skates, a cooked chicken leg (which I took a bite of), etc. exited that hole. No matter what my conjuring words were, I always received something else out of that damn hat! And in between each short burst of "magic," S.S. (Igor), dressed in a striped black-and-white shirt, high water pants, with a hunch on his back and a perpetual disapproving scowl on his contorted mug, would run out from the wings with a large mop and clean up the mess I made. He would mutter and scold and took swipes at me while playing up my idiocy to the audience. Well, the crowd kept roaring and we frequently had to wait for the din to subside before delivering our next lines. Near the end I called for a "volunteer" to join me onstage. The "plant" was Mr. B., the band teacher and one of my faculty frenemies. He was the one who had caught me playing on a piano that had been precisely tuned for Sergio Franchi at a ticketed concert appearance at our school the prior year. It had been an embarrassing debacle for me, and Mr. B. and I did not part that day on the best of terms. Anyway, he had secretly consented to be my stooge knowing full well that most of my class still regarded us as bitter antagonists. He agreed to play the "heel" to symbolically help heal the alleged rift between us. It was ironic, dark comedy, similar to an episode of a WWE championship wrestling-type drama. I enthusiastically thanked him to much catcalling and sarcastic laughter as he walked up on stage. I deftly took off his "expensive" tie, cut it up into pieces with the unwieldy scissors that E.G. had given me through the hat, and proceeded to babble and gesture before placing the cuttings into the hat for a miraculous restoration. Of course, and as planned, E.G. handed me everything except the restored necktie as I feigned panic with Mr. B. accusing me of incompetence and malfeasance. His believable belittlement of me continued unabated as seated fellow students pointedly remembered our previous dustup and crowed with approval. Finally, I gave him back his tie, purposely stapled together incorrectly by E.G. as preordained. I had gotten my "revenge!" But before Mr. B.

could continue his phony outrage, S.S. showed up and physically mopped the "bewildered" band teacher off the wooden stage with a little help from my gyrating and gesticulating assistant, Dave W., who escorted him back to his seat while diagonally contorting his own lips and clapping one-handed. It had been fifteen minutes of mayhem and brought intentionally humorous and sometimes cringe worthy ministrations to a school unused to such slightly decadent debauchery. At the conclusion, most onlookers had at least chuckled warmly, but not all. As I scanned the crowd, there was our high school principal *Shag*, wishing he had a Lucky Strike in his mouth and a tumbler full of Yukon Jack in his hand to calm his nerves. Good lord, thank God that ugliness was over, the visibly relieved *Shag* seemed to say with his shaking head and barely clapping hands. And, then, after a brief but long-awaited interlude, the lighthearted and appropriately whimsical high school play began, with my bestie F. in a title role. The previously wincing and squirming school brass in attendance could now relax, knowing that the following "good-humored" fare would be favorably enjoyed by the many redneck attendees, who unscrupulously pretended to adhere to a highbrow image, at least in public. Oh, well, I had done what I did and received no reprimands, or overt compliments for that matter. But maybe some of those conservative and pouty old ladies in the balcony had laughed a little, too? Who knows? The competitive scholastic German convention was coming up soon and this year, even though most of my "posse" and I were no longer enrolled in German class, we Deutsche alumni were "allowed" to fully participate in hopes of continuing our school's winning ways. And Aussie exchange student Dave W., who did not speak an ounce of the Germanic tongue, also got the nod of approval to join us in Mexico, New York for the much-advertised festival. In addition to the usual events entered, the demanding teacher Frau K. agreed to transpose my recent "magic" act into German and added my small band of seasoned bawdy performers to the newly created competitive comedic section at the multiday spectacle. However, instead of Yur-ass, I called my assistant Yur-nose so as not to ruin our chances at a win. Up Yur-nose sounded better than up Yur-a.... during my German transposed dialogue. And my good bud G.P. was the seemingly unwary audience member who became falsely indignant when I cut up his tie. Our big guy Dave W. goofed around on cue and delivered big laughs, correctly pronouncing his lines in an Aussie accented Teutonic tone, which was hilarious to hear. In addition, E.G. and S.S. seamlessly performed their parts to polished perfection, with much appreciation from a mentally exhausted Mrs. K. I mean, our whole routine was almost R-rated and any bit of unforeseen or unnecessary alleged perversion could have easily sunk us. When we finished, she stopped rolling her eyes and sighed in relief as the three judges clapped vigorously. Immediately surrounded by congratulating fellow teachers from other schools, she visibly gloated and basked in championship triumph as we five *funny* thespians walked off with the inaugural first place trophy for a comedy sketch, much to the amazement and disdain of other schools' student participants who arrogantly thought THEY were humorous. Not. The rest of the convention antics and our school's winning back to back overall first prize State awards will be detailed in an upcoming vignette. And then, the fourth and final taste of comedic senior glory occurred on April 26, 1977. Our "benevolent" reform school decided to showcase our recently successful New York State German performances for the hometown public with a German Show in the high school auditorium. I'm sure Frau K. pushed for a demonstration of our Germanic prowess, and at the same time wanted to put a vindictive and definitive dagger in the heart of the more popular and populated Spanish class, which did not have a similar annual State gala. Perhaps she wanted to keep her job as well? But we did the whole thing in Deutch, the orations, singing, declamations, the play *Aschenputtel* (Cinderella), and with my comedy routine *Der Grösse Zach-Fu* (The Great Zach-Fu) being the farewell finale. The nearly nude Dave W. once again delivered his memorable line Nichts im Armel (nothing up his sleeve) as he insanely ripped off my lightly tacked coat sleeve allowing concealed knickknacks to shower to the ground. E.G. was on point inside the cardboard box, as was G.P., the hapless "stranger" volunteer from the audience whose necktie I fecklessly destroyed. S.S. was a riot as the limping, mop wielding hunchback as he hammed it up for the tittering crowd while continually "struggling" to keep a positive attitude during my deranged number. It was a slice of the same old bunch of crazy lunatics doing an all-male burlesque review onstage for the last time. And the usually comedically-challenged locals in attendance gave us an unpredicted though appreciative sendoff for a job well executed, at least by lowly high school standards. But I'll take it.

78

Taking One for the Team

I don't rightly recall the exact date when my fellow "gang" member J. Logg drew his first puff from a cigarette. Was it when he was a frosh, a sophomore? No one remembered, even he. Nevertheless, he was ardently smoking tobacco by the time senior year rolled around. Pall Mall was his go-to brand and he always had some packs, as well as Bic Flic disposable lighters, stashed in his school locker. Administration shills did not frisk pupils or check for any tobacco related "contraband" in those halcyon *daze*, even though pot and cigarettes were ubiquitous and smoked regularly just outside of school by the "bad element," and on school property! Unfortunately, J. Logg was addicted to nicotine and needed his regular fixes and that played into my scheme one day. Belomorkanal (named after the White Sea-Baltic Canal) is a cigarette brand that has been continuously made in Leningrad since 1932. It is cheap, unfiltered, and popular with a reputation as having the "strongest flavored tobacco" in all the world. It is a *papirossa* in the Russian language, and still in vogue in Russia and the surrounding former Soviet Union republics. Its unique design consists of a hollow, thin cardboard tube attached to the tobacco filled section. Lips compress the cardboard section while drawing in the acrid vapor. My nonsmoking father was given a complimentary pack of those smokes by a sketchy "Russian" truck driver that delivered crushed stones for our driveway in 1977. Because many recent immigrant Slavic laborers still smoked, maybe he assumed my pop also did? My educated professor father had that thick European accent (Estonian) going on and perhaps confused the roughneck "Russian" into thinking he was a fellow smoker. But whatever the reason, my father now had a pack of twenty, foreign-made cancer sticks in his possession and didn't know what to do with them. My Grandpa Pete used to occasionally smoke back on his communist-confiscated farm/estate in Estonia, but it was home-grown tobacco and half of the pleasure was to roll your own shit. He was dubious of lighting up a genuine "store bought" cig. But before pop tossed the pack away, I brought up J. Logg's name. Now even my stodgy and old-fashioned folks knew that he smoked, and they didn't care as long as my sister and I never picked up the nasty habit. J. Logg drove over one Saturday afternoon and pop presented him with a gift: a bona fide pack of cigarettes, straight from that dreaded commie hellhole called the U.S.S.R. It was a novelty item and definitely not commonly found in our neck of the boondocks. J. Logg thanked him as he sparked one up and bravely started to inhale deeply. Then all hell broke loose. The hacking and wheezing continued for at least five long minutes as J. Logg whispered over and over, "Harsh, they are too damn harsh!" I didn't know whether to laugh or cry as my dad and I stood by helplessly watching him cough out a lung. The big show ended with J. Logg pocketing the pack, and with a raspy voice, thanking my father one more time and then hastily exiting our property. Hey, he had forgotten to pick me up. Oh, well. I sincerely hoped he was all right as he left, and I never asked him if he smoked the rest of those killer coffin nails. He probably threw them out somewhere on Elk Creek Road, on the way back to his house to lie down for awhile. Of course, my smug and scolding male and female buds teased him mercilessly after hearing about the incident from me. However, none of us smoked and he did, so who really was *cooler?*

79

The "German" Sequel

I and most of my immediate "crew" were no longer taking German; we all had passed the Regents exam the previous year as juniors and were done with that difficult tongue. Or so we errantly thought. Frau K.'s daughter N.K., who was part of my "group" and taking German IV as a senior, convinced her mom that she desperately needed help if our school was to repeat as state German language champions. I guessed that the current crop of *das Deutche* ding-a-lings were somewhat lacking in the competitive department. Even Frau K., for all her outwardly staid sternness, wanted to win badly. At least that's what N.K. confided in me. Perhaps N.K. just wanted us to go along because she was lonely for our humorous camaraderie? Anyhow, we conspirators were now officially dubbed as German IV students by Frau K. and went along with the gag. And in spite of the scholastic illegality of it all, F., I, and even the non German speaking Aussie exchange student were booked on that trip. Basically, the entire ensemble from last year's winning team was onboard the bus that headed into the setting sun, to Mexico, N.Y. for the annual German convention. And like the prior year, we would be staying for two overnights with suckers, I mean, well-meaning and benevolent host families. However, this time around we were adequately prepared, unlike last year when F. and I "had to" cleverly raid certain classrooms in a strange school to procure props and noisemakers for use during our vaunted sketch-play. No, this time we were ready. We brought a shitload of gizmos, gadgets and instruments to supplement the comedically stylized sketch/play. In addition, my immediate bunch of fellow male buffoons (G.P., E.G., T.B., underclassman S.S., and Australian Dave W.) and I had carefully honed a slapstick/seedy magic act/comedy-short that we had previously and hilariously performed together using the moniker *The Great Zach-Fu and His Troupe*. It had been a heretofore unprecedented warm-up routine for the senior play entitled *Egad, What a Cad*, which my best bud F. had starred in. We then had our skit Teutonically translated by Frau K. and she reluctantly included it as part of the new comic section competition during the upcoming state German festival. She had balked while witnessing the recent live English version and asked me if I could tone it down a bit. I mockingly answered that it wouldn't be as funny then. She begrudgingly acquiesced and gave us the green light to perform it. We were all set, as Dave W. repeatedly practiced his Aussie accented Germanic lines on the bus ride resulting in much laughter and ridicule from the peanut gallery seated all around him. On the westward trek, Frau K. asked me to say a few inspirational words to the raucous underclassmen present. I stood up from the back seat, the crowd instantly simmered down, and I loudly pronounced that we were going to Mexico (Mexico, N.Y., that is) to "clean up," and not just to compete politely. I basically said what our teacher wanted to say but coming from the pie hole of a well-known senior, it carried more weight. Perhaps? My normally long, stringy black hair was in pink curlers for my comic act and I must have looked a sight trying to encourage the underlings with my sincere sounding sentences. But no one laughed, not even a snicker. Getting those coveted trophies was serious business. However, and in spite of my rabble-rousing platitudes we still had to show up and put out, you know. And it would not be easy because the other schools wanted a piece of us after our improbable win last year. However, my sunny and positive forecast for victory bore fruit. Following last year's model, we kicked ass and won first place hardware in events such as the oral declamations, dance (with P.M. as my partner), choir singing, athletic games, costume design and….the comedy routine. Yes, with G.P. being the "random" patsy from the front row, E.G. handing me stuff through my open holed magician's hat that was placed atop the specially rigged box where he crouched hidden from view, Dave W., my nearly naked, cape wearing schizoid assistant, and S.S., the frowning and headshaking Quasimodo-type character cleaning up after each and every "failed" magic trick with a large mop, we slayed the audience and received many accolades for our bawdy and bodacious number. Dave W. had managed to mangle the Germanic language while enunciating his few Aussie-tinged lines and it turned out to be uproariously funny and seemingly part of the act. Frau K. rolled her eyes throughout our number, grimaced at some of the salty and filthy parts but had to give us props along with the three adjudicators who stood up at the finish and loudly proclaimed their support of such innovative shenanigans on stage. Obviously, we took home the first-place statuette, much to the chagrin and outrage of other acts that thought they were politely humorous. WE were the real deal; just sayin'. We still had the *Aschenputtel* (Cinderella) skit/play to act in to nail down our overall number one school status and we did. The same group of seasoned misfits from the previous year, including me, turned "Cinderella" from a typically boring and numb short play into a romping farce, complete with gratuitous, pun-filled German jabber, unwarranted sound effects and obvious pandering to the fully engaged audience. However, this time Frau K.

expected onstage innuendos as well as flatulent debauchery and wasn't surprised. In fact, she had written in some of the "funny" bits herself! The judges loved it as well as we tucked away yet another winning prize. And our tiny, no-account school ended up in first place at the sixth annual Es Sagt's convention! The long ride home was a muted affair. Nothing could have been said or done to top our over-the-top efforts during that weekend's events. Nothing. We were spent yet proud to have delivered the goods when it mattered. And we looked forward to performing the same acts in our own high school auditorium to parents and students in a special future program to highlight our successes, in German, that is.

80

Also Getting the Nod

It was exceedingly rare for two students from the same puny class, and from the same puny high school, to get admitted to the same puny pharmacy college. Anyway, that's what I had heard, but it really happened. F. and I are living proof of it. I had gotten in via a "phone call" placed to the dean of admissions by my giddy guidance counselor in the fall of my senior year. My best bud F. had gotten the nod of admission in the late spring of '77, when students in our "reformatory" generally found out which colleges had rejected or accepted them. However, I don't remember F. celebrating or even making much ado about it. He told me very nonchalantly as I was standing next to his locker one morning, as if it was no big deal. Of course, that's the way F. was; very laid back and optimistic. It was his character and it made perfect sense. We were on our way to do the morning announcements and I was the one who carried on about his fortuitous news. As a matter of fact, his lack of bravado and bodacious blabbing was commonplace in my school, and even among my closest friends. For years we had shared many mental intimacies with each other but when it came time for college selections and future careers, no one seemed to share anything, good or bad. I was hard pressed to have any knowledge from some of my closest comrades about where they were going, what major they would be taking, etc. But why was there such secrecy? They all knew where F. and I were headed. WTF? I thought I had them pegged way better than that. Maybe I was wrong? Perhaps it was none of my business? Perhaps "college talk" was the final high school secretive and rate-limiting-step, kind of like SAT scores, which no one spilled out loud. Contrast that kind of attitude with my kids' approach involving application procedures and ultimate college decision-making processes. My brilliant and athletic firstborn daughter made no bones about trumpeting her intentions when applying to Cornell and McGill Universities, the only ones in our relative geographic area that had entomology/zoology as majors and the only colleges she applied to. Her many friends, teachers, guidance counselor, school custodians, and most neighbors knew of her scholastic business and were all rooting for her. Fortunately, she was accepted to both and decided on McGill University in Montreal because of its superior entomological courses at the undergraduate level. She also saved me a good coin. Most Canadian colleges are still cheaper than American schools and McGill was also ranked higher than some Ivies, at the time. Winning! A similar thing happened to my son. Lots of friends and family members intimated where he SHOULD be going and were privy to his application process. As a visually disabled, three-sport captain/scholar-athlete and valedictorian of his prep school class, he HAD to enroll at an Ivy League college or forever be chastised and embarrassed by "everyone" as a failure. Luckily, three Ivies gave him a shot and he matriculated at Brown University. I won't go into the details of his online applications but suffice it to say that with single digit admit rates Ivies are impossibly difficult to get into. It was then a huge sigh of relief when Cornell, Columbia and Brown stepped up and accepted him because he is not Asian, Jewish, Hispanic, black, a Native American, a Division I caliber sports recruit, poverty stricken, a legacy, an unqualified celebrity (e.g. Emma Watson), an underwater piccolo player, or "connected" in any way. He also wasn't a bleeding-heart hardship case like those feel-good stories of accepted students to Harvard and Yale who were living out of dumpsters, had jailed biological fathers, abusive stepdads, and crackhead whores for mothers. And I didn't "donate" a multimillion-dollar building to any of those eight Ivies, either. No, it was white, middleclass meritocracy based on perfect grades, perfect SAT scores, a brilliantly written admissions essay and blind luck. It was a rare coup of sorts, and "everybody" congratulated him. And I mean everyone, from envious casual acquaintances to honest to goodness people that really cared. It was like winning the lottery; it was a minor miracle. A little showboating was the order of the day, and we parents and grandparents grandstanded as much as possible. However to this day I don't know where my fellow high school "gang" member P.M. went to college. How sad is that? I had known her since the fourth grade, but did I? It just wasn't a big deal back in our day to actively divulge that kind of personal information, and even if it was, no one bragged about it.

81

The Spring of English

After yet another unnerving bout of that tiresome and ineffectual Mrs. G.H. and HER version of Compositional English for the last two quarters of eleventh grade, I was relieved to take Major Authors ll during the first semester of my senior year with a "favorite" of mine, Mrs. L.R. And then I seamlessly transitioned to a female; no, just kidding. I seamlessly transitioned to probably my most beloved course of all time in high school: Creative Writing. It was also taught by that same spindly, white-haired, yet trendy and *hip* oldster Mrs. L.R. She was a real *trip*. This was the second semester course where grammatically proficient (thanks, Mr. G. – eighth-grade grammar teacher) pupils could really shine and frankly express themselves without fear of judgment or reprisal, at least to a point. But over-the-top political satire, morbid and anarchic sentiments were frowned upon and squelched. If you had such thoughts, you had to keep them to yourself. But dark humor was appreciated and that's where I came in. Already somewhat of a teacher's pet in her previous classes, I continued my verbose clowning while producing insightful and intriguing writings time and again. At least Mrs. L.R.

thought so. However, she not only enjoyed my unique brand of levity but also spoke highly about many other pupils in that class, including some of my close buds. Most of my immediate "crew" and I were also involved in the harried yearbook production for our senior year and met with her regularly in the evenings to get the book done. She was the yearbook faculty advisor and received a double dose of us on some days. She got to know us very well, maybe too well. She had become a confidante and friend yet doled out supposedly deserving grades as well. It was a head-rush time for me, finishing up my work in the sports section of the yearbook and finishing up a fantastic year under Mrs. L.R.'s largely hands-off approach to creative writing. Sure she gave us hints, suggestions, tips and encouragement to help us improve as junior authors and made us write something daily in cursive. But mostly she would announce a theme and let us go at it, before collecting our mini masterpieces to creatively comment on and grade. One fine afternoon, after the yearbook project had been essentially completed and I could mentally relax a bit, Mrs. L.R. chose the word spring as the subject of the day in her class. We had free reign to approach it any which way we wanted. Without being purposely flippant but in good spirits nonetheless, I chose my title as "*The Spring of English*," and feverishly began to scrawl cogent lines in blue ink on the blue-lined paper in front of me. No good, as I ripped up the parchment and started over, keeping the same title of course. No good again, as I scribbled out a few unsatisfactory sentences. I had some time left in the period as I rewrote that one-page damn dissertation and handed it in. What was it about? I had taken liberal license to describe a fictional scenario whereby "creative writing" was sprung on unsuspecting English students in the spring and they had no idea what to do. It was a short, sardonic piece of work without much substance, just a few throw away humorous passages and juxtapositional irony. You know, my usual way of approaching situations and life in general. Mrs. L.R. ended up giving me a very high grade and read my "sordid" soliloquy to the class, along with a few other students' works. It was a fun class, a learning class, a class with class and a multitude of writing styles. I dedicated this book to Mrs. L.R. She had inadvertently yet intuitively glimpsed something deep beneath the surface, something more than the overt comedy emanating from the exterior of the class clown and brought out that linguistic creativity into the light. Thank you. In addition, her keen sense of humor meshed with mine and I truly appreciated it. And she more than adequately prepared me for college and future writing endeavors. I miss her.

82

Fired!

My usual bunch of mild lunatics did not think of it first. It had been a yearly tradition for some time now. I'm talking about seniors doing the morning announcements at our boondocks school. I recall listening and laughing as a freshman when previous seniors butchered the five-minute dialogue that was required every morn to give us information, sports reports and plans for upcoming events. Our erstwhile and former gym-teacher-turned-principal *Shag* had taken a back seat and let twelfth-grade chimps make further monkeys out of themselves while orating from the prewritten cue cards. It was all in good fun and I'm sure he got a kick out of it too. Senior year had started, and F. and I were first in line to be the announcement crew for the '76-'77 academic year. We wisecrackers were running the underlying comedic line in school, so it made perfect sense for us to do sequestered "stand-up routines" with a handheld microphone in front of an invisible, rapt, and imprisoned audience at our disposal. But wait a second. Weren't all the materials to be read approved ahead of time and merely spoken over the loudspeaker? Yes and no. Sure we diligently and seriously enunciated the important stuff but when it came to announcing dances, athletic events, birthdays, etc. we went rancid, inserting our sarcastic, politically incorrect horseplay and caustic wit at every chance, much to the consternation of the administration brass. F., N.K., T.B., Dave W. (the Aussie exchange student) and I were the ringleaders and paid a price for our goofy and sometimes bawdy insolence. What we thought was funny didn't always go over well with Principal *Shag* and his minions. We heard rumors of his displeasure with our a.m. antics, but he left us alone. Dave W. used his Aussie-flavored accent to great effect when describing mundane school events. N.K. and T.B. were for the most part the straight shooters and would set me up for the punch lines as needed. F.'s favorite imitation was of Walt Garrison, who was a former Hall of Fame NFL player/rodeo star and Skoal chewing tobacco pitchman. It was his heavy southern drawl that we thought was distinctive yet comedic. My straight-speaking character was Fred Fudpucker, essentially lifted from the *Benny Hill Show*. Ugrass Graboobner was an original dolt I invented, one that was a sarcastic buttinski who interjected humor whenever my friends/co speakers spoke. But it was "Grandpa" that carried the day. I patterned him after *Hee Haw's* Grandpa Jones, complete with a salty southern twang accent but with original last retorts and puns. An example of a typical dialogue sketch was such: "Hey Grandpa, when is the next high school dance?" F. would question me. "Well, ah reckon it's a comin' up on Friday night," I would respond. "Is it expensive?" F. would ask. "Gosh, no," I said. "Will it be fun?" F. would question. "Gosh, yes," I replied. Then F. would proceed to "market" the dance with the time and place and finish the piece by adding, "Don't forget the dance this Friday evening at the gym, or as "Grandpa" would say – that was my cue, "Git down off a yer four-legged mules and stomp around a spell, ya hear?" I heard that we cracked people up, but it was Mr. B., the epileptic band teacher, who cracked, put the kibosh on our foolishness, and got us fired! Of all people, he must have taken umbrage at something off-color that I had said the day before, because he stormed into the tiny broadcast booth next to the guidance office and berated us on the air, before a vigilant teacher intervened and turned off the mic. How ignominious! It was embarrassing as Mr. B. stuttered and pointed his finger at me, calling me names, and saying how unprofessional I was. Fair enough. He may have been correct. My pals and I had been using the speaking platform as a silly farce and perhaps we romped across the line and rankled his serious sensibilities in some way. It was a rude wake-up call for me. At the time I was remorseful and had to take stock of what had occurred. Were we really immature jerks and had asked for trouble all along? I guess so. And I thought everyone appreciated our brand of humor. I guess not. Other teachers finished the dull preaching that morning and we were done. We were asked not to come back. Most students opined their displeasure at our firing, but nothing came of it as Principal *Shag* effectively took over the morning duties with his gravelly, cigarette-smoke and bourbon-conditioned voice. Thanks a lot Mr. B. I thought you and I had buried the hatchet. I didn't know that you wanted it reburied in my bone head! At least my pals and I included ourselves as the Morning Announcement Club in the yearbook because we were all on the yearbook staff and had an "in." Of course the picture shows F. and I dressed as Harpo and Groucho Marx, respectively. We had come to school properly and humorously clothed one day, just for the photo shoot. Nevertheless, I still can't get over our sacking over four decades ago. We had gotten canned because of a few ill-advised and adlibbed one-liners. Oh, well…. Live and learn.

83

Economics and Equus

Why did I take arguably one of the most difficult courses in school? I had smartly avoided British Literature with that needlessly hard-marking and pompous Mr. N. And I did not take Probabilities with Mr. O., the math teacher, because I was too stupid. So why did I so willingly sign up for Economics, a two-quarter class taught by that loud windbag Mr. T., the same blowhard I had for eleventh grade American History? Because of my darn friends, that's why and, the promise of an overnight trip to New York City in May! The latter is what ultimately clinched the decision for me. The senior course itself was a bear and made little sense to me. Mr. T. did the best he could, shouting out complicated concepts while drawing endless cockamamie price lines and supply and demand curves on the blackboard. None of the economic teachings seemed to apply to real world situations, however. Whenever I asked a simple question such as why our village gas stations all charged the same for gasoline and continually raised prices regardless of the supply or demand for oil, he would just glare at me in anger and mumble an unintelligible answer to the floor. Well, now you know how the rest of the year went, academically that is. But now it was time for that vaunted annual trip to the Rotten Apple. It was planned for a long weekend extravaganza and my buds and I were all excited. And who wouldn't be? It was yet another chance to let loose and go nuts, especially with my "horde" in tow. However, there would be another teacher on the trip besides Mr. T., to supposedly help keep law and order. It was Mrs. G.H., that dastardly English Lit instructress whom I had "fought" with during the numerous courses I had with her as a sophomore and junior. I didn't overtly dislike her but had a nonetheless tepid disregard for her. I stayed out of her hair, and she out of mine, when I still had some. The three-hour bus trip downstate was the usual unruly ride with lots of yelling and laughing with my gaggle of pals already plotting pranks and pratfalls during our overnight stays at the cheapo Milford Plaza Hotel. Well, inexpensive by New York City standards! We unpacked, boys with boys and girls with girls, two or three to a room, and then we gathered outside for the "events" to begin. I recall all of us staring upward at the skyscrapers and marveling at the steady hustle-bustle of city life all around us. We were in Times Square, in the very core of the apple. The theater district was just around the block and there were rows of restaurants as far as the eye could see up and down Eighth avenue. The unfamiliar smell of bagels, the unworldly sight of honking Checker taxicabs and the tons of plodding pedestrians scared and intrigued me at the same time. Interestingly and starting in the fall of 1982, I willingly lived in that very same "clotted claptrap of a borough" while attending dental school. But for now it was all new, all "fresh," and I think it showed on our countrified, fresh faces. Besides the prearranged hectic schedule of sightseeing and museum hopping from the moment we arrived on that Thursday afternoon, there were other notable occurrences that bear mentioning. After quickly touring the U.N. building and then getting a figurative taste of New York City by experiencing *The New York Experience*, the unwieldy bunch of us finished the late afternoon in the theater, witnessing the latest Broadway smash hit musical *The Wiz*. You know, the music/comedy that starred an all-black cast and cast major shade on "white" culture by taking African American "cultural" liberties with the original *Wizard of Oz* movie. It was a live, "jive," *Sanford and Son* type of comedic send-up with outrageous costumes, all set to jazzy tunes. It was a riot but at times uncomfortably racially stereotypical, even for a naïve white boy like me. Afterwards, we had a late dinner at Johnny's Italian Eatery. It was always Christmas at Johnny's said the outside signage; the waitresses, the menus, and the rows and rows of blinking lights and miniature fake spruces, respectively, adorning the ceiling and tabletops. Our group mostly slurped down homemade spaghetti and meat sauce and then got ready to hit the hay. However, now it was time for the fun to begin. But wait, we were all bone-weary and nothing happened. Mrs. G.H. patrolled the girls' rooms while Mr. T. played some poker with a few lads before going to bed. The next day saw us visiting the New York Stock Exchange, the Federal Reserve, the Metropolitan Museum of Art and the Guggenheim. Whew. It was too much to absorb, but there was more. That evening we witnessed a serious, mind-expanding dramatic play called *Equus*. Basically the storyline involved a mentally deranged male stable hand who religiously/ ritualistically blinded some horses, was institutionalized, spoke only in jingles, and was unsuccessfully analyzed by a psychiatrist, who had his own issues. The hit play was based on a true story and was kind of a suspenseful thriller. But why did he do it? Why did he blind those horses? It was a plodding tale with a bare stage and mostly a dialogue between the doctor and patient, with nothing getting anywhere fast. The titillating moment came in a flashback scene when the boy finally coherently told the *shrink* that he was in the stable with the horses and was being seduced by a naked female stable hand. Of course, full frontal female nudity was often the norm in plays. But then the lead actor stripped naked and we all clearly saw his parts and pieces under the bright spotlight shown on them. The two extremely shy twin sisters in my class whom I happened to sit next to seemed to faint at the sight. I acted quickly and physically jostled them to make sure they were both okay. And they were. It had been the most emotional part of the play and suddenly there I was touching them on their bare arms. Heaven forbid! What was I thinking? What were they thinking? I just wanted to help them regain consciousness, that's all. Anyway, nothing deleterious happened to me; of course, this was way before the #MeToo movement…. To continue: The convoluted theme of the drama eventually revealed to us that the boy could not perform sexually because of a perverted religiosity and took out his penance for "bad" thoughts and impotence on the horses, whom he could not bear to judge him or witness any possible coitus. It was a fucked-up scenario and probably not appropriate for high schoolers and we left the theater silently and in deep thought. After an all-you-can-eat buffet dinner at the Piccadilly restaurant, where I rather embarrassingly scarfed up platefuls of peel-and-eat-shrimp as if I had never had any before, it was time to get in the water at our hotel's heated indoor pool. At this point I was spending some time talking to S.M., a fellow senior and son of *the* lawyer in town. Why I took up with him I don't know, for we quickly extinguished any notion of friendship upon our return to "Kansas." Perhaps we had briefly bonded over our mutual voracious appetite for that pink crustacean called shrimp? Meanwhile, my stalwart "murder-of-crows" forgot about the monkeyshines we had planned and instead swam, ran about, and then went to bed. After a hearty breakfast, we boarded our familiar yellow school bus and headed for home. After all the running around, noisemaking in the hallways of the hotel and attempts at shenanigans, nothing deleterious had transpired. I and my band of buddies had failed miserably at trying to "overthrow" Mr. T. and Mrs. G. H. with our planned brash antics and boldfaced hubris. We had ample opportunity to do some dirty work but did not. Perhaps fatigue and a sense of maturity had prevailed? Goodness no, I hope not. But, possibly?

84

Prom 2.0

How often do two best friends go out on a double date with two other best friends? I don't know but it happened to me and my best bud F. in June of 1977. It was time for the junior prom and being seniors F. and I were asked to go by H. and V., two eleventh-grade gals who had also been pals since grade school. Now, I had dabbled in dating the previous year with my on-again and off-again senior sweety, J.D. We had gone to my junior prom together. However, she graduated and left me bereft of a girlfriend when I became a twelfth grader. F. had also dabbled in the dating department, and his senior paramour and prior prom date J.J. also graduated and left him sans romantic female partner. So basically, we were two available males at the time. Maybe that's why H. and V. jumped at the opportunity to snag us and drag us to the prom. On second thought, it wasn't all that mercenary on their part. We all kind of knew each other and unanimously agreed to attend as a foursome. It wasn't awkward but at the same time there were no sparks in the air. Although both girls were cute enough for dating purposes, F. and I agreed to the deal because we wanted to have fun and not necessarily to become sexually or even platonically involved with them. I'm sure the ladies felt the same way, but I could have been mistaken. We sat at our table making very small talk and neither girl seemed to be having a good time. Sure, we danced, we laughed, we gossiped about other couples; however, the atmosphere was one of stilted contrivance. As a lark, F. and I even went so far as to pose as the faux king and queen along with Aussie exchange student Dave W., who mugged with us for a few hilarious photos. Other students expected that kind of tomfoolery from us and roared with appreciation. Not so much our dates, who sat at our table looking on disapprovingly, the way fiancées would glance at future husbands who needed to be "tamed." That famous 1954 flick called *White Christmas* comes to mind, when Rosemary Clooney and Judy Haynes had serious designs on Bing Crosby and Danny Kaye, respectively, although it took a while for the "boys" to get the hint. Not us; we were seventeen-year-old jokesters and took no hints from anyone! The prom ended and all four of us ended up at an after-party in a farmhouse on the outskirts of town. The beer and booze were flowing, and the talking got ever louder as I sharply surveyed the scene and tried to locate H., my date. I found her schmoozing up to J.P., the tall, senior, farm boy and varsity basketball stud who was the first baller to have dunked a ball in our school's history. I was sitting there in the high school bleachers in awe when he did it. His steady girl and prom date, C.L., was a junior and seemed pissed that H. was horning in on him. I sort of confronted the trio in the kitchen and H. snubbed me and brusquely told me she was going home with J.P. I was slightly dumbfounded but gathered myself and went to look for a ride home. I don't know what C.L. did after I left. Did all the drinking cause hidden feelings of love and lust to surface among all parties or only from H.? Did a cat fight ensue later? Was my date just biding her time to finally get her claws into a "real" man and not some stooge called Mayputz? All those questions, with no answers. F. and his date V. took me home with neither sadness nor elation on my part. It was a neutral ride to my house and little was said about the evening. As a corollary to this vignette F. and V. never hooked up, but they did remain good friends. Basketballer J.P. attended the junior college in town and joined his daddy's farm. Duh. He married C.L., his dark-haired hottie high school girlfriend and got down to farming and living large, well, at least she did. As to H., who never made any inroads on J.P. at that prom party, she disappeared from my orbit. But then I literally bumped into her one summer night after my first year of pharmacy college at a crowded liquor lounge called Zanzibar, one of many that had

suddenly sprung up when our village became legally "wet."
I said "hi" to her and she snubbed me once more. What
the hell? I had a steady girlfriend in college (Tumbleweed)
and wasn't about to hit on her, but she could have at least
said hello. Nothing. Maybe she was still embarrassed about
that incident with J.P. that I had witnessed or perhaps she
was ashamed for ever having gone to the prom with me in
the first place? It was probably the latter. Oh, well; women,
what can I say? Having an inherently empathetic and
intuitive nature, I thought I would be able to figure things
out like that. Perhaps not.

85

Senior Trippin'

High school was almost over and there was one more thing to do as seniors. Not senior citizens, but as seventeen-and eighteen-year-olds! That's right; it was time to go on a sanctioned class trip, and not to the Catskill Game Farm. We had already done that as third graders. And not to the Farmers Museum at the outskirts of our farming town, either. We had already gone there on a field day in first grade. No, this time we had to go somewhere special, to some sort of spa. But where? Our student council nerds and vice president V.F. proposed some places among themselves. The class president G.B. couldn't partake in the discussions or decision-making process because he was in and out of the pokey during the senior year. My wiseacre pal G.P. jokingly spread the rumor that we were going to Grohinger's, a mock-out of my bud E.G.'s last name and a take-off on the famous Borscht Belt Jewish resort called Grossinger's. But our class couldn't afford Grossinger's and it was probably solidly booked, even for a day trip. So a date was made with the Hotel Gibber, on Kiamesha Lake. It was also a Jewish lodging, so everything was "kosher," so to speak. To drum up support from the class our vice president ginned up the rhetoric to make it seem like the Hotel Gibber was THE place to go. Was it? How could we know? We were ignorant country trash and didn't know one Hebrew *ha'rbenik* (inn) from another. We were also told that there was in indoor skating rink, an outdoor heated pool, tennis courts, shuffleboard, a lake nearby, and room to roam. Subsequently my best friend F. and I went ballistic with our packing. We took our ice skates, hockey sticks and pucks, tennis racquets and balls, Frisbees, Jarts, swim trunks, sunglasses, etc. We would be more than ready for a super fun adventure. It was going to be amazing. A whole day to fool around to my heart's content in the Yiddish "promised land." But the anticipation was killing me. Finally the day arrived and we boarded two yellow school buses to bus us downstate a bit, and into the "Jewish Alps." My best bud F. and I had trundled our heavy load of accoutrements onto our bus to much laughter from N.Z., that obnoxious and pretentious asshole who just happened to sit by my bud and Aussie exchange student Dave W., in the seat behind us. N.Z. thought he was a funny guy but most kids in our class disliked him, including me. He was such a jerk at times. Anyhow, with our playtime accessories tightly wedged around us, F. and I could barely breathe but suffered in silence while sitting together toward the back of the bus. I scanned and scrutinized the multitude of familiar faces in front of me and thought that this might be the final time we were all together as a large dysfunctional family unit, with individual members who would someday thrive and some who would not. Nevertheless, if this was going to be our "last day in the sun," then nothing could ruin it! I smiled as I saw the pairings on that bus. My immediate cohorts were seated as expected: T.B. with J. Logg, L.B. with P.M., E.G. with G.P. and F. and I together, once more. Only N.K. defected from our "gang" and sat with her gal pal and class "blonde hottie," C.V. N.K. didn't really abdicate from our tightknit and ancient group, she had merely expanded her horizons and gained C.V. as her "new" best friend. Whatever, we would all soon be leaving each other and as far as I was concerned, to each his/her own. At the same time, I'm sure a lot of us "gentlemen" fantasized about getting into C.V.'s pants at least once before we graduated. But how? You would have thought that N.K. could have helped me out. You know, brokered a sexual tryst between C.V. and me. No such luck. Nothing happened. Thanks a lot, N.K.! But like they say, if you don't ask you don't get. Maybe I should have asked for it? Anyway, there was B.H. with his shirt off as usual, gesticulating to no one in particular, just like he did in my sixth-grade class. And there was sporty J.N., my former

English partner in seventh grade, sitting beside burly E.T., another multisport athlete whom I had known since kindergarten. School super-jock J.M. sat with his cheerleader/violinist/intelligent girlfriend M.E., A.H. was with E.B., G.B. was with K.A., D.F. was with J.F., I.P. was with her equally shy fraternal sister S.P., etc. And K.P., although E.G.'s current squeeze, *platzed* with her twin sister F.P. The trek was uneventful save for the yelling, screaming and name calling going on. You know, the usual. Our female chaperone, and mother of K.F., tried to quiet us down periodically but utterly failed to squelch the din. At long last we arrived at our destination. All eyes peered out the bus windows at the dilapidated, antiquated and generally rundown hotel buildings in front of us. What the eff? I hoped things were better inside. Nope. Before unpacking our stuff into our designated rooms, F. and I ran to see the pool and indoor rink. The cobwebbed ice rink hadn't seen frozen water since the late '60s and the supposedly heated outdoor pool was a cold, algae-infested body of swampy liquid, with broken lounge chairs ringing the fractured concrete edges. Yet we saw a few older guests sitting by it as if part of a normal ritual of vacationing. Holy Hell! We were duped, swindled, bamboozled and any other derogatory adjective you could think of. I was really steamed. The Hotel Gibber was a dump! F. and I sullenly dumped our gear into a large room, reluctantly picked up our tennis racquets and balls, and walked into the blazing sunshine to check out the two knackered courts. Of course they were overgrown with weeds, the nets were sagging, and it appeared as if they hadn't been played on for ages. There were no scuff marks on the surface indicative of recent sneaker traffic. Oh, well. I opened my new can of optic yellow Wilson extra duty balls and started to hit a few across the net to F. N.K. politely joined us but then others spontaneously horned in on us, using the hotel's shitty racquets. At one point, there were five unathletic and inebriated people per side slamming balls in all directions. This was not tennis, it was bullshit. I walked off the court wondering where all the liquor had come from. I should've figured that concealed flasks of brew and booze would be quaffed at a poorly supervised outing such as this. As I was disgustedly heading toward the pool, I happened to glance over to the lake front only to witness my close bud J. Logg attempting to get into a rowboat and head out into the drink. "Where are the fuckin' oars," he drunkenly bellowed, while puffing on his usual, a Pall Mall cigarette dangling from his lips. "How am I supposed to paddle this goddamn wooden tub?" he further yelled. This was the same upstanding young male citizen who had recently been selected to attend the very prestigious Boys State and had recently traded in his standard-shift Chevy Chevelle and bought a brand new silver Chevy Vega for the occasion. The unanimous Boys State candidate swore like a trucker and smoked like a chimney, but I loved him like a brother from another father and mother. Mrs. F., a female parent and one of our favorite chaperones, rounded up some implements for him and then roughly shoved him off into the dirty lake. I laughed hysterically, as I'm sure others did, watching J. Logg try to maneuver a leaking skiff with a mop and broom as makeshift oars. He was not pleased and cursed up a storm as T.B., E.G. and G.P. finally extricated him out of the shithole of a lake. He was still swearing and drunk as a skunk as he belligerently boarded what he thought was a non-functioning golf cart and pretended to turn it on as a joke, while posing for a picture by E.G. However after he stepped on the pedal the cart lurched forward and before he could stop it, ended up nose first in the lake. And E.G. had missed the photo op. Crap, another deviant debacle that we had to run from. And we did. But first my comrades and I sprinted over, pulled J. Logg from the "sinking ship" and then literally ran away. I never did take a dip in that green-colored frap inside the outdoor pool, however. And I don't think others did either. Finally, it was time for chow. Great, maybe the food would be good? We were expecting some tender vittles such as a succulent cut of braised Jewish brisket with all the trimmings. Instead, we got a slab of beefy gristle with gobs of lard around the edges of our paper plates. Okay, there were a few boiled onions strewn about next to the meat to make it appear like a legit meal, but, all in all, it was a paltry presentation by the chef, if the Gibber actually had one. We ate, our stomachs convulsed, and F. and I went back out into the fray to play some Frisbee. We tossed the disc and others joined in. Most were wasted and continually laughed throughout the afternoon, without doing much except breathing and drinking. Toward dusk, it was time to go home. I'm sure there were episodes of barfing, diarrhea and personal hijinks that I had missed but everyone got their respective shit together and boarded our buses on time to head back north. I think we had traumatized the resting adult guests long enough and they were most likely happy to see us depart. A rowdy bunch of overzealous "hooligans" had taken over the place for a day and our immature shenanigans were definitely not in their daily holiday schedules of eating bagels and lox for lunch, Matzo Ball soup for supper and then seeing a Jewish comedian for dessert, with a goblet of Manischewitz wine as a nightcap. Nonetheless, we tiredly got on the buses and that's when I noticed that the existing order of things had profoundly changed except for B.H., who was still topless and flaunting his hairless body in all directions. Now, granted, I can't vouch for what transpired on bus number two, but my bus had some personnel changes worth noting. Most flagrantly, N.K. was no longer sitting next to the hottie C.V., who was busy cuddling with J.N. It's funny; I didn't notice them the whole day. Were they in fact doing "the nasty" in one of the rooms the whole time while my infantile chums and I were naïvely prancing around the Gibber grounds? Nobody knew for sure but there they sat, cheek to cheek, as if they had been seriously dating for a while. Was it lust at first sight? I mean, they had known each other for years. Was it a last gasp flirtation and consummation before high school ended? I don't know as I witnessed N.K. sitting dejectedly between R.T. and C.B. And then there were my "posse-mates" T.B. and P.M. They were holding hands and cooing to one another. I had known that they had a thing for each other, but it had always been on again and off again. I guessed that this time it was game on, at least for the ride home. J.M. and M.E. were more than smooching, but they were the class couple and were "allowed" to do such PDA. F. and I sat together and bantered humorously back and forth. We rehashed the day and remarked that we had been assured Shangri-La but got a boffo experience instead. However, we had our tainted fun, had a few mishaps and gained some gossip in the process. And, as an afterthought, none of the aforementioned couples worked out in the end. Even J.M. and M.E. divorced after a brief marriage. However, was the trip successful? I guessed so and perhaps the Gibber was the perfect place for us to desecrate and further destroy. Just an aside: It is now a hotbed of Ultra-Orthodox Hasidic Jewry, complete with a temple and brand new buildings. No more is it a Catskill hostel for reformed Jews and Gentiles to vacation at. It's just as well. The whole area is no longer a recreational retreat, having gone bust years ago. Luckily we roughnecks from *farm country* had gotten our last licks in and called it a day.

86

Prognostication?

It was graduation day at my putridly small high school. Roughly 114 of we remaining stalwart students got ready to receive our commencement diplomas. There were some early graduates among us who I did not really know, as well as some over-retained dumbasses that should have left years ago. However, dressed in the familiar maroon and white school colors, we were all lined up and ready for the festivities to begin. Our respective parental units were seated in the bleachers of the gym as we now "former" classmates solemnly took our seats in steel, fold-out chairs lined up in tight rows on the floor of the newly built gymnasium. It was interesting to note that the vast majority of students who were going to stay in town and nix a college education got the most applause and adulation from the crowd and their respective redneck parents. However, moms and dads whose offspring were going on to further educational endeavors just sat there silently with dour expressions on their faces. Maybe thoughts of future tuition payments danced in their heads, unlike the happy-go-lucky local farmers, whose graduating kids were headed out to pasture without a dime to pay.

Our beleaguered and stupid class president could not speak at our "prestigious" ceremony because he was in the slammer at the time. What else was new? He had been unanimously elected by our crass class as a cruel rebuttal and comeuppance to a longtime female friend of mine who had deliriously desired the presidency and was obviously the better candidate. But life isn't always fair; it can be fairly funny, but not fair. So after Reverend H.'s invocation, V.F., our good-natured and capable vice president, gave a stirring and rousing oration that I misremember to this very day. He was immediately followed by Dave W., the Australian exchange student and member of my "gang," who muddled through a long thank-you list and humorous short stories in his unique Aussie accent before launching into *Waltzing Matilda*, the unofficial national anthem of his home nation. Our woebegone school did not have a valedictorian or salutatorian in my day as most normal high schools did. I'm not sure why, however. Then, after the hackneyed bromides flung about by our local assemblyman in his deluded version of a keynote commencement address, it was time for the awards; and, of course, there were petty politics involved. Much like the previous and secretive National Honor Society induction process, which F. and I were left out of and of which I was still seething about, the awards were a goddamn joke. Poor pupils, teacher's kids and politically connected progeny received the bulk of the generous monetary prizes for basically doing squat in high school. My best friend F. and I had busted our butts not only to entertain the "troops" on a daily basis, but were involved in sports, theatre and musical and artistic productions while also maintaining a solid A scholastic average from ninth through twelfth grade. But, no, there were no big congratulations for us. Sure we were both Regents Honors graduates but where were our rewards? But wait, I heard my name called. I stood up, tall and proud and proceeded to the podium as required only to receive the Driver's Education Award to much ridicule and laughter from the entire gym crowd. I turned beet red and quickly retreated to my seat. Then I received the I Dare You Award, a non moneyed 2 x 3 inch certificate for "trying hard" in high school. What? Really? Come on. I deserved better. I dejectedly sat back down to tepid applause. However, I garnered one more prime pick that day: The Wayman Prize of $10 offered by Dr. Leon H. Wayman and Dr. John M. Wayman to the senior who planned on entering some phase of dentistry or its allied profession. I shook hands with Principal *Shag*, pocketed the envelope with the measly sawbuck tucked inside, walked back, and plopped into my chair. I was going to pharmacy college in the fall, not to dental school. What a feckless and wrongheaded award to give me, I thought at the time. Was pharmacy really that close to dentistry? And a lousy ten bucks at that. They were supposedly rich orthodontists in the city over the hills, and that's all that they could afford? And ironically dentistry was definitely NOT in my plans; I never once even casually considered it as a viable or likely career. Fast forward more than a few decades and here I am, partially retired after a thirty five-year stint as a dental specialist, a prosthodontist to be exact. But how did the Wayman brothers realize that ahead of time? Did they have a premonition about me? They didn't even know me, or did they? Perhaps fate had thrown one of them a knowing and philanthropical punch in the middle of the night or, alternatively, they may have astutely sent out ten-spots and hokey certificates as slick business propaganda to all the teeny places of learning in our geographic area. The award would then be doled out by the individual school's brass to a "deserving" senior of its choosing. I think it was the latter scenario; a win-win-win for orthodontist, school and student. Anyway, a much belated shout out and thank-you to them for at least allotting me some money with which to purchase a sweatshirt from my pharmaceutical college as an incoming frosh. But although I successfully graduated from pharmacy college and passed the state board exam, that

"allied profession" never stuck. Dentistry would be my
ultimate calling and future bread and butter, for better or
worse.

87

Pharmacy Buds

As previously mentioned, my best friend F. also received a positive nod and got into pharmacy college in the spring of our senior year, when you were supposed to. He was relieved. It was a minor miracle because the college usually picked only one candidate per small town/village, which was its MO in hopes of the graduates returning to said hometowns to set up shop. That way, New York State would always have an evenly spread bevy of pharmacists, from corner to corner. Those, of course, were the olden days, with privately owned drugstores. The chain pharmacies were just starting their insidious encroachments; their explosion in the years hence changed the archaic and parochial approach to pharmacy manpower (and it was mostly men in those days, too). Anyway, two best buds would be enrolled in pharmacy college together; how cool was that? But seriously, as the summer dwindled down, my housing situation search was just not materializing. Many anguishing phone calls to the college's sole housing officer produced leads but no leases. Perhaps I was asking for too much? I finally realized that because the college had no dorms, I had to find private accommodations myself. I had to do the legwork, and fast. My father, although a college professor, always seemed put out and feigned ignorance of my dire plight. I desperately needed assistance and he did the ostrich thing. I'm not sure why. It's as if he didn't quite believe I was actually leaving. Whatever, and I needed help. We should have gotten into the station wagon, driven the two hours, stayed overnight and really beat the pavement until I found a place to live. No such luck. I had also forgotten that my parents were extremely allergic to hotels, motels and restaurants. I was a young driver and didn't have a car, didn't know the way, and didn't have a checkbook, etc. Otherwise, I would have gone myself. I was doomed. I called my best friend and *he* helped me, thank goodness. He had found lodging in a small house, on a quiet street and about a 20-minute walk from the school. He recommended me to the landlord, who would be living there as well, and he acquiesced. The extra income was also appreciated by him. The landlord cleaned out an outsized closet, fumigated it, and it became my new bedroom. I was very grateful. The landlord also promised to cook dinners and feed us if we bought the food. This was sounding better and better. Although I hadn't seen the place or met the leaseholder, F. assured me that things were on the square and I would be okay with it. I trusted him. So, there would be two of us, plus the

landlord and his dog. My parents were clueless but elated.
I was all set. My friend did say that the landlord was the
cantor and senior music director at a major Catholic
church in town, and a bit strange. What? Strange in what
way? We would both find out as time unfolded, but for
now I had a place to live. I couldn't cook, wash clothes or
clean a house, but, so what. I was thinking of what
rock-and-roll records to bring; this college gig was going to
be great! And it was.

88

One Last Fling

High school was over with, my aggravating college housing situation was finally resolved, and the summer was fast waning. My thoughts were squarely focused on preparing myself mentally for pharmacy school and all that collegiate life entailed. Having practically "lived" at the junior college in town where my dad, and later my mom, was a tenured professor, it had given me a snippet of what living away from home COULD be like. Granted it was a somewhat skewed snapshot of reality, but that's all I had to go by. My best friend F. would be attending the same college as I and we would be living together as roommates in a private house on Morris Street. How sweet was that deal? Very sweet. With obvious trepidation, I was nonetheless looking forward to a logical progression in life, at least as thought by a slightly naïve seventeen-year-old. It was a time for seriousness, of thoughtfulness and composure for I would soon be gone from familiarity, comfort and parental guidance. There was no more time to fool around and be lighthearted. Serious studies were just around the corner and I had to steel myself rather quickly. Then I received a rather humorous phone call from a gentleman I had never heard of before. He introduced himself as a local would-be thespian, musician and director of "events," and asked whether I would be interested in participating in a local summer theater group and its upcoming presentation called *Summer Magic*? He told be enthusiastically that he had seen me perform at the high school and wanted me in his show. It felt good to have my ego stroked; to be wanted and recognized. But wait just a second, Mac. Was he looking for seasoned volunteers or suckers? Was he desperate to fill a pitiful and inexperienced roster after broadcasting the upcoming show around the village? I don't know, and probably never will. I was slightly suspicious at his true motives and it was kind of late notice, but I agreed to become part of the ensemble. Why not? One more funny gag wouldn't kill me, now would it? Well, after many phone calls I managed to get F. on board, as well as his younger brother. The cast would be a mixed bag of recent graduates and theatrically unknown and untested underclassmen, with rehearsals to be held at the First Presbyterian Church on Clinton Street. Although the overall logistical plans looked great on paper, F. and I had to get together in a goddamn hurry and think of some funny routines to do. And of course, they HAD to be humorous; *continuous comedy* had been our forte throughout our long, high school sentence together. We just had to deliver, one last time; a few final gestures of "witty shit" before we departed our sleepy town for good! F. was working full time at the town's lone drugstore and we could only meet in the evenings, which made for sometimes futilely frantic get-togethers at his house or mine. Nevertheless, we cobbled together a few sketches and roughly presented them at our first scheduled rehearsal at the First Pres. Church. When our turn came other kids reverently parted and observed our nascent routines with unmitigated but appropriate laughter while the unnerved "director" and musical accompanist P.N. looked on in awe. We weren't THAT good, however even our lowbrow and primitive outlines more than surpassed anything that anyone else had come up with. Most of the other acts were tired, "unprofessional," and somewhat silly, even by my cornball standards. It became readily apparent that F. and I had to once again wade in and take over an entire production to get it sharpened up and polished for the paying public. I wished that more of my former "gang" members could be with us but, alas, most of them had already "moved on." It was up to F. and me to get things done, again! No pressure there. We encouraged, we criticized, and we cheer led the scurvy lot that had signed up or been duped like us into burying their insecurities and then to willingly strut around onstage in front of strangers. Granted, some were better than others but after numerous trials and errors F. and I made sure that each musical number, skit and dance was ready for applause. Oh, and F. and I were also the designated M.C.s and were introduced after the opening remarks by the director. And so the expose' began on a sweltering August 24th night, in the Little Theater at the junior college up on the hill. It was a packed house with some of my best buds hogging the front row and familiar townsfolk scattered throughout the wood paneled enclosure while riveted to velour seats. There was E.G., with his girlfriend at the time, sitting right in front of me. And there was N.K., T.B. and J.Logg. What the hell? They all told me they were "too busy" to help us out yet there they were ready to laugh at F. and me again, as usual. And I'm sure the rest of my "crew" was somewhere in that darkened auditorium as well, minus that Aussie Dave W., who had flown the coop back to his home country. Basically my "posse" was still intact, supportive and covalently bonded to F. and me, but WE two "merchants of mirth" had to do the jerky work of would-be comedians, not them. Oh, well, we were already practiced up so we might as well get 'er done. And we ultimately did. We announced the acts, the performers hit their marks, people clapped, and the pomp moved along. Then our turn came. F. and I donned black tights and white face makeup during intermission and then slayed the crowd with a pantomime routine that even Marcel Marceau might have barfed at. However it was original, set to music and looked authentic, with no lip syncing. It was silently done; duh! We received a thunderous ovation for our efforts and then quickly changed modes into being M.C.s again, comedically bantering with one another between the two mics set up on opposite ends of the stage. We stood barefoot, in skin-hugging leotards and with white face paint on. What a sight. After introducing a few more uproarious numbers that we had previously fine-tuned such as *Week-End Update*, plagiarized from *Saturday Night Live*, and *The Mating Game*, a send-up of TV's *The Dating Game*, it was time for F. and I to execute our featured performance: a violin/piano "concerto" loosely based on musical slapstick previously done by Borge Rosenbaum (Victor Borge) and perhaps Laurel and Hardy in their respective heydays. A grand piano and a metal violin stand with music on it appeared in front of the curtain. Still in our mime garb but without facial makeup, I sat down to finger the ivories only to notice that the lid was stuck. F. came over to help me open it as the laughter started to build. After frantically failing, we pushed the "uncooperative" piano behind the curtain, proceeded to run a live buzz saw for sound effect and then wheeled out the opened Steinway while wiping off fake sawdust from the keys. At last we could start our duet. But wait, why was F. flailing out incorrect tunes on his fiddle? Darn it, his music booklet was upside down. No wonder our beats and notes didn't jibe. After bawling him out and ripping up his notes in a foot-stomping temper tantrum, I "angrily" started to play solo, but F. kneeled down and played bits and pieces from the scattered and shredded papers on the ground. The tomfoolery continued with more pratfalls, more insinuations, gesturing to the crowd, and more false starts. Finally, just when we were about to mutually asphyxiate one another on top of the keyboard, a "plant" from the audience raced onstage, separated we quarrelsome "fiends" and gave us each fresh sheet music to play from. F. and I glared at one another in faux distrust, tepidly tapped out the tempo and then proceeded to enthrall the hall with a difficult and much practiced selection from Beethoven, which was in our wheelhouse. It was a showstopper. People clapped; hopefully none had crapped or hurled. The laughter and appreciation were tremendous, and we had succeeded one last time. One last fling at something that we both loved to do: comedic entertainment. The extravaganza wrapped up but not before one final salute and send-off to summer vacation: a slide show focusing on photos of graduated high school seniors set to the melancholy and bittersweet song *We May Never Pass This Way Again*, by Seals & Crofts. Even I got misty-eyed while sitting in the back row and reminiscing about all the good and bad times that I had growing up in my bucolic village and interacting with my friends. Though not overtly nostalgic, I became choked up seeing my very close buds, some for the last time. F. and I took our "brotherly" buffoonery to the same pharmacy college, split up as roommates and a comedy duo after the second year, cast aside pill counting after becoming duly licensed pharmacists, and then embarked on vastly different career paths. F. became a brilliant pharmaceutical scientist, which the world needs more of. I became a Doctor of Dental Surgery, as well as a "doctor of dental entertainment." I am a prosthodontic dental specialist still trying to inject levity alongside Novocain into nervous patients. Some things just never change….

89

Disclaimer

Did I really mean to offend so many people for so long? Probably, and it started in grammar school. However, I have to sincerely apologize to the few who were seemingly victimized by me, regardless of my fun-loving nature and intentions. High school was a time of growing up although some succeeded at a faster pace than others. Some of my fellow classmates would argue that I was left behind; some might say that I was ahead of the curve. Maybe I was both, at the same time! It's difficult to reminisce without an ounce of regret or hindsight. Life in the late '70s was tough for all of us, in spite of the burgeoning comedy zeal on TV and in the movies. I muddled along with my peers and tried to wiggle out of difficult mental situations with levity and wit. Sometimes I succeeded and sometimes I did not. I want to thank all those that put up with me and my shenanigans during yesteryear and to remember that it was nothing personal, just business as usual. On second thought, it WAS personal and none of your business. Ha!

90

Last Words

High school, my high school, my alma mater. But did it matter? I think so. With the slow abatement of prejudices against me, I managed to gain many acquaintances, learned multiple factoids, exploited my artistic, athletic and musical talents and had a lighthearted scourge of pals to pal around with for the duration of our confinement. Saddled with an oft addled sense of humor, which I liberally dispensed to family, friends and foes alike, I'd say that grades nine through twelve were an "education" for me. Was I ever greatly disappointed? Yes, when I did not become elected to the National Honor Society in eleventh grade, when I was supposedly an odds-on favorite and a shoe-in for inclusion. It was a bitter pill to swallow, especially when realizing that many of the inductees did not belong in that hallowed group. I also probably ruined my best friend F.'s chances of getting favorably honored as well because of our close association throughout the years of imprisonment. It's fair to say that it is the only award of recognition that I was ever willfully denied, while so obviously deserving of it. Being omitted was a terrible blow to my psyche and it still irks me to this day. Anyway, was I ever greatly pleased during high school? Yes, when Mr. T., my harried guidance counselor and former shop teacher, who also doubled as a summer house painter, got me into pharmacy college with a single phone call to the dean of admissions of said college. He had uncharacteristically stuck his neck out, pleaded my case, and then sent in all my required application materials as an afterthought. I deserved to be admitted but marveled at his *chutzpah* for vouching so vociferously for me. Thank you, Mr. T. I was also pleased at my ability to organize and execute a few comedic adventures on stage involving my likeminded and stalwart buddies. We had a hoot performing our unique brand of funniness for the whole school to see on numerous occasions.

At this time, I would like to thank my former immediate friends who stuck by me through thick and thin, and vice versa. Although we dissected everything and everyone, and everything about everyone, for some reason intimate discussions about our sexual desires, religious beliefs and grades were off-limits and taboo subjects. Nevertheless, we managed to hang out together as "brothers and sisters" for the duration of our public school tenure and only slightly crossed the line into interpersonal relationships. Also, I'd like to acknowledge that although I let you readers peek at

the allegedly humorous and often dysfunctional state of
my own life, some of the truly physical and emotional
horror stories of the people I knew were not mentioned
because they were not funny at all; the stories, that is. I
tried to share the bright side, the comic side, with only a
side of the depressive disappointments that befell many of
us as part of growing up. Everybody had shit going on,
including townsfolk, teachers and parents. This was
supposed to be a comedy book; I hope I achieved that goal
without belittling the psychological battles that were
silently but bravely fought all around me all those years
ago.

Most of my fellow graduates and I were about to leave
home and embark on new journeys whether collegiate or
not, and, whether we stayed put in our hometown or went
out into the brave new world. Moving on from high school
was as much mental as physical. But we fervently promised
to keep in touch with each other. And, did we? Yeah, right!

I started my "education" as a shy, dark skinned and
black-haired kindergartner; a *dirty Russian*, a *foreigner* in a
"white," rural village although born in western New York
State to intelligent immigrant Estonian parents. However,
gradually with humor, wit, guile, with book-smarts and

legs that could run, I survived and then thrived. I even graduated and was bestowed a Regents Honors diploma. Having an ounce of brain, a few ounces of talent and a pound of ambition has been the story of my life. And, so, it continues…. one laugh at a time.

Thanks for the read.

About the Author

Dr. I. Mayputz (not his real name) graduated with highest honors from high school, from pharmacy college and summa cum laude from dental school. After completing a master's degree in prosthodontics at a then prestigious institution, he embarked on his dental career in private practice. He once briefly toyed with the idea of earning a Ph.D. to become an actual entomologist, but ultimately decided on a dreadfully stressful albeit lucrative career instead. In addition to being an elite master's athlete, author, naturalist and part-time naturist, he is also known as a caustic wit and provocateur. He wrote this book to entertain family, friends, and any curious sod willing to relive the *daze* of high school.

For more alleged levity by Dr. I. Mayputz, please read:

Dental School: A Bizarre Comedy

Pharmacy College: Crazy Daze and Hazy Nites

Elementary School: Wits and Twits

Junior High: The Muddle Years

WHO
DAT?